D1590021

POISONING

THE ANGELS

Also by Marguerite Shakespeare

A Question of Risk
Utmost Good Faith

Marguerite Shakespeare

POISONING

THE ANGELS

St. Martin's Press New York

Design by Basha Zapatka

Library of Congress Cataloging-in-Publication Data

Shakespeare, L. M. (L. Marguerite)
    Poisoning the angels / Marguerite Shakespeare.
        p.   cm.
    "A Thomas Dunne book."
    ISBN 0-312-09895-2
    1. Chemical industry—United States—Corrupt practices—Fiction.
    2. Toxic wastes—United States—Fiction.   I. Title.
    PR6069.H285P65   1993
    823'.914—dc20   93-11468
                                                              CIP

First Edition: October 1993

10 9 8 7 6 5 4 3 2 1

For
Jocasta Shakespeare
My daughter
With much love

POISONING

THE ANGELS

*I*n the Mojave Desert in California the wind, encountering no obstruction, blows without a sound. At its passage the sky, like a stretched kite of thinnest silk, seems to quiver and pull tensely at its moorings. A crow flies—absolutely solitary, absolutely silent, absolutely black—across this pale expanse. When it settles a hundred yards away on the sparse skeleton of a cactus tree, the silent and invisible wind bends back its wing and tail feathers.

This wind comes in from the popcorn civilization ten miles away on the desert's borders, smelling of hamburgers and chemically scented polishes and diesel fumes. But now space has already bleached, the desert has stripped it of all human memories. Like other winds in other deserts, it blows into a person's nostrils nothing but the smell of their own soul. For the man who stands leaning against the hood of his truck, who sees the bird and watches the invisible wind, that is not a pleasant experience. He takes a restless pace to one side, and his boots crush the gray desert floor. It is half past five in the afternoon in early spring, and in the last two minutes already the light has changed. The sun has lost its gold for a metallic color, and night will fall fast. In another five minutes the heavy bulk of the truck will have begun to blur with shadow, and the metal to go cold.

"C'mon, Ash" he says to his companion.

Ash is leaning against the passenger door on the other side, staring across the desert. Something has caught his eye.

"What is it there? You see something?"

Ash says nothing but points with a jerk of his head and a narrowing of his eyes. The twilight, now so rapidly drifting down over the landscape, helps, rather than hinders, in making clear what it is that holds his attention: a little handful of flames that fatten themselves on the deepening shadows. Someone has lit a fire. It flickers far away like a candle in a darkened room.

Both men stare at it in silence. On Chuck's face the fretful expression has been replaced by a half smile, like a man anticipating something good to eat.

"Who can that be?"

"Dunno," Ash says. "Let's go 'n' find out." And he climbs into the driving seat of the truck and switches on the engine and the lights.

Far away by the fire someone looks up and marks the beam of the headlights with a quiet unworried eye. The flames of the campfire gild the dust, the stunted bushes, the pleasant curves of the camper's skin, with a fitful glow. The light catches a loop of fair hair, the glint of liquid in the eye, a jet black shadow darting out from a spiny tuft of bush, or a long black line from a single grain of sand.

The camper seems undisturbed by the sudden headlights on the horizon and the approach of the truck. On a small makeshift table an arm's length away from the fire, six sample jars containing what looks like dust are neatly arranged. The camper, with the same undisturbed gestures as before, now screws the lid onto a seventh jar and puts it with the rest. She does that despite the fact that, in the very moment of her reaching out to place the jar, the truck, fully lit, has charged the remaining distance before the fire and roared to a stop.

Chuck Barber jumps down while his friend Ash is still dealing with the engine. Once that is cut, it is quiet again. For a moment before Chuck nervously breaks it, the desert's tensile silence has already reformed and isolated the three of them.

"Hi there," Chuck says.

"Hello," she says. And smiles.

Chuck bites his lip, his eye glittering but guarded.

"Where you from?" he says.

"Barstow. I teach in the school there."

Ash hangs back. He looks at her with his head bent slightly on one side and then at Chuck. Chuck says, "Excuse me, ma'am, but you shouldn't be all alone here. It could be dangerous."

Ash would have laughed at that, but when his mouth has opened slightly and he turns from Chuck to the girl, he holds it back. There is no trace of that in her expression which would have prompted his next move. His smile dies, and he gives the side of his cheek an uncertain scratch.

"Don't you worry about me," she says just as politely as if Chuck were offering her a chair to sit on when she wasn't tired. "I know what to look out for in the desert, and there's nothing dangerous around here."

"Yes, but . . ."

She waits silently and then says, "You mean men?"

"That's right," Ash says abruptly, and looks at Chuck to see if he approves.

"Well, you're men, aren't you?"

"Yes ma'am," Ash says, still uncertain.

"Well then . . ." She gives a small friendly shrug and smiles at him, appearing to feel that that sums it up. Although her face only shows dimly in the half light, there is no shadow of duplicity—or fear—in it. The men are nonplussed. Ash opens his mouth to say something, but then with it still open he turns his face to Chuck, as if his friend has to put the words in there before he can spit them out. But Chuck says nothing. He has a patch on the side of his jeans where Goldie has sewn a jagged square of emery cloth so that he could strike a match on his pants, and he has a habit of running his thumbnail on it when he is thinking. He does it now, and that quiet grating sound is all that can be heard between two gusts of wind on the fire. And then all he comes up with at the end of it is to say, "Well. Goodnight, ma'am."

His voice sounds puzzled and confused. It isn't much to produce after all that thinking.

"Are we going?" Ash asks. He divides his own tone between respect for Chuck's decision and incredulity at leaving that figure by the fire. But his friend is already getting into the truck.

"Goodnight," the girl says.

Ash clambers round in his great boots and gets up into the driver's seat. "Night, ma'am," he says over his shoulder, and crashes the gears forward before cutting a great curve in the powdery ground and dry scrub with his wheels and heading back for home.

For several minutes the truck plunges along the parallel tracks of its own headlights and the men inside say nothing. Ash, his great hands that are meaty and padded out with flesh gripping the wheel, looks sullen. Chuck calculating. When they are some distance off, they start to argue. Chuck says something. Ash raises his big heavy chin. Chuck's lips move, and he jerks his thumb over his shoulder. The engine roars as the truck hits a small sunken hollow, and one wheel spins while the machine bites into the sand with the other three.

The men are arguing about the girl. Now that the mysterious quietness of her gaze no longer confronts them, Ash wants to know why in hell they turned tail. Chuck, like a drunk being told of an episode of unconsciousness, tries to reconstruct his reasoning at the time, but without the girl in front of him, he can't remember what it was that made him decide to leave and to call off Ash. For that matter, with her in front of him, he hadn't quite known either.

He must have thought of some way of diverting Ash from his frustration because he says something, and suddenly they both laugh. They are ill at ease still, but they laugh.

All at once Ash hits the rim of the steering wheel with the flat of his open hand and jams on the brakes. The tires tear into the dust, and the off side wheel slews out half a yard. Chuck, simultaneously thrown forward in his seat, turns toward Ash with an angry question that dies on his lips as he catches the glint in his friend's eye. He starts to laugh again with relish. Ash laughs with him, and this time he uses the gears to turn, throwing the truck into reverse and then spinning the wheels round and heading back toward the fire and the girl.

When they have finished laughing, they both still smile, or at least, their teeth are bared and their eyes are shining. They look intensely toward the distant fire, which they soon locate still burning in the place they'd left. Pitch-black night has settled on the land. There is no moon. The lit carcass of the cab lurches along the track and the headlamps throw rock-sized shadows from the pebbles in the sandy dust.

"Kill the lights," Chuck says.

Ash kills them.

At this point, between them and the fire, a slight rise in the ground hides all but the glow of the flames. The truck prowls more slowly forward toward the little rosy nipple of light. In five more minutes they have it back in full view. The flames still dance a lively pattern all alone in the darkness. The table and the girl both seem to have gone.

Ash draws up within ten feet of the fire. "She's hiding," he whispers. You can tell that he is smiling as he says it.

Chuck leans over without a word and switches on the lights. They hit the darkness like a bomb. The whole landscape goes up, each bush, each crease in the earth. But nothing moves. There is no sign of the girl.

"Swing the light round," Chuck orders. Ash cuts an arc from east to west. He then locks the lever back into position, switches on the ignition, and swings the truck round, harvesting the landscape, scything it down to a whisker with the flashing blade of those lamps.

"Which way'd she go?" Chuck says. "She didn't have no car."

Ash nods, still smiling. "We'll find her," he says. "You bet on it!" And using the fire as a center, he begins to mark out a wide circle with the truck.

Twenty minutes later they are still there circling the fire, like some hideously engrossed moth that has eaten the flame that attracted it. With headlights blazing, the truck goes round and round the dying embers in ever-widening circles, but the girl has gone. They never catch her. She has vanished without a trace.

CHAPTER 2

So you come home in a filthy temper, honey," Barbara said. "Warram I supposed to do? Ten years ago I'd have taken my clothes off, but what do I do now?"

Clothed, she looked the picture of American elegance. Her short blond hair immaculate, her face as discreetly and tastefully painted as the blush ivory walls of the open-plan living room in which she stood, she faced her husband across twenty feet of carpeting as he turned to mount the stairs.

A woman who could say what she had just said deserved some appreciation, but Dale was not into being fair and especially not to his wife. He said curtly, "Don't try to be funny, Barbro. You have this house full of servants, and I ask for one small thing and can't have it."

Never mind what it was that he reckoned he couldn't have—it could have been any one of a number of things, a new arrangement for his shirts or an extra cleaning for his pool—just so long as it gave him an opportunity to vent his feelings and assert himself. Barbara stood there nonplussed. Although she would have been the last to say it, she ran this fifteen-bedroom mansion in Los Angeles with as much skill as the manager of the Ritz Hotel in London ran the Ritz. Nevertheless, it is a truth universally acknowledged that the latter is a highly paid skilled executive and the former is only a housewife. She stood there in her uniform, which came free with the job—new Japanese designer suit, Gucci shoes—and watched her husband slam off to change without another word.

Dale went up the broad fan of the staircase with his mind back on other things; back where it had been before. His inner eye dwelt on the boardroom of Santhill Chemicals and the five men grouped in various attitudes of frustration and anger around the table. The shining boardroom table was built to accommodate forty but for crisis occasions like this one they kept it in the family. Dale stood now in the long window of his dressing room, loosening his tie, and below him the grass and flowers and even the water posed for him, their glossy greens and radiant colors calling silently through the air, "Look at us!" But his eyes had that boardroom table clamped to the retina. He saw nothing else. He gritted his perfect teeth and cursed the Environmental Protection Agency. He saw their latest document lying flat on the polished mahogany. The thumb resting on one corner of it belonged to Jim Faber, accountant, of the sort a firm listened to when they were in trouble; when they had to get it right. Charles Seaford sat at the head of the table, slightly baby-faced, his rounded features crumpled by time, but sanctified in every detail—his chair, his suit, his hands—by wealth. On his left sat Zack Webern, the lawyer, in whose intellectual mind ability and agility were closely linked. If the law had turned its back on something which a client of Zack Webern's needed, he could turn the law around with a neat flourish like someone spinning a piano stool. Dale should have remembered this, but panic had somewhat blinded him for the moment in spite of the way he outwardly squared his shoulders and hardened the muscles round his mouth. He himself had nothing if he did not have Santhill. The number one chemicals firm on the West Coast and an industry leader for the whole U.S.A., Santhill was the basket into which some of the men around the table had put every egg they'd got. They could be about to see the Environmental Protection Agency smash the entire clutch.

Charles Seaford, who was the president of this firm and whose father had started it up, shifted suddenly in his weighty chair, pushing it abruptly sideways and bringing his fist down on the table. "I won't stand for it!" he said. "By God, the methods we have used for the disposal of toxic waste since 1968 have been beyond reproach. Beyond reproach."

Vincent Cordoba, the sales director, who made up the last of the group around the table and who had, like the others, stock options and other financial interest in the company, responded to this cliché in a threatening drawl that showed his own temper. He was the only man at the table who smiled; but a stranger, told he was going to be locked up in a room with one of them, would not have chosen Vincent. He said, "We know that, Charles. We've been through it already. It's not the point they're making. They don't care about 1968. It's 1958 they're bothered with."

Seaford glared at the younger man. He heard the contempt in Vincent's words, but his brain lagged behind his instincts and he ignored the warning. Someone—probably Vincent himself—had sold Charles the idea that the sales director could be trusted.

"I don't need you to tell me that," he said. "In my father's day, when he started this company in 1952, there were no laws governing the disposal of toxic waste. And my point is that it just can't be legal to invent them retrospectively now and allow the Environmental Protection Agency to slap this demand for prohibitively expensive remedial treatment"—he slapped it himself, bringing the flat of his hand down on the document lying before him—"this outrageous cleanup order on us. We just can't afford it. Jim here says it will wipe out our investment schedule for five years, and I believe him. We lose our place! We're minor league!" He allowed a brief silence, but he obviously intended to carry on. "That toxic waste dump of ours in the Mojave Desert has been there forty years. It does no harm. It's on our own land. It's fenced and guarded. It's not poisoning the water table. But this damned Environmental Protection Agency orders us, in the name of the government of the United

States of America, to make it disappear. And what I don't understand is how the hell they've got the right to do that when the cost of cleanup will ruin us and comes off our net profit!"

Jim Faber, pointing at his spread sheet, said unnecessarily, "Those are the figures, I'm afraid."

He really was afraid. On his cheekbones a slight flush, like the human version of high tech graphics, gave his blue eyes a hectic stare. He looked unreliable; something he hadn't done in years.

There was an unhappy silence in the boardroom, and Dale participated in it again in retrospective silence as he stood looking out over his garden. Without moving the rest of his body, he dropped his coat onto a chair and reached up again to further loosen his tie. It was interesting that Zack Webern had nothing to say. The law was his province. But Seaford soon put that right.

"What do you have to say, Zack?"

Seaford came to a complete stop there, and Zack drew his head slowly up and back like a man focusing on a heavy object being lowered through the air. He said, "I still think we'll look around for someone else to pay the bill."

"I thought Dale had established there was no usable insurance cover in place," Vincent Cordoba said, "so how can we get someone else to pay? Have I missed out on something? Have you guys come up with an angle on the old general liability insurance cover?"

This was the moment that really riled Dale Falcus, since as second in command to Charles Seaford, he was the one who should have foreseen and provided for this development by updating retrospective insurance cover. These Washington do-fucking-gooders whining about the planet Earth and the environment like a new breed of Holy Joes with their snoopers and analysis charts had been around for some time. A more astute vice president might have thought about the toxic waste site in the Mojave Desert before the EPA did it for him. This is what Vincent Cordoba, the handsome, dangerous bastard, was really pointing out, getting the knife in with a dexterity that rivaled that of his own grandfather. Dale thought of himself as young, but he was fifty and lacked the resilience to start picking up old mistakes or the flexibility to dodge the blame.

Charles Seaford came to his defense with the spurious charity of a man too upset to resist giving an insult. He said, "I blame myself." Noblesse oblige! And everyone could see he blamed Dale. He even looked at him there and then with that infuriating mannerism of lowering his chin and directing an upward-slanting weary gaze. Dale felt himself blush, or thought he did, but it was from rage, not shame.

At last the garden registered on his office-weary stare. Good Christ, it was amazing, sometimes, how little pleasure the rich got out of their achievements. The damn pool, the landscaping, all the fruits of power failed to soothe when the power that earned them was itself at risk. He cast his mind about for a means of cheering himself up and realized he hadn't had a drink yet. With his tie half off his neck he turned from the window just as Barbara appeared in the doorway. She thought the slightly softened expression of reawakened appetite was for her.

CHAPTER 3

*I*n the dusty streets of Los Angeles as the heat of the same day simmered down toward evening, Zack Webern walked alone from his parked car toward a turning off at St. Vincent Boulevard. No one knew he had come here. In the gap between the working day and the other life that began when he reached home, just occasionally some alien life would flourish. In such a way he would, to himself, describe Jeannie, and in such terms he would also refer, if refer he must, to the brief history of his deal with Senator Quant over the contingency account and to the time when he got Danny Meyer out of trouble. This was another.

Zack Webern was an emotional man. His sparse legal frame and dry manner formed a screen that inadequately concealed cares, passionate opinions, and affections. For looks, he rather resembled a mixture of Woody Allen and Soames Forsyte. He was a brilliant corporate lawyer, but the dimension of repressed and at the same time nervous dynamism that characterized him was his Achilles' heel. And like Achilles he managed extremely well in spite of it until it came to the appointed moment in his life.

This was the appointed moment in Zack Webern's life. He

had left the boardroom of Santhill Chemicals pierced with the poisoned arrow shot from the bow of the Environmental Protection Agency. Not his life, but his professional integrity was about to leak out of the wound. He wore a dark gray suit of very fine cloth with a subdued check pattern, that did its best to mask the fact that he held one thin shoulder much higher than the other. Half an hour before this, the driver who had brought his car up from the underground carpark beneath Santhill Century Hall was surprised when Zack dismissed him and took the wheel himself. He drove out into the main stream of traffic with unexpected quietness. It was not a desire to conquer in the field of who drives first and fastest that motivated Zack Webern. On the contrary, it was the need to protect the gains he had already made; his fortune, his reputation, his company. He and Charles Seaford had created Santhill Chemicals together. Seaford senior might have started the firm, but under him it had been a small enterprise; its projection was small; it had cast a niggling little shadow. Out of this they had created one of the top-ranking companies in America, and the man wasn't born who was going to take that from Zack Webern. Failing all else—and all else had failed—this was one occasion when Zack was prepared to turn his back on the law and fight dirty.

He drove now along Sunset Boulevard, past front garden after front garden crammed with flowers under the all-embracing American sun. He reached Brentwood and momentarily lost track of which way he should go next. Another car went by fast and open, the radio firing on all cylinders. He hardly heard it. He turned left just in time and shortly afterward parked his car and began to walk.

As he drew near to the house, George Cash, on the lookout from within, turned and said to the boy in the kitchen, "Okay, Hugo. Close the door."

"Look. I object to this!"

The bell rang.

Hugo came right out into the hall. "I object to being hidden," he said with a sulky smile, "like this!"

George gave him a shove but whispered something, and

the boy let the door be closed on him again; by which time the bell rang for a second time.

Zack Webern, the minute he stepped into the hall, got the hang of the place. It had an air, a style about it. His first meeting with George Cash had been conducted in neutral territory, namely a restaurant downtown, and Zack had been too preoccupied with putting his proposition in exactly the right way to notice personal details, such as whether or not George Cash was homosexual. But now, the house was a giveaway. There was an extreme artistic deliberation in the way things were placed, and somehow you could just tell without asking, that there was no Mrs. Cash. This was a new dimension, but it was not important so long as it did not involve any compromise over discretion.

Cash was making some effort to behave as if this visit of Zack's was a social meeting. He was himself quite a young man, about thirty-two. He had a compact rather badly proportioned body, and red hair that waved in awkward contours. He stood now smiling in the sitting room like a salesman with a bottle of scotch in his hand, not realizing how surprising it was that Zack Webern had accepted his offer of a drink. Once he had it in his hand, Zack held the glass distastefully and didn't drink from it. George Cash said "Cheers," pointing at the sofa and sitting himself in an armchair nearby. Still dry lipped, the lawyer sat down. The basics of the business between them had already been settled at that earlier meeting in the small Italian restaurant.

"I need a document," Zack had said then, and to give George Cash credit (or discredit) where it was due, the young man had been very quick on the uptake. His profession as an archive archaeologist consisted in combing public records and private archives such as the stored paperwork of certain old companies, banks, and public archives, and seeing whether there were any papers of value that had been overlooked. Archive archaeologists had recently become quite a respected new form of professional life following the high percentage of finds and the value of some of them. Share certificates, bonds, insurance documents, wills—the archive archaeologist could claim from the owner or beneficiary a percentage of the value of the find.

In this case Zack Webern, on seeing an advertisement placed by George Cash in the professional services column of a local paper, had had an inspiration. If forgotten insurance documents were sometimes overlooked in the overcrowded archives of large companies, why not Santhill? Why not the very insurance document for general liability covering the years '55 to '62 they needed to pay for the EPA cleanup order?

You might say that the answer was simple. A person could not find what was not there. But Zack Webern had thought carefully and come to the conclusion that the right person might be able to find what was not there. The right person might be prepared to forge it, and use his professional activity to "find" it. And so Zack Webern had put it very delicately to George Cash that he might be that right person, and George Cash had said yes.

Zack now put his drink down untasted on the glass table and took from his briefcase the one potentially incriminating document that he would be obliged to part with in order to enable George Cash to perform his commission. His hand was not quite steady. He laid the paper down and said, without looking at George Cash, "These are the details. Will you look at them and see if you need any more information."

George Cash took up the paper that had been in this way passed to him via the table rather than hand to hand. He leant back and read it, making sure that he gave to the gesture all the ease of a legitimate business situation. He saw there the name of the firm—Santhill Chemicals, Inc., U.S.A.—and the details for the type of general liability insurance that Zack Webern wished Charles Seaford's father had taken out at the time. He read all the other details.

"Lloyd's of London!" he said after the silence spent reading. Zack Webern's mouth tightened slightly until the edge of his bottom row of teeth showed above the lip. "You've got it down as being insured through Lloyd's?"

Zack Webern still didn't answer, but turned his face toward George without saying a word, and George, with a slight and cryptic quarter smile, angled his head until his eyes were slanted like a spirit level on a crooked wall.

"Lloyd's of London," Zack Webern eventually said, "would have been a natural taker for that insurance, and I'd sooner they paid than an American firm."

"Oh, sure," George said, "you want to be confident of getting your money."

An irritated and bitter expression crossed the lawyer's face. "That was not my point," he said, "although no doubt most of the world shares your opinion." He said this very sourly, and added, "Lloyd's leads the insurance markets of the world, does it not? And I know two things about them. One: They're rich. Two: They keep—or at least they did keep—lousy records."

George nodded, but he wasn't so sure.

"Look, young man, I've worked on at least a dozen court cases involving insurance awards. I could just about claim to have invented the deep pocket. Now, the deepest pocket is usually Lloyd's, one way or another, and I always try and get in there. My experience is going to stand me in good stead. I know what I'm talking about."

"I don't doubt that," George said politely. "But they've got one hell of a reputation."

The lawyer made an exasperated noise in the back of his throat.

"Well—"

"Look here." Zack leaned forward and put one finger on the table. "Their reputation is largely romantic. Everyone thinks it's so damn romantic that the backers who pay the claims are all private individuals who run the whole organization like an independent private club. Do you know how it works? It is like a private club. An underwriter at Lloyd's gets together a group of rich backers—the Names—to form a syndicate. He then commences business by underwriting insurance risks and charging premiums, and the members of the syndicate share the profits or the loss, right?"

He looked up briefly. George Cash nodded. It was the first time he'd heard of it in fact.

"Until 1982," Zack carried on. "I won't go into why things changed then, but take it from me, until 1982 they kept only the sort of records a gentleman"—and he spat out the word in a way that conveyed just what he thought of the idea—"might consider appropriate when entering into an agreement. Do you get me? A gentleman keeps his word, so he doesn't go in for a lot of paperwork. I tell you, your hair would go gray if you knew the sums of money that bunch have paid up without so much as one single enforceable document, just because the underwriter's initial appears—in pencil even!—on the insurance slip."

George said, "You surprise me. Why does so much American business go over there in that case?"

The lawyer made a dismissive gesture. He wasn't going to go into all that. He wasn't going to go into the whole British myth, which he intensely disliked. He said, "Never mind all that. My point is simply that if you produce a document that looks like the real thing for the years in question we won't have any trouble."

George Cash nodded.

"Do you know how to go about it?"

Cash had lost his salesmanlike bonhomie. "Research," he said. "No trouble." He picked a small piece of paper out of his breast pocket and handed it to Zack. "As it happens, by coincidence . . ." he said.

Zack looked at it. "What is it? A phone number?"

George held out his hand for it again and with a ballpoint added a name and handed it back.

"Charlie Grimmond? Who is he? Am I meant to know him?"

"No way," George said. "He's a junkie. Don't worry. I don't take the stuff." He leaned back in his chair again, but the gesture deprived him of all pretense of relaxation. "Let me tell you about Charlie Grimmond. He's the son of the chairman of one of Lloyd's biggest agencies that owns and manages several syndicates. They put him to work when he finished college, as a deputy underwriter in one of his father's outfits—syndicates,

I suppose I should say—but he got hooked on cocaine, and his own father sacked him and threw him out. That's his phone number. He lives here now, in downtown L.A. I met Charlie through some friends who took him up when he first arrived here." There was a brief pause. He added chillingly, "He's on heroin now."

Zack said, "I see."

"He can give me any information I want on details of authenticity for the insurance document. He's quite well-heeled, but junkies always need more, and he'll do it for the money." George made it sound like a concession and guarded at that, as if the lawyer might expect him to discount his charges.

"I leave it to you, young man," Zack said. "I don't want to have anything to do with it."

He realized as he said it that the remark lacked credibility or even sense. George Cash kept his gaze tactfully averted. The lawyer seemed to remember suddenly that he hadn't taken any of his drink. He picked up the glass and swallowed half of it, and then left.

CHAPTER 4

*C*harlie Grimmond had an apartment on Spring Street near Fifth in a house built to last. That's how he described it when he first got there, and it was effective shorthand for a building erected on nineteenth-century European lines. It had stood in the path of many human lives like a complicated drainage system through which the dregs of human existence filtered into various parts of the city, including the crematorium. It didn't need, and didn't get, the delicate maintenance of the jerry-built executive villas that changed hands at half a million dollars plus elsewhere. In this house the window frames were correctly jointed, the walls were built of brick. It had more in common with Dale Falcus's mansion in Bel-Air than George Cash's villa had, or Zack Webern's for that matter. But it was nevertheless the sort of house that nobody wanted. Just like its owner, it's original soundness of structure and classic elegance was overlaid with dilapidation. They had both sunk to the bottom of the market.

On an afternoon two weeks after Zack's meeting with George Cash, Charlie Grimmond, with no idea what time of day it was, climbed the stairs and tried to unlock his front door. His hands were large and strong-looking, and yet he couldn't hold the key firmly enough to get it into the lock. He held a grocery bag in the crook of his other arm and towered unsteadily over the latch patiently struggling like an athlete caught in an invisible net.

To the man and the girl who were already inside the house, the sound of Charlie's key misfiring and scraping against the lock came as a welcome interruption. The girl got up from where she had been sprawling on a large cushion and walked unsteadily out into the hall. The room she had left was like a haphazard index of Charlie Grimmond's life. There were scattered books, which he had never finished reading, cushions, and bits of upholstery. The original curtains had been torn down, and the intention to replace them had been lost in some hiatus between hope and collapse that had resulted in drapes of cloth pinned to the frames. The cloth was rather good—a detail that George Cash had noticed the first time he had called round. He had reached out and touched them and taken a few minutes to ponder on whether it was really worn silk damask, gritty with age, which he felt between his fingers. But then, the light fittings were unchanged; a colored bulb, a paper ball, and so on. Clothes brought from the bedroom had been dropped and never returned; ditto, cups from the kitchen. The armchair on which he now waited had once been a fine example of French bergère, but the double cane had exploded in two places and under the litter of dead cushions and filth it had become an unsuitable place for even George Cash to sit. He sat on it, nevertheless, watching Marianne through the open door as she came back from the hall with Charlie behind her, neither of them too steady on their feet.

"Hi," he said to Charlie.

Charlie Grimmond gave a slight laugh in reply, which to anyone who understood the patois of despair translated as hello. He was carrying an armful of plastic bags, not by the handles. A milk carton fell out and crashed on the floor without breaking open and without focusing Charlie's distracted gaze. He turned his head repeatedly from side to side, as if he felt his spine or something else was out of true. He was having trouble coordinating the conflicting ideas of arriving home and doing what he had to do next. Eventually he put everything down on the flap of an old desk and said, "Coffee, baby. Just coffee. Oh, Christ!"

"She's gone," George said. "She's doing it. Hold on here." He got to his feet at last to catch the disgorged contents of one of the bags as Charlie crashed into a small upright chair.

"Why don't I open a window?" George wrestled with the catch and flung open the casement so that after an instant's delay a draft of air blew in, laced with the peppery seasoning of traffic noise. When he turned, Charlie was sprawled as much as he could be over the uncomfortable frame of the chair, but he was trying to behave with some semblance of normality like a courteous man desperately struggling to remember how to do it. He reached up and tried to comb back his hair with his fingers. He turned his face as he did so toward George, who was standing again by the sofa. A slight frown crossed his blue eyes, but he was beyond really remembering whether he liked or disliked George Cash, or indeed why he was there.

"These guys wouldn't let me have . . . ," he said, and lost the thread of his sentence. "I don't feel too good."

George looked at him, wondering if he might do better to spend the rest of the afternoon trying a different contact. The trouble was that Charlie was an essential contributor to the paperwork he was concocting for Zack Webern, and time was important. He decided to stick it out for another five or ten minutes. He said, "I'll go and get you some coffee." But as he turned, he saw Marianne hurrying back through the door. The fevered fragility of her movements bespoke some urgent purpose, and she took no notice of George. Her jersey fell in loose, black, threadbare folds over her jeans in a way that emphasized the emaciated grace of her body as she hurried unsteadily across the room. She bent over Charlie and excitedly whispered something, so that with a painful effort he staggered loosely to his feet, and before George could say a word, they had both bolted. No doubt someone had come up with the missing fix.

George looked at his watch. It was half past two. He was always conscious of the cost of time to a self-employed man.

You spent an unproductive hour, and it cost you money. He looked down at the front of his white shirt and flicked a speck with the back of his fingers. He'd done well so far, considering he'd had nothing to start with, but he was determined to make real money. If he had had the advantages of a Charlie Grimmond, he'd have been ahead of the game. Even now, even disinherited and thrown out by his father, Charlie was in the enviable position of having a subsistence in the form of an inheritance from a great-aunt, the sister of an American grandmother. Yes, sir, Charlie had got the basics. He'd had an American passport from way back—some dodge to do with having been born in Philadelphia. Otherwise it wouldn't have been that easy for a druggy English aristo to hole up in the U.S.A. But even there his problems had been solved for him. If he hadn't invented a few problems for himself, he'd have had it made.

George Cash, with the intention of catching up, waited, deep in thought and looking out the window until a sound behind him made him turn. Charlie had come back, in more than one sense of the word. He stood in the doorway, and compared with fifteen minutes ago, you'd have thought—and you would have been right—that his body had received some rejuvenating infusion. He stood, not upright exactly but with a stoop that was casual rather than debilitated. Heroin had made his hair thin a good deal but it was still blond, and when occasionally he had it cut, as now, he looked the way his mother always thought he would—a tall blond Rupert Brooke, a poetic T. E. Lawrence.

Charlie didn't mind seeing George there. It had always taken him a long time to mind anyone. He said, "Sorry, George, have you been waiting for me? Or have you come to see Spencer? He's out."

"No. You," George said. "Are you okay?"

"I'm fine now, fine."

That was an overstatement, but they say judgment is a matter of comparison. Charlie walked across the room and smiled. His haggard features lit up amazingly. "Have a drink. There's whiskey somewhere. Marianne. Marianne!" There was no answer. He laughed. "Girls. Bet she's lying down. You know . . ."

He fidgeted with a pile of papers on the desk and unearthed a cigarette packet. It was empty. "Marianne!" He walked over to the door. "Where . . ."

This could go on forever, George thought with a flash of irritation. What always amazed him was that drugs and all the fallout was so bloody boring. But George always knew when to move in on a situation and get a grip on things, so when Charlie finally came back again, he said, "Look, pal, I've got to go in a minute, but we must talk about that business proposition I made you the other day. Marianne said you were a bit short of cash."

"Damn right," Charlie said. His blue eyes clouded over again. George had just witnessed one tortured bridging of the gap between sickness and well-being, of a sort that only lots of money could buy, and Charlie himself had that fact in mind all the time. "Damn right," he said again. "Very."

"Well, if you're very short," George said impatiently, "get on with this commission, for God's sake. I'm depending on you."

"Oh, Christ!" Charlie had obviously forgotten, but now he remembered, the scheme for the reinsurance document that he was helping with.

George said, "Did you get your friends to send you the blanks from the Lloyd's policy signing office?"

"Yes, I did. I put them . . ." Charlie turned to the desk again and opened a drawer. He was rummaging, not looking. "Marianne!"

"Don't call her again," snapped George. "Think. Where did you put them?" Charlie clawed back his hair distractedly, half leaning on the desktop. A flush had appeared on his cheekbones like the first stain of mortality on a pale flower. Young, old, decrepit, and athletic. In other circumstances George might have had an eye for it all, and then again he might not.

"In another room," George asked, "or in here?"

"Here."

"The desk then? Or . . ." he searched the room with his

eye, seeing only chaos. "You wouldn't have let it get messed up in some pile of rubbish on the floor, would you?"

"No, no. Calm down. It's in the drawer." And Charlie bent and opened the lowest drawer in the desk and took out the papers straight away. There were several blanks. George picked up his briefcase and carefully stored the sheets away, then glanced again at his watch. Should he or should he not attempt to make a date with Charlie in advance for the next stage? The chances were he'd forget anyway. For now he seemed in such good form it seemed a shame not to take advantage of the opportunity. He snapped the briefcase shut and straightened up.

"Would it be a good idea to draft the schedule now?" he asked. "I've got time if you have."

Charlie shook his head. "No point." He took a long drag on the cigarette that he had managed to find. His fingers trembled so much he didn't want to waste the opportunity once he had got the cigarette to his mouth.

"Why not?"

Instead of replying, Charlie said, after a pause, "Spencer's leaving. Did I tell you?"

George tightened his lips in something between a wince and a smile. "We're talking about the job, Charlie. To hell with Spencer. Why not draft the schedule now, while you're in the mood?"

"I'm not in the mood, you jerk. What makes you think I'm in the mood to do a crap thing like that just when I have the chance to get a little peace?"

"Okay," George said curtly. "I thought you needed the money, but if you don't, that's okay by me."

"I do want the money."

"Well, you can have it when this thing's done," George said.

Charlie laughed, a mocking peal that deteriorated into a fit of coughing, which brought a sweat out on his brow and finished with him reaching out with an unsteady hand and saying, "You win, George boy. You always win. Give me one of the blanks."

George undid the briefcase again, counted the sheets, and separated one. Charlie snatched it, staggered upright, and turned the chair round to the desk. He cleared a space, and before he could start looking for one, George handed him a pen. For a moment he collected himself. He looked at the familiar paper and his mind cleared. He said in a voice one or two brokers still working in Lloyd's would have recognized, "All right, we'll do it."

He went on, "The insured is Santhill. It must be printed here. You know where all these entries go? You've looked up other similar documents?"

"Yes, but carry on. Sketch it in."

Charlie did so, pointing out as he wrote, "Here are the dates between which the cover ran; you told me '55 with renewals to '62? And premium?"

He was silent for a long moment, and George thought he'd gone off again. When he was about to say something, Charlie made a peremptory gesture for silence and finally wrote down a figure. He was about to hand the paper back when something occurred to him. Whatever it was, it obviously fired him up. He started to laugh, shaking his shoulders and at the same time playacting at having to hold back the joyless mad sound of his own amusement. "What are you doing?" George asked nervously. "What are you adding there?"

"Syndicate number," Charlie said. "That's all you really need me for. You could have got all this from the records. But you need a syndicate number. See? The syndicate that underwrote it, that 'led the risk,' as they say. I've given you one there. It's got to be a real number that will pay. And it's got to be appropriate. I've given you one!"

"You mean you've remembered an accurate number. You sure you've got it right?"

"You bet I have!" Charlie said, starting to laugh again, his voice cracking as if the joke was too much for him. "Be sure the man who draws all this up gets it right. That's the number of one of my father's syndicates. That'll give the old bastard something to think about!"

CHAPTER 5

*C*harlie's father—"the old bastard"—deserved something of the kind. Perhaps he deserved worse. To see him, shortly after the time of Charlie's latest meeting with George Cash, emerging one morning from his superb house in Knightsbridge, London, and getting into his car, you might think he was a typical member of a wealthy upper-class business community and harmless in his way. His chauffeur held open the door as he stepped into the Rolls, and if you were watching from a certain distance you would see that Sir Adrian Grimmond—he was a baronet—was tall and upright, extremely well fed and rather graceful and leisurely in his movements. He had a slightly supercilious air of being pleased with his surroundings, and unless you stood nearby at a moment when something had occurred to annoy him, you might miss the steel in his eye. Lofty good humor characterized almost all his dealings, but he did not suffer inconvenience from any quarter. No one got the better of him in the City, and he wasn't inconvenienced at home, because his genial bullying had long ago utterly subdued his wife. And, as already mentioned, when his son went to the bad, Sir Adrian got rid of him.

To return to that matter of his son, picture Sir Adrian as he proceeds on this particular morning toward his office in the City, and imagine him not as he is, amply and elegantly suited, with an open copy of *The Times* on his knee, as he sits at his ease—but naked. He is rosy and smooth in spite of being sixty, but there is a sensitive point—say, between the third and fourth rib on the left side—that reacts painfully to certain thoughts, as if prodded with a sharp stick. This area of his heart has a definite sore patch like an old bruise, and he can still feel it if provoked.

Charlie caused that. His son, Charles, going to Eton and cutting quite a figure, was a source of pride to Sir Adrian once, an absolutely necessary rounding off of his own prestige. He loved his son. He was proud of him. He'd been used to speak of him with a dismissive indulgence that was more revealing than overt pride. He'd say, "Yes, he's going up to Oxford in October," as if everybody's son went to Eton and Oxford, and in a sense they did, from his point of view. Everybody who mattered.

Sir Adrian and his wife went regularly to the school's celebrated yearly open day, the fourth of June, and ate their picnics on Agar's Plough and met their friends and their friends' children and watched the rowing. You could even have called Sir Adrian an indulgent father. He was never anxious to talk much of Charlie's occasional problems. Sir Adrian would say that Charles was growing up, and as long as whatever it was didn't inconvenience his father, there was no need to talk about it. On occasion it happened that Charlie had badly needed to talk, but the opportunity had not been forthcoming.

When Charlie's three years at university were over, the move from Oxford to the City was another step that should have been as smooth as all the rest. Sir Adrian opened another bottle of champagne, and Charlie, like a tall, blond, thin sheep, went meekly through into the next field of endeavor. He appeared for his first morning's work in the Room in Lloyd's without having once caused his father the tedium of serious discussions of the work that might really suit him. Sir Adrian arranged everything in the best possible way, and what could be wrong with that?

Following that sharp jab to the heart (or the amour propre,

in his case the two terms being interchangeable), Sir Adrian's sense of well-being on this particular morning faded slightly. He sat with his copy of *The Times* unopened, while James drove with faultless calm down West Halkin Street and into Belgrave Square. Through the car window Sir Adrian looked at the still bare but budding trees and the daffodils in the square, which were beginning to break open their yellow trumpets in the grass.

Nowadays he made a point of never thinking of his son. It was not that he had completely forgotten the charm that Charles had had when he was a boy, or the promise of his early youth. But he had the sense, as he pointed out to the boy's mother and as he reminded himself now, to accept that the boy had turned out to be no good. It was better not to remember Charles as he had been when, as a little fellow, with such a good sporting sort of look and fine blond hair, he had first gone up to Eton. Better to put all that out of mind. He had turned into a weak, ill-disciplined youth who couldn't keep his fingers off the dirty little drugs some wastrel had introduced him to at Oxford, and that was that. Nevertheless, as the memory prodded Sir Adrian on this occasion, the sensitive place reacted, and he looked up sharply and stared out of the window with an expression of grim disapproval. A woman drawing level in a Ford Fiesta glanced his way and happened to catch his eye. For an instant the brooding grandee and the startled housewife looked at each other, before the flow of traffic separated them forever.

Sir Adrian deserved to be called a grandee because of his title, his figure, and his wealth. He was no jumped-up modern baronet, but the ninth in direct succession. Although he had inherited wealth, he had greatly increased it by his own efforts. His chosen field in business was Lloyd's of London. As a young man with money and connections available, he had preferred it to the Stock Exchange. Anyone could work on the Stock Exchange, and make a fortune too, if the ability was there. But Lloyd's had a special cachet.

He tried now to turn his thoughts in that pleasing direction in which his own special talents—the clubman's enjoyment of comparing personalities and the scholar's and moneyed man's skill at assessment—could have free rein. But for some reason on this occasion the subject of Charles continued to obtrude. When Sir Adrian found his thoughts on the brink of reliving that disgraceful scene when Charles, newly appointed to the box at Lloyd's, was found at work in a state of collapse from an overdose of cocaine, he slid open the glass between himself and the driver and said, "Can't you get us out of this traffic, James? I'm going to be late if this carries on."

"I'm sorry, sir," the man said. "There's been an accident on Westminster Bridge."

"What sort of an accident?"

"Builder's crane, sir."

"Where did you hear that?"

"On the radio this morning, sir."

"Really!" In that case, Adrian thought, why hadn't the fellow changed the route and gone via Trafalgar Square. But he said nothing. Can't make a silk purse out of a sow's ear. James was paid to drive, not think. He opened his copy of *The Times* at last. Charlie was forgotten.

In due course—a little late but the idea had ceased to annoy him—Sir Adrian's car drew up outside his office. James came round to open the door, and Sir Adrian got out and walked grandly up the broad steps and into the building. As he passed the commissionaires' desks both men acknowledged him with that flourish of respect reserved for distinguished men, and smiling, he stepped into the elevator being held open for him. And if the racing tips that Carter was giving him as they glided up to the fourth floor (Sir Adrian was adept at small, flattering attentions paid to working men if they were on his team) had been replaced by a whispered account of Charles's latest misdemeanor in L.A., Adrian would merely have pursed his lips with scorn at the idea of his son having the power or the wit to do him any harm.

And indeed, although Charlie might have wanted to give "the old bastard" a setback, it was by no means a foregone conclusion that he would succeed. Take this forged document that was on its way from America. Following the wise practice of old Lloyd's hands, Sir Adrian always reinsured old years from his own to other syndicates on a regular basis, in much the same way that a bookie lays off a bet. Several of his syndicates went back to the 1930s, and as a matter of course he regularly looked at all the main headings of past business with the underwriters with a view to weeding out any years that might contain items of cover still capable of causing trouble and reinsuring the risk elsewhere. At Lloyd's this established practice of pass-the-parcel was called buying a "run-off." And it so happens that the forged Santhill document would fit neatly into the bundle of a number of years that Sir Adrian had, in this manner, passed on to someone else. It was not a syndicate of his that would have to pay. And so the elevator glided ruthlessly up to the fourth floor, with Sir Adrian safely inside.

*7*here are worse places to be than the city of London on a sunny morning in spring, but not according to Rachel Grimmond, B.A. Oxon., twenty-four, broker, and niece of Sir Adrian, arriving late as usual at her desk in the offices of Steiger and Wallace.

The divisional director of American nonmarine reinsurance, a man named John Grise—torn between the need to take her to task for her lateness and his own desire for approval from the owner of those heavenly legs and that beautiful little backside stretching too short a skirt into too shapely a shape—had been watching the clock. About nine hours after Dale Falcus arrived home from work in California, Rachel, in a mood as blistering and downhearted but for different reasons—in her case due entirely to an uncompromising contempt for business life and a coltish, unbroken attitude to the desk and the office—arrived in the broking room and came to an abrupt halt just inside the door. John Grise had beckoned to her through the glass wall of his adjoining office.

The other brokers, who had been at their desks for more than an hour, made the odd gibe as she passed, in several cases combined with ill-timed attempts to get her to have lunch with them. John Grise's opening remark was not all that different. He said, "Good afternoon, Rachel."

She acknowledged the quip with a short and threatening smile, and he floundered. From among the various papers on his desk he took a firm hold of one, glanced at it, and turned it over. The gesture had no significance. It was a device, like the tight-rope walker carrying a pole. He said, "Sit down a moment."

She sat.

"It's about this difficult syndicate reinsurance run-off that's been going the rounds. I gather from Miles that he couldn't get any underwriter to accept it, and he's passed the slip on to you."

The paper he had under his hand was the latest bundle of run-offs from the Grimmond syndicates. There was no outward and visible sign of the little bit of semtex Charlie Grimmond had attached to the package; or of the claim for $25,000,000 that would shortly follow it. But all forms of excess risk business especially to do with America were unpopular at the time.

"How did you get on?" John Grise now asked. His manner was friendly, but he had an ulterior motive in questioning her, and this particular slip provided the pretext; namely, that if it turned out that yesterday was one of the afternoons that Rachel had spent in her health club in Fulham or having lunch in a restaurant in the West End, as usual, with her friends when other brokers were industriously combing the market for business, he'd have her—as far as work was concerned—where he wanted her. The gentlemanly traditions of the City did not easily allow for giving the officer class the sack, and as a broker working for Steiger and Wallace, Rachel came into that category. But he hoped to be able to shame her into conformity.

He was out of luck.

"I got Bob Keats to take it," she said.

"Bob Keats!" He was incredulous. "At Lloyd's? Syndicate TT4? Surely Miles had tried him?"

"I believe he did," Rachel said, "but I got Bob to change his mind."

"How?"

He accidentally let an admonitory tone into his voice as if

he were accusing her of prostitution, and in fact, a girl like this one (he had one sister himself who was working in a flower shop while waiting to get married) was so totally beyond his ken he did, for an instant, wonder.

She read his mind and laughed. She laughed heartily with just a hint of cruelty and recrossed her legs. He blushed.

"Well, how did you persuade him?"

The answer was that Rachel had gone to Bob Keats's box and stood there for half an hour in the broker's queue reading *Frankenstein* by Mary Shelley. When she got to the head of the queue, she put her book back in the slipcase and took out the slip. Bob Keats should have given it all his attention. He pretended at first not to notice her legs as she sat down beside him on the bench, and then he found a pretext to keep her waiting by asking a question of his deputy, Nigel Store-Smith. Rachel's mane of blond hair was tied up that day but not, needless to say, in a smooth tycoon chignon. Bob Keats noticed that too. He noticed everything about her: the beautiful eyes, the long lashes, and the rebellious aura that, subdued by her politeness, tantalized his volatile cockney heart. He turned back to her with a matter-of-fact air and took the slip in his fingers. He looked surprised.

"Is this the business John Grise rang me up about?"

She nodded, leaning toward him and looking at the paper over his arm. "Uh-huh." He looked sideways at her, taking full advantage of the circumstances to let his stare linger with a deliberate challenge on her profile, poised so close to his eye.

"You've written a number of run-offs for 23TZ," Rachel pointed out.

Bob pressed a key on his computer to check a file on the screen.

"Adrian Grimmond's agency?"

"Yes."

"Aren't you Rachel Grimmond?" he said after a pause.

"My uncle," she said with a wicked smile that widened her eyes and curved the corners of her lips right over. "Steiger and Wallace broke quite a lot of business for his syndicates. I happen to work for Steiger and Wallace."

"Well, well."

He pretended to get to work, but you couldn't say he was fully concentrating as he certainly should have done. Run-offs, although there was a fashion for them just then, were high risk.

"What can you tell me about this?"

Miles had briefed Rachel on the run-off on the basis of what was known at the time. She relayed the various assurances to Bob Keats, and he enjoyed listening to her. "I'm not keen," he said. In fact, he had got his business and other interests thoroughly confused, and when he said that, he thought that he was lying. "What can you offer to persuade me?"

She blushed.

"Lunch?" he asked.

"Can't afford it."

"Well, I'll have to pay then, won't I?"

She was taken aback. She laughed, although she didn't really like it. "Okay."

And he took up the syndicate stamp, thumped it on the inkpad, stamped the slip, and signed it.

Rachel now recounted an edited version of this scene, and John Grise said, trying not to sound disappointed, "You did very well."

She said "Thank you" crisply. Negotiating such a sale came low on her list of life's achievements, but John Grise couldn't understand her attitude. He thought she was quick-witted, beautiful, badly behaved, very well-educated, defiant, and vulnerable, and he certainly couldn't make head nor tail of her.

She left his office, and for a moment he watched her cross the room outside. She walked between the shoulder-high partitions between the desks, seeing through the far window the ghost of the sun shining grimly on the gray walls of the building opposite, and within the broking room the school clock on the wall and the fluorescent light fittings with the corpses of dead flies trapped inside.

The men looked up as she passed, as did the two girls, also brokers, who happened to be better at getting out of bed in the morning. "Not better at getting into it, though," the men would wittily observe, given half a chance. Melissa Cole, with her shining bob of tycoon hair, the earring off her right ear lying on the desk as she held her phone clamped to her head, waved at Rachel simultaneously smiling and mouthing the word "lunch." Rachel nodded back to her and smiled as she picked up her own receiver, which was ringing. She had time to throw her bag on the floor, sit, open the left-hand drawer of the desk with her free hand, and pull out her slipcase before at last a voice at the other end said, "Rachel. Is that you, Rachel?"

It was not, after all, going to be a totally ordinary day. This was not a broker in Arizona trying to lay off an infestation of mite on chicken farms, or another with an equally fascinating bit of business on, say, catastrophe re-insurance. Past experience told her that the voice, sounding distant and confused but which she nevertheless recognized, was being hampered in its communication not by the limitations of modern technology but by the build-up of drugs in the system of the caller. It was her cousin, Charlie Grimmond, calling from Los Angeles. With the familiar pang of simultaneous compassion and irritation, she nevertheless said warmly, "Hello, Charlie. What's up? How are you?"

There was silence. The line seemed to have gone dead. She pressed the bar impatiently, risking making it go deader. Now that she was at her desk, she was acutely conscious of the time and of work needing to be done. She suddenly remembered an unattended memo from the day before still between the pages of her diary. She was about to put the phone down when Charlie managed to say, "Rachel!" again. Then, "Listen . . ."

"Go on, Charlie," she urged him, in the teeth of another silence. "I'm listening."

She bit the inside of her lip and waited. Talking to Charlie hadn't always been like trying to have a conversation with an insect stuck on its back. He had even been one of the adolescent heroes of her childhood, and between that laughing, friendly boy and the pathetic drug addict who went to live in L.A., she had no prejudice to interpose as a barrier. Just an affectionate, irritated, bored tolerance—and pity.

"Charlie?" she groaned. "For heaven's sake, I'm at work! Are you still there?"

"Rachel." He laughed, not quite meaninglessly. "Rachel! How lovely to hear your voice. How are you, Rachel?"

"Okay," she said. "How's America?"

"I've got something to tell you," he said. "Listen."

But when he started to assemble the words to describe the forgery and the way he'd managed to remember one of his father's syndicate numbers to pick up the bill, he started to laugh again before he could get a single word out, and couldn't stop.

She let him go on for what seemed like minutes, not liking to snap the thread and send him back in such an obvious state of collapse into the oblivion of an unconnected line. As soon as she had a chance, she said, "Look, Charlie—"

"Wait. Wait! I've got to tell you. This insurance document for general liability, you see, and I put . . ." He couldn't stop himself. "This missal is a missile. I know it's not a sacred text, but all the same—get it?" He laughed again and yelled in an American accent, "This missal is a missile!"

She cupped her hand over the mouthpiece and shouted discreetly down it, "Charlie!"

No one else in the room looked up. They were all engrossed, working away as if their lives depended on it. Charlie came to his senses.

"Sorry. But I must tell you . . ."

She wasn't really listening anymore. John Grise was coming out of his office.

"I've got to go, Charlie," she said. "Are you all right? Are you thinking of coming over?"

"Yes. Yes. I might one day. I can stay in your flat, can't I, baby?"

She said yes.

"But don't go. I had something to say. I wanted to warn you about something. What was it, Rachel?"

"Search me, Charlie," she said. "How should I know? Hello? Hello?"

But he had disappeared back into the twilight world of drug addiction. Anyone in normal circumstances might have thought that the biggest warning that he had to offer was not to take cocaine.

CHAPTER 7

*7*he broker's blond hair, the polished wood under the paper, the feel of the bench beneath him, and even a glint of gold from the ring on his own finger as he brought the syndicate's rubber stamp smartly down on the slip—like a man meeting his death in a sudden accident, Bob Keats saw all these details flash past his inner eye when, three months after the event, the run-off reinsurance that Rachel had broked to him went up in smoke. For about sixty seconds he tried to take it calmly, as John Grise and his claims manager, Jack Colehearn, having arrived by prior appointment in Bob's office, proceeded to describe the details of the Santhill claim.

But it couldn't be done. At the same time as he concentrated on what John Grise was telling him, Bob Keats was momentarily tormented by these visual memories of the circumstances surrounding his acceptance of the business. That moment had cost his syndicate—or apparently was going to cost his syndicate—$25,000,000, and he literally couldn't, for a moment, take it in. And yet, at the same time, since he was an underwriter and dealt in such reversals of fortune, that "couldn't" had more of furious unwillingness in it. If it had been about somebody else, he could have believed it easily enough, and the process of mental assimilation would not have caused this burning and throttling sensation that he was experiencing now.

He managed to ask his deputy for the relevant logbook, and while he held out his hand to take it, he looked, with his stocky figure in the suit that had recently become a bit tight, as phlegmatic as anyone could expect. Only it wasn't going to last.

John Grise eyed him with wary stoicism. He knew this loss would be a bitter pill for Bob Keats to swallow and he half expected, what with Bob's reputation for falling back on the habits of his cockney childhood when roused, to have it spat back in his own face.

"Show me this so-called policy," Keats demanded.

Jack Colehearn held out the forged paper. Bob Keats took it and pinched it between his fingers. The paper held its lying face still under his scrutiny; all the slightly archaic wordings, the rather pretty random stamps from the Lloyd's policy signing office, and so on. A thin sheet of india paper attached to one side of it in the old manner of those days listed all the Lloyd's member's names in minute print. All there. All present and correct.

"Is there something wrong with it?" John Grise asked suddenly in a sharp hopeful tone.

"No, no. Nothing like that," Jack Colehearn said thoughtfully, and the misguided assurance dropped from his lips unnoticed.

Bob Keats lowered the paper and said venomously, "Show me the valuation."

Jack Colehearn took it out of the file that had been compiled, neatly summarizing once again the details of the EPA's authority as he handed it over.

As Bob surveyed it, his perspective shifted. He had been on the verge of blustering, but the more he took in this situation, the more his anger distilled in the heat of its own fire.

"You assured me," he said with hatred directed at John

Grise, "that this old run-off year from one of the Grimmond syndicates was clean, so what's this Environmental Agency charge against Santhill Chemicals doing in it?"

John Grise, pale and unhappy but correct, nodded. "As far as we knew, Bob," he said. "You knew, I knew, that records on an old year like this are always incomplete and that from thirty years ago something always *can* emerge that was forgotten. In this case, it has."

He finished the sentence with his head, his body, poised tensely in an attitude of anxious conciliatory firmness. His face slightly poked forward, his eyes fixed earnestly on Bob Keats, he held the pose for a moment in silence, hoping for reassurance, but none came.

"What about the underwriter on the Grimmond syndicate who passed this on?" Keats finally spat out, almost ignoring him. "Remind me who it is, Nigel."

Nigel Store-Smith and Jack Colehearn replied in unison, "Stan Lacy."

"Didn't he know something of this when he decided to buy the run-off? I don't believe he knew nothing of this. Get him on the phone, Nigel."

John Grise was shocked. "I can assure you, Bob," he said urgently, as Nigel Store-Smith picked up the phone, "Stan Lacy was under the same impression as that which he passed on to me—no serious risks to come. Speak to him by all means; but I assure you that this particular combined general liability policy wasn't included in the business he knew about or notified to me. But the wording of the overall cover given at the time made no exclusion that can be said to cut it out, so we're stuck with it. And look at the date. The EPA have only just slapped the order on Santhill."

Bob Keats made no response to this long speech except a stony stare, and all three of them listened to the deputy making contact with the Grimmond Managing Agency on the phone and being told Stan Lacy had already gone to the box.

"Ring him at Lloyd's then and tell him I want to see him at four this afternoon."

The message was duly passed on, while Bob Keats sat with every line of his body signaling combat, from the set of his mouth to his back muscles to the flex of his fingers and the direction of his gaze, which had lost the matter-of-fact ellipse of normal times and hit its targets—first Nigel completing the phone call and then the hapless John Grise—in a straight hard line. "I'll tell you this," Bob Keats said, "for nothing. It's a pick-up!"

Both John Grise and Jack Colehearn looked at first as if they didn't understand what was being said, although a "pick-up" was a familiar Lloyd's term.

"You know what I mean by pick-up," Bob Keats said. "You've heard the expression, I take it."

"How do you make that out?" Jack Colehearn eventually said in tones of frigid disgust.

Bob's face was no longer pale. His eyes sparked with aggression. He leaned forward and the movement looked as if it might almost tear the taut bracken-colored tweed of his suit. He had one hand flat on his desk. His short fingers were manicured, and he stabbed one of them on the leather twice as he repeated "pick-up!" He paused but not long enough to be interrupted. With his mouth pressed shut, he rubbed the inside of his bottom lip with his tongue. "It was a clear case of deliberate nondisclosure," he went on. "Someone knew and didn't tell. A Grimmond syndicate needs a run-off. They know damn well something's in the pipeline. Look at the EPA report! It was already active when I accepted this rubbish. And who do you send to my box? Rachel Grimmond. Don't tell me that's a coincidence. Or that a nice juicy morsel like her wasn't used to keep my eye off the ball." He seemed unaware, in his fury, of having very nearly made a rather terrible pun. "All tits and blond hair, not to mention John Grise's pious reassurances, and I sign something that's going to cost my syndicate twenty-five million dollars! Well, you can think again."

"Look, Bob . . ."

"I don't want any contribution here, thank you, Nigel,"

Keats said without even deflecting his eyes from their target. "My mind's made up."

"Don't you think you should make a few inquiries first?" Jack Colehearn asked in a mild tone that was meant to have a cutting edge to it.

"Certainly I'll make some inquiries," Bob said, "but if I don't know a rotten egg when I smell one, where do you think I've been all this time?"

A quick flush of anger momentarily lit up John Grise's prosaic features. Bob Keats's temper hardened at the sight of it.

"That's all I've got to say for the moment." He rapped out the words with a dead nonreturnable spin. "I'll let you know." Nevertheless, he went on as his two visitors got to their feet, "if anyone pays on this one"—and he gave a last contemptuous flick to the document—"my guess is that it will have to be the original syndicate that issued it. And I don't take kindly to the attempt you've made to pass it on to me. I'll tell you that for nothing!"

He didn't get up to see his guests out. When the door was closed behind them, he picked up the document again and spent three seconds staring at it. And the glare of his eyes rested, like a cigarette burn, on the syndicate number that Charlie had put there.

CHAPTER 8

*S*arah Grimmond, the wife of Sir Adrian, sat by the looking glass in her bedroom trying to fix an earring in the pierced lobe of her ear. Whether she herself embodied the gray shadow in the glass or vice versa was a moot point that few would have thought worth working out. She was the sort of woman whose real existence, on casual inspection, was entirely vouched for by her clothes and her belongings. Behind her or in front of her—whichever way it was—the flesh and blood figure of Sir Adrian loomed up, ruddy with life and that version of good humor that has to do with habits of wealth and power.

He put a glass of champagne down on the embroidered cloth and said, "Here you are, my dear."

Sarah said thank-you in the same perfectly satisfied tone with which another woman might accept a library ticket. At last she fitted the little gold butterfly clip onto the back of the single pearl earring. "I meant to ask Jonathan to dinner," she said, as she took hold of the glass and lifted it, "for Rachel. You remember she's dining with us tonight?"

"Thank God you didn't."

"You like him don't you?" She sipped the champagne.

"Oh, he's all right. But he's too dull for Rachel. Rachel's got a bit of zip in her."

Sir Adrian was fond of his niece, who had also been his ward since her parents had died in a plane crash during her last year at school. Just before getting up, Sarah checked once more on her appearance. She was immaculate. In her very conventional way she was elegant, with her thick gray hair, cut short, her jewelry, manicured hands, silk underclothes, while her mind was an inventory of polished silver, thank-you letters, menus, the general management of Sir Adrian's home life.

Adrian had now gone back into the drawing room, and Sarah was about to follow him. At this time of year the light was very pretty around half past seven, and drawing one of the bedroom curtains, she paused to look through the large windows out over Cadogan Square. Rachel, who was just walking from the Knightsbridge underground, had not yet come into view. There were still daffodils in the square, and now the subdued glow of windows shining to the right.

Sarah arranged the curtains neatly before turning her back, picking up her glass, glancing with satisfaction over the room. Nothing was out of place. She walked through to the dining room. Everything received her attention: the dove-gray carpet, the flowers, the lamps that were on and those that were off, the time in relation to the food planned for dinner, and then Adrian speaking on the phone in the drawing room, and the muted sound of the television from the library next door.

It was not that the evening was designed for anything more than a quiet family supper, but Sarah marshaled all the details with care. If she was watchful enough, there would be no gap in which to remember Charlie. In the drawing room she set down her glass and turned to pick up the *Evening Standard* from the table where Adrian always left it for her; even so, it was as if some ghost plucked her sleeve as she calmly sat, unable to dodge the remote sting of grief.

Her mind was like her house would be if there was one room in it that, unlike all the other well-ordered, fragrant rooms, stank to high heaven with the corpse of her only child. Charlie might not be dead in the real sense, but he had been declared dead to all intents and purposes by Sir Adrian. And all the nice arrangements of Sarah's existence were conditional upon that decree being endorsed without fuss. She could neither talk about Charlie nor try to help him nor have news of him. All her colorless arrangements—her housekeeping, her social life, her home, her friends—were ordered with exactness precisely to circumvent that one unopened room, the existence of which was never out of her mind.

Rachel, now walking across Pont Street and starting down Cadogan Square, looked forward to the conversation before her for the evening, calculating that the uproar over the run-off with Bob Keats would provide a lively subject for discussion with her uncle.

Sir Adrian himself opened the door and welcomed her in. As always, and rather gallantly, he kissed her and walked through with his arm around her shoulder in a way designed to make it plain that despite his age and kinship he could still appreciate a beautiful young girl when he saw one. To Sarah, who rose humbly from her chair as they came into the room, the two of them looked dashing and brave in a way that she shrank from but with simultaneous gestures of admiration and affection. She kissed Rachel almost with warmth, while recoiling from the smell of daffodils and spring twilight that seemed unbearably to cling to the bodies of the young and reminded her of Charlie.

"Sit down, dear," she said. "You must be very tired after running about all day."

"Tired?" Adrian said. "You're not tired are you, Rachel? I shouldn't think they give you enough to do in that office of yours to tire a flea!"

"Oh, no!" she laughed.

He handed her a glass of champagne, and she took a sip from it before deciding where to sit. "You might have a different idea of it, Uncle Adrian, when I tell you what's been going on there today."

"And what may that be?"

"One of your syndicates used my firm to broke some dud run-off years that were described as being harmless—and there's hell to pay."

He looked up from refilling his glass with the familiar expression of quickened interest.

"Really. You don't mean T6SM?"

"No. Stan Lacy's syndicate."

"Ah." Sir Adrian stood there for a moment holding the bottle delicately out with his right hand, and with his left meditatively fingering the buttonhole of his coat. "Now I remember. Dead years. American liability but nothing live. Nothing could go wrong with that!"

"Not even when the underwriter in 1958 left the cover open ended and renewed for five years in succession?"

He considered that but still dismissed it.

"Why did you buy the run-off then?" Rachel asked.

He put his head on one side with a humorous lowering of the eyelids at this challenge. "Well now . . ."

From where she was sitting, the lowness of the armchair having apparently doubled the length of her legs so that she was hard pressed to know where to put them, Rachel kept her eye on his until he resumed his sentence.

"I rather go in for it," he said with a bit of an air, as if he was talking about racing or the opera. "It's a routine precaution with old years of account. It looks good to member agents. Just in case."

"In case of what?"

"In case." He looked mockingly at her. "Are you going to tell me what this is about?"

"A claim for twenty-five million dollars."

"Twenty-five million dollars!"

He widened his eyes and looked at her with the exaggerated expression of a genial adult listening to a child's account of a goblin. She was used to being teased by him and merely waited in this case, with a dry look.

"You're not serious, I hope," he said eventually.

"Yes, I am. Stan Lacy gave the years to John Grise to broke, and I actually took the slip around the Room in Lloyd's, as it happens."

"Successfully?"

"Oh, yes!" she said. "Twenty-five million dollars' worth of toxic waste pollution. All included in that package of old years that your underwriter said was harmless. I got Bob Keats to take it."

"More fool him," said Adrian.

Sarah looked at her watch and stood up.

"Come along, you two," she said. "I won't have you arguing about business all evening like you did last time. The soup will be getting cold."

They both obediently rose and started to follow her, but Adrian said, "Where did this toxic waste come from?"

"An American chemicals firm called Santhill."

"1958 you said. Pollution wasn't heard of then."

"Exactly. Your underwriter of the day didn't think to exclude it."

"And you've seen the original insurance document?"

Sarah waved her niece to a chair and went over to the alcove where Cook had left the soup on a hot tray. As soon as she had her back to them, Sarah stopped listening to Rachel's account of the EPA and Bob Keats. She rarely listened to the content of any conversation that Adrian was involved in. She listened only to the general tone in order to keep check on his humor. It wasn't that she herself was capable of doing a thing about it on the rare occasions that his masterful equanimity was disturbed, but she needed to know about it, like a prisoner of war monitoring the humor of his guards. She took the lid off the soup tureen and started to fill the bowls with a silver ladle. When she was a girl, she had longed to go to the university, but her father thought that educating women was a waste of time and money. Now in middle age, this woman of society whose soup bowls were Spode and whose husband gave her champagne to drink before dinner had been persuaded to repudiate all contact with her only child. She stoically dressed in tidy clothes and cared about being neat in serving up the soup. "Thank you, dear," she murmured, as Rachel appeared at her side to hand the plates.

"Bob Keats is that East End fellow, isn't he?" Adrian's

voice chimed in, as he circled the table with the mineral water and continued his uninterrupted conversation with Rachel. "The bright one, with that namby-pamby Old Etonian deputy, Squeaky Smith's son, Nigel."

"That's right."

"And you say he won't pay?"

"He says someone must have known about this more serious risk buried in the old years—either Stan Lacy, my boss, or me—and whether it's conspiracy or nondisclosure, he won't pay."

"Don't want to, you mean!"

"He says *won't*. He's going to law."

"That's bad," Adrian said. "There's far too much of that going on."

"You don't seem very worried, Uncle Adrian," Rachel said after a pause when they were all seated.

"I'm not." He smiled his quirky superior smile and crumbled a piece of bread with the tips of the fingers of his left hand. "I'm not, m'dear. Yet."

"Well, I am," she said. "I leaned on Bob to get him to take that run-off reinsurance. It's not as if he was keen."

"Susceptible to a pretty girl, is he?" Adrian laughed with a knowing glance directed at her over his glass.

"Not anymore, he isn't," she said.

The story of this run-off reinsurance from one of his own syndicates to Bob Keats kept Adrian amused from the beginning to the end of dinner. He took the view that the arrival of girls as equals working in the City—clever graduates of the best universities like Rachel—was an asset, and something his generation would get used to and would enjoy if they had any sense. He reflected on the matter of Bob Keats's response to the fix he was in, and a small judicious smile gave his broad face, his short bony nose, his hooded eye, an air of slightly playful seriousness, as he considered the question. His attitude was that of a habitual winner who has succeeded once again in getting rid of a rotten apple out of his own basket just in time. As for his beautiful little niece, she was in a man's world now, my dear, and he would watch her deal with it with interest.

When he said as much, she took it in good part. If she had been talking to one of her own contemporaries, she'd have made some biting comment, but to her uncle she trimmed her sails. She always suspected that in spite of his liberal talk his good nature was partly dependent on the certainty that as a man among women he would always win.

"I will deal with it," she said. "Bob Keats is not so different from you, you know, Uncle Adrian."

"Indeed!"

"Yes. He also looks on pretty women as privileged interlopers, provided that in the last resort they know their place."

Sir Adrian gave an exclamation of laughter and then said,

"You give Bob Keats a run for his money. Don't let him get away with anything."

"I'm the one doing the running just at the moment," she said. "They say in the great book of Chinese wisdom that the female fox walking on thin ice needs to beware of the especial danger of falling in and being dragged down by the tail."

CHAPTER 9

A few days later—on the Wednesday after he had informed his lawyer that he was denying liability, and news
of the claim and his response to it had already begun to spread
in the market—Bob Keats stepped off his train from Kent in the
morning, threw his copy of the *Daily Mail* in the litter bin as he
walked down Eastcheap and backed straight into Rachel Grimmond.

It gave him a start. As far as his other colleagues were
concerned, he knew where he bloody well was: no concessions,
no mealymouthed compromises from Nigel Store-Smith. Bob
Keats was built for fighting.

But now, backing off from Rachel on the sidewalk and
looking up at her, he flushed and, with an involuntary touch of
artificiality like an old stagehand, apologized profusely.

"Rachel!" he exclaimed, "I wasn't looking where I was
going. I'm so sorry. Did I hurt you?"

"No," she said. "Not at all."

In fact, the sole of his shoe had cut a scratch on her instep.
She wore high heels and no stockings.

"I'm terribly sorry."

"Honestly, I'm all right, Bob."

"We're going the same way, aren't we?" he said. "I need to talk to you about that run-off. Not now. But how about lunch?"

She was taken aback. Her immediate reaction was dismay, although she didn't show it. And she felt she couldn't refuse. As she walked along beside him, she was at the same time reassured and slightly uneasy at his manner. If he wanted to discuss the Santhill claim, she would have expected him to make an appointment in the office. But as she simultaneously realized, through the official channels he would get John Grise or Jack Colehearn, or even Archer Brandon as he had already done, but not her.

"I can do that," she said.

"Good. How about Pratt's wine bar, one o'clock?"

"One o'clock then." She assumed he wanted an informal exchange on the subject, and to do it in a way that showed he had no hard feelings.

If Bob had no hard feelings, then the red double-decker bus that passed just as he reached his turning off and drowned the sound of his voice as he said good-bye to Rachel was driving on its roof with its wheels in the air. He had hard feelings all right, and now that the moment of inspiration that had led him to conceal them for ten minutes was over, these feelings reasserted themselves and literally drained the blood from his face. He looked exhausted as he continued on his way toward his office, locked in bitter thought. And the reflection hurting him most was that any woman could have the power to injure him in a way he couldn't immediately sort out with the back of his hand. Until he reached the very door of his own office, Rachel stayed in his thoughts. He ground the memory of that bit of business she'd led him into in the teeth of his mind. The objective he had for this lunch was to give himself an opportunity to wring out of her an admission of complicity—with Stan Lacy, Grimmond's management, John Grise, or the whole lot. He didn't care, just so long as he got her to admit that someone knew, someone at least suspected, someone used her to sweeten the hidden pill.

Bob Keats spent an unpleasant morning in his office. He had to go down to the box for half an hour before lunch, and from there in due course, keeping a sharp eye on the time, he went to his rendezvous with Rachel. The wine bar was crowded. He managed, after some shoving, to get a table and install Rachel at it. But around the bar itself, their voices clanging on the hard red-tiled floor, a mixture of City muckers and bright young financial types ate their sandwiches and knocked back their drinks standing up. It was only the wish to lull her suspicions and avoid any embarrassing sensation of déjà vu that had led Bob to choose this restaurant. He liked the more sophisticated places himself. He looked back from the bar, where he was thrashing about getting food and wine, and saw Rachel, with her long legs with the high instep and slim ankles crossed and to him she looked at ease. She had it all her own way.

He measured her. He unconsciously measured the distance between them like a predator, a restless shadow circling its prey among the chairs and tables.

When eventually he returned to her with a bottle of wine and two glasses, a mess of conflicting feelings, among them despised but irrepressible class consciousness and the desire to conceal his purpose, prompted another unintentionally grotesque parody of gallant manners.

"I'm sorry!" he said emphatically. "I really am!"

"What for?" she said. "This is great."

"Drink up," he said. "I'll be back in a minute."

She poured herself a glass of wine and drank it like lemonade while she waited for him to fight his way back to the food counter. After ten minutes he returned. She said, "Bob! You should have let me help you."

"Why?" he said, looking down at her. "A lady like you, in that scrum?"

"I'm perfectly used to it."

He didn't believe her. But he wished he could. If he had had time to follow his dream mind through a few frames, he would have watched her drag an iron bucket across a cement floor and scrub that floor hard, and the sight would have been balm to him. And yet, at exactly the same time, he felt an exaggerated respect for the fact that such an experience would be outside the realm of possibility. It was the mixture of the two that curdled him. It was why he was about to behave in the way he did.

"Right! Let's talk about it!" He sat down. "Pâté, olives, bread, smoked salmon. You can have cake later if you're a good girl."

Like any woman, from a double first graduate in physics to a prostitute, Rachel swallowed the remark about the cake without gagging or even appearing to notice. She flashed him a smile, which was what she knew she was meant to do. So far, inwardly savage with rebellion but outwardly compliant, she could go. Toward Bob she was more chivalrous than she would have dreamt of being to Nigel Store-Smith, for example, if he had tried the same tack.

"Now. This bloody run-off—excuse my language. Have you any idea what it's going to cost me?"

"I have," she said. "Of course. I was at the meeting."

He plunged into his prepared approach, and all the time he was thinking to himself as he talked and she talked back, "She's bright. She's bright as a fucking button. All the more reason why she knew what she was doing." He refilled her glass and his own. A waiter happened to be passing, and with a telepathic dynamism that was remarkable in the circumstances, he penetrated the boy's "need to know" defenses and commanded another bottle.

"What beats me," he said to Rachel, when he'd got it and done some more pouring, "is the timeliness of it all. You've got to admit it."

"How do you mean?"

"Stan Lacy. Don't you think it was an extraordinarily timely bit of off-loading for his syndicate."

She began to reiterate her assurances, but he suddenly cut her off. He leaned forward and did what he had been meaning to do the whole time: he put his hand on her leg. She repressed her reaction. There was always another reason to make allowances. Her father, when giving her advice about men, had once said to her, "Remember, a man always knows where his hands are." But the joke lies in the apparently irrepressible tendency on the part of women to think that, on any given occasion, he doesn't: that somehow it's not his fault his hand has got where it has: that it's some kind of accident.

Rachel imagined that in the enthusiasm of the discussion Bob probably thought he had his hand on the table.

He said, "Come on now, Rachel. Between the two of us. I won't let you down."

"What do you mean?" she said. She hadn't the faintest idea what he was getting at.

He bit his lip and tried to look coy. Then he sat back. "Just the truth," he said. "You knew." He waited. "Just that. You knew. I'm not saying it was your fault. Pressures . . . But you're an extremely bright girl. You knew what you were at."

"You mean you still think I helped them to pull a fast one on you?"

"Got it in one."

"Well, I didn't," she said. "And really, Bob, neither did anyone else. That piece of business wasn't on record. I think it was arrogant of the old market not to keep better records—if you want my opinion."

"Oh, yes, I want your opinion!"

In spite of his tone she took no offense. "What else is this sort of cover for?" she asked. "Everyone knows that old years of that sort of vintage can contain dynamite so no one keeps too many. Every now and then a syndicate like 23TZ gets rid of a few in the reinsurance market just as routine, and that's all it was."

"So it was just my bad luck."

She still wasn't hearing any warning. "Yes," she said.

He let her run down to nothing, waited, and then said, "I don't believe you."

This time she couldn't mistake the unpleasant edge that had got into the tone of his voice. She blushed.

"I think," he reiterated, "that it was a pick-up. You may have forgotten, young lady, but I took you out for lunch that day as part of the bargain. Well?"

"That wasn't part of the bargain," she said. "For heaven's sake, that was just a friendly joke. Apart from anything else, no one pays twenty-five million dollars for a lunch date!"

"Did I or didn't I?"

Even if he was drunk, she wasn't going to humor him to the extent of answering that sort of a harangue. She started to get up.

"Sit down!" he said. He lunged forward and grabbed her wrist where she had stretched forward to take her bag. She froze, taking in too late the now frank viciousness of his expression. After a second she bent her knees and sat again.

"What if I was a man who'd broked you some business you regretted?" she asked with tense logic and in a voice that barely shook at the edges. "Are you going to start having punch-ups with them?"

"No," he said. "But no man is going to come to my box with his tits jutting out and his whole body flashing 'come on,' is he?" Her face went white with shock. "You. With your legs and those little hips you jammed up against mine on the bench while you got me to stamp the line." He said this very fast and quiet, and then caught himself up and held his breath pulling himself together for the final stretch.

"Let go my hand!" she said, and half stood again.

For an answer he jerked it tight against the table. The movement attracted fleeting attention from one or two of the crowd. She waited, glaring into his inflamed face, her body half standing braced against her trapped wrist.

"*Sir* Adrian Grimmond"—he emphasized the title with an angry slur, although he was still keeping his voice low—"Sir Adrian Grimmond is your uncle. One of the syndicates belonging to his managing agency stands to get this balls-breaking claim. You are the lady who snuggles a package into my hot little hand, promising there's nothing nasty inside when in fact Santhill's time bomb is in there. And I say—"

"Is there something going on here, Rachel?"

The voice coming unexpectedly from behind Bob made him start, and he lost, and then tightened again, his grip on her wrist.

"There's no need for anyone else to interfere," he said, without looking round. "I've nearly finished what I'm saying."

"Then why not let go her wrist first."

With deliberation he did that and stood up to take a good but unsteady look at the intruder. He said, "Who are you?"

"David Cooper. I work with Rachel."

"Is that so!" There was no shaking of hands.

"So what's the problem?"

"I don't know what the hell it's got to do with you," Bob Keats said, "but listen in if you want to. This"—he paused, as if he was going to bring out a real insult, and then, in a revealing tone of loathing, said "girl" as if he had found exactly the right word—"this girl used all her powers of persuasion to get me to put my syndicate stamp on a line."

"Well, she's a broker, isn't she?" David said. "That's her job."

"Not that kind of persuasion," Bob said. "I fancied her and she knew it. She played on it to get me to take something she knew was going to turn belly up in the water." He ignored David's expression and turned to Rachel. He kept his voice low. He said to her, "Just you remember this, darling. A promise for a promise. If you stick to your story and I have to pay up, so will you." He looked at her for an instant longer. "You know what I mean."

The chaotic activity around them had not abated. In the momentary silence between the three of them a sudden chorus of laughter from a group near the bar sounded like a playful intrusion from another world. Then Bob Keats turned sharply away. He maneuvered himself quite deftly through the furniture and the people, only clipping the odd corner or elbow like a car being driven by a drunk down a side street, and finally disappeared up the stairs.

once well-known children's verse runs as follows:

> *The rain it raineth every day*
> *Upon the just and unjust fella;*
> *But more upon the just because*
> *The unjust hath the just's umbrella.*

Charles Seaford, standing on the terrace of his house in Bel-Air, California, did not know that he had hold of anyone else's umbrella. All he knew was that one minute his company was about to be swept into obscurity by a deluge of crippling compulsory expenditure, and the next Zack Webern had opened this umbrella over his head, this missing insurance cover that had miraculously been found. As of now, the microclimate of Santhill Chemicals had reentered a halcyon phase. The sun had come out again. Charles Seaford, with a glass of champagne in his hand, looked up at the blue sky with profound satisfaction. He had a clear conscience. Let it rain somewhere else. He and his wife, Joannie, were giving a party.

Lee Wexford, the man standing at that moment beside Seaford, was privately amused (in a way, that it was characteristic

of him to be privately amused at something) to feel the vibrations of well-being bouncing off his old friend. He knew that
Seaford had almost been washed up in the recent EPA crisis, and
he was glad his friend had survived. He surveyed the elegant
throng of guests grouped below them on the grass, under the
clipped trees, between the rose beds, with almost as much satisfaction as Charles himself.

"Now, look there," his host said, and made a discreet
gesture with his glass at a group, among whom a slight dapper
figure in a beige suit formed the center. "That's Harvey Sanger,
the property developer, who's come over from New York to
make the deal the papers have been carrying on about."

Lee looked. "Will he sew it up?"

"No!"

Charles said that no in a short clipped way but with a
twinkle in his eye, and Lee threw back his head and laughed as
was intended.

"You know something I don't?"

"Now why should you think that?" Again, he delivered
the playful cliché deadpan, and Lee responded.

"Well . . ."

He was taller than Charles and the skin between his cheekbones and earlobes was puckered in a network of symmetrical
creases that it would have cost a fortune to put there on purpose.
When he mimicked an expression of judicious laughter as he did
now, the creases deepened. Michael Tolyer, a good-looking,
insignificant young man of limitless ambition made, at that moment, to go past the two senior business tycoons with his senses
alert for a break in their conversation that might let him in.
Charles spotted him.

"Come here, Michael," he said, and like a genial cardsharp
he palmed the interesting gossip about Sanger International so
that Lee saw the ace disappear back into the pack, to be replaced
by this shortish dark young knave, who stood waiting to be
introduced.

He shook Michael's hand good-naturedly, but he wasn't
staying. Patronizing keen young men, a benevolence so much

enjoyed by many older men, was not his style. He took in briefly the respectful straight-eyed look, the immaculate clothes of a future savior of the human race—or at least its business community—and left.

"That's Lee Wexford for you," Charles said, shaking his head with smiling disapproval and flattering Michael Tolyer with a confidence. "From one of the oldest and richest families in the States, and he knows it. But he's smart. You remember that." The young man accepted the admonition as if it conferred on him a smattering of the filial protégé's role that he was after.

Lee made good his escape. He thought to himself as he went from the terrace down the flight of stone steps, fifty feet across, imported from some ruined garden in Europe, that he'd pick up that rumor about Harvey Sanger from some other source. On the bottom step he paused to survey the field. He himself was benefiting just now from the same influx of government-guaranteed investment which had launched Sanger, but he didn't depend on it for survival. Governments give and governments can take away, like God. He toyed now, as he stood on the bottom step glass of whiskey in hand, with the idea of the present mood of government changing, in which case Harvey Sanger would be about as comfortable as someone standing on a chair with a noose about his neck who sees a blind and deaf man coming in his direction.

Lee picked another large whiskey off a passing tray. He preferred it to champagne, and so did Zack Webern's son, Daniel, who Lee now realized was standing just beside him.

"Hello, Daniel," Lee said. "How're you doing?"

The youth acknowledged the greeting without smiling, and although he opened his mouth, no sound came out before he reapplied it to the rim of his glass.

"Is your mother here?"

Daniel, in reply, cast Lee a sidelong look of mixed suspicion and gloom. Lee answered himself by spotting Jane Webern among the guests. She stood not far away—chic, thin, and lovely—her straight black hair tied in a knot on the nape of her neck, talking in an animated group of film folk. Although she was thirty yards away across the grass, Lee knew that it was no coincidence that her back was toward her son. Her shoulder blades habitually moved, like those toy windmills that children used to carry down the street, to present themselves at the correct angle with her back toward the unwelcome draught of her son's presence. It was not that she was hard-hearted, but she liked pleasure, and fate had given her a son whose company only a social worker could really enjoy.

Zack felt the same. He also, from time to time, looked up from where he was engrossed in conversation with Dale Falcus in the shade of the Kashmir cypress and cast a furtive resentful glance toward the boy; just checking. Reluctantly he acknowledged Lee's greeting at the same time. He just raised his glass a fraction in mid-sentence and then, catching sight of something over Lee's shoulder, turned his own. Lee looked round. Vincent Cordoba stood on the step above him. The sun also being in that direction, he to some extent blocked it giving to Lee a fleeting impression, before he turned back, of darkness where it hadn't been expected.

"Well, well," Vincent said, "what have we here?"

Both Lee and Daniel continued to stand where they were, shoulder to shoulder, looking out toward the lawn and drinking their whiskey, but Lee said, without again looking round, "Afternoon, Vincent."

Vincent fetched up at the other side of Daniel and said, "Here's looking at you. We whiskey drinkers gotta stick together."

There was no opposition, but at last Lee spotted someone he wouldn't mind talking to.

"What were you two guys talking about before I butted in?" asked Vincent to Daniel, looking after the retreating back of Lee Wexford as the snotty bastard drifted elegantly off across the grass.

Daniel didn't bother to reply.

"Let's see if I can make out by guessing what you were looking at," Vincent said with insinuating friendliness. "There's Isobel Falcus?"

No reaction.

"And there's her brother Bobby, who's younger than you, isn't he?"

No reaction.

"And what about your mother? Where's she? Ah! There she is. Beautiful as ever."

At least Daniel had followed the line of his eye even if he still said nothing.

"She must be proud of you, Daniel, now you've joined your dad's firm, isn't that right?"

The hapless young man shifted his feet and took a huge gulp from the tumbler of whiskey. His fingers were reddened as if he spent his time digging in the garden, and as they gripped the glass, they shook it, although not much. Doing everything by halves, as if he could avoid compromise in this stinking world by withholding some consent even from the simplest commitment, he didn't raise the glass high enough to reach his lips, and had to crane down his neck to drink.

"You were right, you know," Vincent said, watching him. "You were right to dump college and get started at the job. Good thinking."

He'd got his knife in at last where Daniel could feel it. The youth shook his head.

"What do you mean?" Vincent said, as if he'd spoken out loud. "Dad hard to work with?" And he laughed and slapped his arm round Daniel's shoulder. Instead of recoiling, the young man felt a little glimmer of warmth lap at the ice-cold sack of his heart.

"Jeez," he said, and from the corner of his lowered eye he cast Vincent a grateful look.

"Well, see here," Vincent said, "all dads are hard on their sons. You don't want to take too much notice."

"Too much notice! He says if I don't pay a little more attention, he'll throw me out."

"He wouldn't do that," Vincent said.

"You're wrong!" Daniel had got going now. Zack and Dale Falcus had walked off to have a look at the tennis and no one was watching Daniel, and now he'd got this friendly ear, he was going to be as difficult to stop as he had been to get started. "He thinks I'm useless, and he says so right there in front of everybody."

"You mean in front of other staff in the office?"

"Sure." He took another gulp of whiskey. "I'm his son, and he just treats me like shit. I can tell you, he's got no cause to do that. He doesn't have the right."

Vincent was interested. He liked to get under the skin—anyone's skin. There was a climate under there that always interested him.

"Well, look here," he said. "You just stick it out. Your dad's been having a hard time lately. I expect you know the firm was in serious jeopardy there with the EPA. Your dad is the one who found the solution."

The answer came back in a long adolescent sneer. "Yeah," said Daniel Webern. "I know."

Vincent pricked up his ears. "Well, that's something to be proud of, isn't it?" His face wore an expression of wholesome inquiry, like a wolf in sheep's clothing just attending to the sound of a distant shepherd's whistle.

"That depends," said Daniel.

"On what?"

He had to wait for it. As he waited, he inadvertently held himself with extraordinary stillness. Even a sudden small gust of wind that made a snatch at Lindy Packer's short lightweight skirt and caused a ripple of laughter seemed not to blow on Vincent Cordoba.

"On what," he asked again, "does it depend?"

"How he did it."

"What do you mean, how?"

Daniel's gaze shifted anxiously from group to group across the grass in fear or hope of a monitoring parent on the alert to catch his eye, but for a brief interval he was truly alone. The interest he had aroused in Vincent excited, as well as alarmed, him.

"I get a lousy time," he said. "They just keep on at me without . . ."

"I know, Daniel." Vincent sealed up that line of escape and sent the quivering youth back to basics.

"Well, he got in touch with this guy, but you know that. George Cash. But I know . . . I'm telling you"—he turned round now on the stone step to face Vincent, managing his feet clumsily and damn near spilling his whiskey—"he paid that guy."

"I know that too, Daniel," Vincent said, allowing a measure of chill to escape his eye. "These guys, these archive archeologists, they get paid for their work like you and me."

"Don't get sarcastic," said Daniel with unexpected lucidity, "I'm not the fool you all think I am."

"I don't think you're a fool."

"Well, I'm not. I don't mean that sort of payment. I mean more. Much more."

"What is 'more,' Daniel?"

"I don't know exactly." The boy angrily jerked his glass toward his lips and jerked it away again. He jabbed his left shoulder in a gesture either copied off some video of a roughneck or natural. As Vincent watched him nearly spill his whiskey down his jacket again, his eyes had almost a yellow tinge in them. At the same moment, through the arch in the clipped hedge, Jane Webern emerged, but Daniel's head was down and he didn't see her before, as Vincent watched her out of the corner of his eye, she swiveled predictably on her delicate feet until her back was to her son.

"Well, if you don't know, Daniel, what's the fuss about?"

"I said I don't know exactly how much he paid," Daniel said in a sullen but decisive mutter, "but I sure as hell know he paid that guy to forge the document. He didn't find it."

Vincent didn't move. "Forge it?"

"Yeah. What else? I'm telling you. But you'd better not tell anyone else."

"No."

"Right!" Daniel said, not quite knowing what to do with the silence Vincent let fall on him. After a while he asked, "Are you going to tell him what I said?"

"Your dad, you mean?"

"Exactly."

Vincent paused for long enough for the boy's nervousness to break out again before answering. "That's a very serious allegation, Daniel," he said.

"Aw, Christ, forget it!" the poor fool burst out. "I made it up. I . . . got a grudge against him. I fantasize."

Vincent steadied him with a look. "We both know that's not so."

Daniel hesitated. It seemed he was in trouble either way, coming or going. He made one last desperate effort to choose.

"Look here," Vincent said. "Don't go all childish on me. You're a man now. We've had a man's conversation. Okay?"

Daniel waited, looking at him suspiciously.

"I'm not going to tell anyone about this conversation," Vincent said. "Not your dad, not anyone. You understand?"

Daniel nodded.

"It's the best way."

Daniel nodded again.

"And be patient." Vincent patted him at last with a friendly hand on his arm. He was demonstrating that quality himself to the last degree as he soothed the boy's nerves and tied up all the loose ends before going straight over to the telephone and ordering a private check on what had just been told him.

"Stick it out," he said. "You won't be working for your dad forever, you know. There'll be other fish to fry."

CHAPTER 11

*T*hey say that in any large gathering the public eye tends to be on the rich, famous, and beautiful, but when Vincent Cordoba left Daniel to go indoors and make his phone call, he was carefully watched, even if it didn't amount to quite the same thing.

Senator Kabe Geary, for example, who on account of this distraction had not heard more than one word in ten of Sanger's conversation for the last five minutes tuned in again, and immediately the edge of his resistance hardened against the argument that was being put to him so that even years later the property developer was still convinced that in that moment he had made some fatal blunder. Although Sanger reconstructed the conversation piece by piece, searching for the moment when the California development seemed suddenly to lose its attraction for Senator Geary, he could never complete the picture. The vital fragment in the jigsaw puzzle—that piece on which was shown the hand of Senator Geary putting something in a pocket, probably his own—was not there for Harvey Sanger to look at and put in place. But this, and not anything else, was the clue to the whole conversation. The local politician had listened to fifteen minutes of wind-up about the projected development on the hill simply because he was preoccupied the entire time by watching that snake in the grass, that saturnine, blackmailing, manipulative, evil bastard, Vincent Cordoba, and wondering who he planned to talk to next.

Zack Webern also. Although he had not witnessed his son's long tête-à-tête with Vincent Cordoba, or Vincent's retreat into the house, he stood now alone, for a moment, on the edge of the swimming pool with his glass in his hand. The unaccountable, sharp pain he felt between the shoulder blades was perhaps actually caused by what was going on a hundred yards away, out of his sight. With antennae subtler than the mere human eye or ear, he was aware of something going on behind his back.

Since his involvement with George Cash, Zack had enjoyed no peace of mind anyway. His thin face, which had always had a tendency to fall into an expression of anxious thought, was noticeably more strained these days. He knew it himself. Jane remarked on it. But, temporarily at least, he couldn't help it. When he looked inside his mind, the Cash episode, which was meant to have solved, not created, a problem, would jump out at him like a bogeyman jumping out of the shadows of his own conscience. It would make his heart leap and a darkness crack down on some area that formerly, without his having been aware of it, let some light into his soul. The practical results of the forgery vis-à-vis Santhill were beginning to seem as nothing compared to this unexpected mental backlash—this sensation as if a stone had been rolled over the opening of his mind and shut him in, in darkness. Then he would set himself to prizing it away again, using the following arguments: George Cash was discreet; no one could find out about the forgery unless Cash told them, and he could be relied on; the document could easily have been there in the first place; the EPA was unfair. Bit by bit he'd fit the fingers of his mind under the edge and heave at that stone of guilt that shut him in, and bit by bit he'd shift it until first a crack of light and then some more would be let in.

"Hi there, Zack. All alone?" Jane's sister, Betsy—the one he liked—came up behind him, and he turned to her with something on the brink of a smile. She was wearing a dress of cherry-red silk with tiny blue high-heeled shoes printed all over it, and on her feet she had the identical shoes in blue leather. While he took this in and said his hellos, and his attention was necessarily distracted from with his own inner state, furtively the stone started to slide back into place.

"This is a party, you know!" said Betsy. "You're meant to talk to people!"

"I've been talking."

Surreptitiously—masked by the pleasant sensations that had to do with Betsy's still firm and curvaceous cheeks, top and bottom, and the scent she wore, reminiscent of expensive airplanes and parties like this one, and the way her manner was always so special to "family" even though she was so famous—surreptitiously and temporarily unheeded, the foul burden of guilt slid back over Zack's heart until with one telltale, muted shudder it once more locked into place.

"Oh, come on!" Betsy said. She had brought up the subject of Daniel, and the mention of his name happened to coincide with the secret reassertion of Zack's inner burden. "He's not that bad!"

"That's what you think," Zack said wryly. "You don't have to work with him, Betsy."

Not only did Betsy not have to work with Daniel but she didn't actually want to talk about him much, either, although she had brought the subject up herself. She began to look for a way out. Her mouth and eyes and the angle of her face all expressed sympathy and attention to what Zack was now saying, but with a well-practiced skill she managed several swift peeps out of the corner of her eye and spotted an escape via one film producer and two bridge partners, which would bring her up to the tennis court in time for the end of her son, Steve's, game.

When she had accomplished this, Zack found himself alone again. His thoughts returned at once to their sickening obsession. As he once more marshaled the liberating arguments—Cash's dependable discretion, the EPA's unfairness, and so on—the light, when it began to penetrate once more past the evil obstruction revealed, or half revealed, the outlines of something new. With his mouth stretched with apprehension and his glass forgotten in his hand, Zack Webern chased the new shadow in his mind. The shadow was cast by that conversation that he had seen begin between Vincent and Daniel, but his conscious mind couldn't quite grasp it. If his senses had not been rendered almost supernaturally alert by habitual nervous tension and now honed to penetration point by this dangerous secret enterprise with George Cash, he would have noticed nothing. As it was, this blacker shadow leapt into his mind, just for an instant, for the twinkling of an eye, before escaping the grasp of his thoughts.

He tried again. He couldn't get it. His consciousness was crammed with little splinters of observation among which were included Daniel talking to Vincent, and Vincent walking across the terrace, but he could not identify the connection with this new fear. He let his breath out in a muted groan of exasperation. He felt terrible. He felt threatened. He began the mantra—Cash reliable, EPA unjustified. But when he had finished, the sense of a new and blacker danger persisted. He stood by the swimming pool for half an hour trying to catch this shadow by the tail, to examine it, to know it. But the essence of it was that he was no longer in control of who or what might choose to feed off the carcass of his integrity. The idea that an evil deed could put a man in such a position was new to him. He hadn't thought that crime, like a piece of putrefying flesh, might attract sharks. He only sensed the presence of a scavenger in search of carrion— and saw Vincent Cordoba coming back out of the house.

*I*t was at that same party that Barbara Falcus first tried to introduce everybody to Finn Garrett.

When Zack Webern had reached the point in his thoughts that coincided with the reemergence of Vincent Cordoba from the house, he searched with his eye among the nearest guests for someone with whom to find refuge and saw her standing in a group of three men and a young woman, with Barbara doing the honors. Barbara Falcus saw Zack approaching but continued to talk, like someone on a stage carrying on despite late arrivals in the audience. When Zack came within range, she drew him into the circle by putting her arm around his shoulder, but as for stopping talking, that was right out of the question.

"So you see," she said, pointing to Finn, "we've got a celebrity here, and my feeling is that we have more—we have a spiritual leader. Oh, yes! I know what you're thinking. We don't expect to follow in the footsteps of a mere girl, not in our society. I know, dear"—she referred back to the young woman—"you don't need to remind me. It's not a question of following. But still . . ."

There was a pause for breath, but the group was locked in listening mode and displayed the inability to profit by her momentary silence that so often encourages inveterate anecdotalists to think that, but for them, social gatherings would be silent.

"Even so," Barbara carried on, "you *are* teaching, Finn, and I happen to think that your teaching is the most important thing I've heard in my lifetime. No! I mean it! And don't forget," she remonstrated with the three men, who stared back guiltily at her, "Jesus was murdered when he was only thirty-three."

Zack looked to see how the girl was taking this tirade. He expected to see an ugly girl, or a modest beauty with one of those sublime expressions, but he saw neither. Instead, she looked friendly and thoughtful and, in so far as she was suffering from Barbara's determination to be her acolyte, her eyes held an expression of patient intelligence that at once aroused Zack's respect in spite of the rubbish Barbara was talking about her. She was tall and thin with wavy dark blond hair. She wore no makeup on her skin, but her eyes were faintly outlined. Her thick lashes grew at an angle that caught the light on their ends and made a line, like a line of sunlight, across the gray-blue of her eyes.

She was the girl whom Chuck and Ash had encountered in the desert.

"Now, honey," Barbara continued, "I want you to meet Zack Webern, Santhill's lawyer. Zack, this is Finn Garrett. Finn is also a scientist with an important job in local administration, you know." Barbara, in introducing her protégée, had no intention of abandoning her or of leaving gaps in the conversation that other people could waste by not asking the right questions. "Tell Zack about your TV program, honey. Have you seen her, Zack? Have you, Vincent?"

Zack hadn't realized that Vincent had just come up behind him. He half turned. The other two men showed signs of wanting to abscond. Poor Barbara had got the wrong end of the stick in thinking she could sell spiritual enlightenment to them. Finn Garrett didn't appeal to them. Playgirls were more their type. "Have you seen her classes on TV? And," (to Finn) "do you remember the dancing children, honey? Did any," turning round, "did any of you see the dancing children. Absolutely amazing! It was a demonstration to do with the spiritual importance of being able to make yourself unavailable, and I'll have to tell you about that another time, or maybe Finn will tell you. Anyhow, what was amazing was that one moment a group of children were all dancing on this stage, and then they turn their backs to the audience and, literally, *disappear!*" Barbara held her ten fingers rigidly in the air for an instant. Each nail was perfectly polished with Desert Rose. "The backs of the children's costumes all match, exactly, to bits of the stage set, you see. This child at the exact spot by a tree, that one by a certain boulder—absolutely *still*—and one moment the stage is full of children and the next—they've disappeared! Magic!"

Finn had still not said a word. Not that she was trying to rise above poor Barbara's sales pitch, but the only two men in a radius of five miles who would have been really interested were Chuck and Ash, who had damn near run out of gas looking for her that night in the desert, and frightened themselves with ghost stories into the bargain.

"How do you do," said Vincent. He'd just decided that he was rather interested in this girl, and he cut callously across Barbara's tirade without ceremony. "My name's Vincent Cordoba."

Finn took the hand that was held out to her. His fingers closed around hers.

"I'm gonna leave you for ten minutes, honey." Barbara broke in. "Can you come with me, Zack? Jane said to ask you to fetch Daniel out of the bathroom."

They went; and in the moment that her hand lay within Vincent's grip Finn's equanimity, which had withstood an hour of Barbara's enthusiasm, wavered.

"I'm very interested," he said, "in what Barbara was just talking about. Do you teach dancing then?" He had missed the bit of Barbara's sales pitch that mentioned Finn's professional scientific background.

"Not really," she said. "It was a one-time thing, just a device to demonstrate an idea of mine."

"What idea is that?"

She cast a look up at him. "Unavailability."

You could say one thing for Vincent, he was quick. He couldn't immediately do anything about the expression that his face, somewhat rigidly, had fixed upon it expressive of admiring interest in a new acquaintance. But his eyes narrowed.

"Unavailability," he deliberately repeated.

"Oh," she said. "You mustn't let me become a bore on this subject. Barbara is very interested in a course of spiritual extension classes I have been teaching."

"On TV, did she say?"

"Yes."

The girl smiled openly for the first time as if at a shared joke, and Vincent repositioned himself. He asked himself if perhaps she was friendly after all.

"So this is what you do," he said. He made a circular gesture with the flat of his hand, smiling. "You enslave rapturous housewives with your philosophy!"

Waiting for her answer, he looked carefully at her face, very even in color and rather pale, which seemed to hover on a level with his own against the dark backdrop of the trees edging that part of the property. Something about her—perhaps the monochrome ensemble of her clothes or her skin being pale, made her look appropriately like a garden statue. In contrast with the other guests, who collectively vibrated to the meaty shove of men and women in pursuit of money and power, she definitely stood out.

Vincent might like that. The attractive fold that cut down the side of his mouth and from the hollow of his cheek deepened as he looked at her and waited for her reply.

"No," she said. "It's a sideline."

"What do you do for a center line?"

"I'm a jack-of-all-trades."

"Is that feminist-speak for housewife?" he said. "Have I got a rival? Where's your husband?" He pretended to look around.

It obviously crossed Finn Garrett's mind that it was a pity

no one else seemed likely to join their group at that moment. She looked at her glass, which was empty.

"Would you . . . ?" she said.

"Oh, no!" Vincent shook his head, laughing. "You're not getting rid of me that easily." But he held out his hand, and she put the glass into it.

"Come on."

"I'm not married."

"I'm glad to hear it. And you work teaching what?"

"Science."

"Oh!"

"Can I have my drink now?" she asked with a smile.

He playacted at considering, said "I'll be back," and was just turning away when Senator Kabe Geary nearly collided with him.

"Oh, hello, Senator," Vincent immediately said in the respectful tone of a comparative stranger. "I'm just off to fill a glass. Now, do you know Finn Garrett?"

Immediately, Senator Geary wished he had not come over. It dawned on him that perhaps Vincent Cordoba had not known who Finn Garrett really was—in which case he could have kept out of it. Too late now, though.

"Hello, Dr. Garrett," he said.

"Doctor Garrett?"

"Yes indeed." Kabe Geary said that with his chin slightly lowered and moving his head from right to left over the three syllables and then coming to a dead stop like a train that has just crashed slowly into its terminal.

"J. F. Garrett?" Vincent said, working it out.

If Kabe Geary's tone of voice could have implied some history that might make this meeting embarrassing, Vincent at once, or almost at once, put that right. He said again in a yet more convincing tone of surprised pleasure, "You're J. F. Garrett? I always thought J. F. Garrett was a man!"

The young woman gave a half smile.

"J. F. Garrett, the scourge of the ungodly," Vincent went on. "Special adviser of the California district of the U.S. Food and Drug Administration Agency, and chairman of the committee on toxic waste disposal? My, oh my!" And he fixed his brilliant smile at an angle so that the bite of his teeth was set across her line of vision where her eyes could not get past it. "Does Charles Seaford know you're here?"

"I'm his guest, naturally," she said, "but Barbara Falcus brought me."

"Dear old Barbara," Vincent said, and in the alchemy of his tone the meaning of the first word was drastically changed. "But she said you did these"—he hunted for the word with a flourish of the hand that held the empty glass—"these philosophy programs on television."

"Spiritual extension," she said. "And if you remember, I said I was a jack-of-all-trades."

"And mistress of none?" he capped her.

"I hope it depends on which sense you mean that."

"Fast. Fast."

His own mind was working at breakneck speed. He had lost, or a firm he had a controlling interest in—ExMetals, a toxic waste disposal unit dealing with poisonous metal dust biproducts—had lost a deal worth $20,000 because J. F. Garrett had blocked the license. The name of Vincent Cordoba appeared on the letterhead of ExMetals, albeit in the smallest print that could be considered legal. Nevertheless, perhaps she'd noticed and remembered it. The loss of that contract because of his failure to swing the license had been partly blamed on Kabe Geary, and Cordoba had threatened to cancel Geary's retainer, or publicize the fact that he was getting one, if he couldn't look after the interests of his friends a little better.

"But does Charles Seaford know you're here?" Vincent persisted. "He's likely to be very sensitive just now." He threw a conspiratorial glance from Finn to Kabe Geary and back again.

"Because of the EPA ruling over Santhill?"

"Of course," Vincent said. "We're insured, but we had an anxious moment there, and Charles took it very badly."

She looked unhappy and gave Kabe a rueful glance.

"Who'd be an expert on toxic waste disposal and pollution?" she said. "No one wants to know you."

"Oh, I'm sure that's not true!" Vincent exclaimed, as if to utterly reassure her. But his tone of voice didn't quite hit the mark which, considering the general accuracy of his aim, was no doubt deliberate. "Here's Barbara for one, heading back to take care of you. And I must be off. 'Bye, Senator. Good-bye, Dr. Garrett." And with all three of them looking after him, he went away across the lawn.

As he walked, his thoughts soon reverted to the phone call he had made half an hour ago in which he had initiated a very private check on Daniel Webern's story. And he smiled to himself. If it turned out to be true and Santhill's insurance was forged, Vincent was not going to sneak on anyone. Not he. But he would use it for his own ends. A certain very profitable Italian contract for the disposal of poisonous waste was going begging, one that plenty of people knew about but no one could place owing to the exceptional toxicity of the product. What better home for it than a dump already blacklisted by the EPA and scheduled for clearance? When the legal clean-up operation started, there would simply be a bit more to be cleared. And no one need know where it came from. It would be done very discreetly. Vincent's name would be kept out of it. And in the meantime, when the rest of Santhill's senior management heard—as inevitably they would—that illegal traders had turned up and were dumping on their site, he need only arrange for an anonymous threat in connection with the forged insurance document, and they would keep as quiet as mice. Just as quiet as little, frightened mice.

As Vincent set his foot on the first of the stone steps leading back up to the terrace, a quiet private laugh escaped him, and Dale Falcus, standing nearby, heard it. He fidgeted with the stem of his glass as he looked sharply at Vincent out of the corner of his eye. He missed the punch line of the joke that was being told to the group around him, but the small sacrifice went without recompense. His glance stopped short at Vincent's buff linen jacket, which covered the heart that held the secrets.

CHAPTER 13

The Italian dealer seeking to dispose of that consignment of ultratoxic waste heard from Vincent Cordoba within the hour after the private investigator confirmed Daniel's remarks. Three days after the Seaford's party Vincent arrived in Italy to negotiate the details of the contract and arrange for the shipment of the toxic waste to the U.S.A. He landed at Naples airport and booked himself into the Vittorio Emanuele Hotel in Sorrento. It was raining. By twelve o'clock Italian time he was sitting in the window of the public reception room downstairs drinking a cup of black coffee. The rich surroundings of bergère work, crumpled green silk, paneled walls, and glass suited his 1930s matinee idol good looks. And so did the prospect of the deal he had come here to make. If he could promise a safe haven to this shipment once it was unloaded in the States, he could virtually name his own price to the dealer, who had so far found every obstacle put in his path. But it needed management. In this business an illegal transaction—which this one was fated to be—was as complicated and meticulous as a legal one, and Vincent had plenty of experience of both: the Santhill dump gave him a special opportunity, that was all.

He looked at his watch. It was still raining but only just, and the sun was beginning to strike the wet flags of the terrace that overlooked the sea. A woman in the party of Americans in the opposite corner looked up as Vincent rose to his feet. He unconsciously posed for her as he weighed the pros and cons of fetching his raincoat from his room or going out without it. A minute later she spotted him again outside the window, walking across the terrace toward the outside elevator connecting the terrace with the beach far below.

By the time he got out at the bottom the rain had stopped. On the soaked gray sand of the tiny beach lay a storm of oranges that had been thrown up in the night. As Vincent passed on his way toward the town, a filthy man crouched in a boat, mending something. The road led around to the small harbor square, cobbled and planted with shaped olive trees. On one side a restaurant with a corrugated, transparent plastic roof was crammed between the road and the retaining wall. Vincent crossed the road and went in.

When he stood inside the door and looked around him, the occupants, bathed in a greenish light from the rain-soaked trees and the faint green tinge of the transparent plastic roof, looked back with varying degrees of interest. It was a shabby place for someone of Vincent's sartorial elegance. But then again, there were some English tourists at a far table who had got lost enough to find their way here for lunch. On the left of the door at a long table there was a group of what looked like local fishermen. None of the clientele corresponded to Vincent's expectation of the man he'd come to meet. He experienced that sharpening of anxiety that comes when the idea first occurs that some simple but essential preliminary can go wrong. This consignment of toxic waste was a dangerous, negatively charged oxide sulfate compound that had to be handled with extreme care. The price of the contract for disposal would be high exactly for that reason. It was higher yet because European conservationists had mobilized public opinion against the waste material. It had to be tactfully reduced to a shadow of its current presence. It had to disappear twice: once from public scrutiny while making its way to the country of disposal, the U.S.A., and once within that country, again. Vincent's plans involved skillful manipulation of shipping documents and licenses before the load would even get to America. Once the waste arrived there, he knew how to key it in to the black market network of illegal trucking, but the whole scheme was a write-off if it began with a man who couldn't even turn up on time. He checked his watch again, and at that moment the door opened behind him.

CHAPTER 14

*B*ob Keats was as good as his word when it came to fighting. The law might, and it might not, protect Rachel Grimmond from a revenge that Keats considered absolutely fitting to her sex. He kept that in the back of his mind. But more immediately he was determined to sue his way out of paying the claim. His contention was nondisclosure on the part of Stan Lacy or of his brokers, who had tried to pass the booby-trapped run-off onto him. They could think again. He'd make them fight for every penny.

On the day after Vincent Cordoba's mission to Sorrento, a steering committee, set up in London to examine the case of the Keats syndicate, was due to meet in Lloyd's. A small group of harassed members agents, whose Names stood to lose heavily on the claim, were gathered together under the chairmanship of Giles Aston. And a small man now walking down Lime Street was on his way to join them.

He wore a suit of country cloth that distinguished him, if that was the word, from the conventionally dressed men that thronged the pavements and alleys in the immediate vicinity of the Lloyd's building. The suit itself had been tailored with great care by the crippled son of the postmaster of the Welsh village of Llangwenny. The cloth held today exactly the same cut and fall that it had in the first place, being constructed on those lines that don't wear out. It was a suit that would not release its owner from the obligation to wear it for at least another twenty years, and whether as a result he looked distinguished or eccentric was an open question.

He stopped to buy a paper on the corner before turning toward the Lloyd's building. The broad flight of steps constructed like a concrete ladder leading up to the main entrance was intermittently crowded with the comings and goings of the market. As he put his change back in his pocket, it flashed through his mind that the last time he came here, it had been to report on a case that had ended in a once-revered underwriter being killed in the back streets of Baghdad. As he took out his temporary pass to show at the top of the steps, it was that scene and not this one, that was most present to his inward eye. For an instant he smelled the smell of the hot banks of the Tigris wafting through a rotting window frame, and whether it came from Regent's Park or his memory, his ears caught the yell of a distant call to prayer.

He held out his pass for inspection. The identification photograph showed him looking into the camera with an expression of unreal solemnity, and under it was printed his name: MALDWYN HARRIS.

"Mal!"

For a second the sound of the voice, while that vivid splinter of memory was still in his mind, confused him. He waited for her to shout his name a second time before he turned with a smile to the tall, young woman emerging from the main doors almost at a run, and said, "Hello, Celia! Fancy seeing you here! I thought you said you'd never darken their doors again."

"I'm not darkening them. I'm collecting some money."

"Good God!" he said with exaggerated incredulity, "you must be the only one then!"

"I don't mean on my underwriting. I've been doing some articles for the magazine. Come and have a cup of coffee with me," she said. "Tell me what you're up to. I suppose it's another scandal. They ought to ring the Lutine bell when they see you coming up the steps."

"I can't," he said. "Have coffee, I mean. There's nothing confidential about my appointment. It's a plain loss assessment job this time. Shipping Investigation Securities does take on routine jobs as well as fraud these days, you know," he said, referring to his employers. "It's not all beer and skittles."

"Beer and skittles! Is that what you call jobs like Baghdad?"

"We tough men," he said self-mockingly looking up at her, "have a different view from you girls."

She looked at her watch.

"Well, make it lunch then."

"All right."

"When will you be out?"

"Let me see. . . ." He paused, calculating. "It's a steering committee. I don't know if they'll want me to sit in on witness interviews."

"Steering committee? You don't mean Santhill?"

He looked at her in astonishment, but before he could speak, she had already seen that her guess had hit the mark, and her incredulous laughter cut him off.

"I just knew it!" she said. "You would! It's about the syndicate that collected a twenty-five million dollar loss and the underwriter who bought the run-off threatened to rape the broker who planted it on him."

"I can see you're still friendly with Ossie Hollander," Mal said dryly. "There's no other way a person could be so steeped in City gossip unless they'd just had dinner with him."

"But you must have known."

"Not really. I've been on another job abroad, not connected with Lloyd's. Shipping I.S. investigates insurance fraud worldwide, you know."

"So you admit it's fraud."

"Not at all in this case, I believe," he said. "Just a complicated, unexpectedly large claim, and someone called Giles Aston asked me to take on the assessment on that basis. Look, I'll be late, Celia. One o'clock at Bubs?"

"All right. I'll see you there," she said.

Mal Harris walked over to the bank of elevators set in the outside wall of the building, and when it came, pressed the button for the eleventh floor. The glass-sided cage soared above the tops of surrounding churches, until it came to the level that housed the top hierarchy of Lloyd's. Mal stepped out and walked across the bridge to the main body of the building, where the committee rooms and the chairman's office were located. Here the style of the interior marked a sudden break with the industrial design of the floors below and a swing over to the classical. When the chips were down, the top men got their classical, elitist surroundings—and to hell with the Marxist principles that fathered the proletarian imagery below. Here were the columns and the marble and the stone: the entire eighteenth century Adam committee room, complete with paneling and plaster work set up like a doll's house in one corner: and in the middle of the floor the glass-sheeted internal wall around the central atrium, with its spectacular view of the drop down to the underwriting room on the ground floor.

Mal Harris walked around to where the chairman's waiter, seated at a desk in front of his office, looked up and recognized the visitor. He smiled and half stood to lean across the desk and shake hands.

"Good morning, sir," he said. "I don't know if I can say it's a pleasure to see you, sir. What's the trouble this time?"

Mal smiled at the familiar witticism. He had a way of raising his eyebrows as he smiled, while something in his eye gave to the inoffensive mildness of his expression the same sort of subversive kick that chili gives to carne.

"I don't think it's serious this time," Mal said. "It's not the chairman who wants to see me. It's Mr. Giles Aston."

"That'll be the steering committee for TT4 in room eight, sir," Fred said. "Not likely to be the beginning of another one of your spectacular involvements with the market then?"

"I couldn't say until I see Mr. Aston," said Mal. "Perhaps a posse of Names are on their way round to shoot the lot of you. I read in the papers they've lost a lot of money."

Fred tried not to laugh. But not so hard as to do himself an injury.

"That'll be Mr. Keats, sir."

"You're not on his syndicate then, Fred?"

"Me, sir!" Fred quipped. "My wife would never give me another cooked breakfast. Yes, miss, can I help you?" He turned as Rachel Grimmond approached his desk, her slipcase on her hip with her makeup bag clamped between the press studs. She wore stockings and a skirt that was a good two inches longer than usual.

"I have an appointment," she said, "with the steering committee headed by Mr. Giles Aston. Which is Room 8?"

"Second along to the right there, miss," he said. "But if you'd like to wait until Mr. Aston rings through, I'll let him know that you're here. Who shall I say it is?"

"Rachel Grimmond."

He inclined his head politely and waved his hand toward a chair a little way off.

Mal Harris betrayed no reaction as he sat down and prepared to wait for his summons to the committee room. He looked thoughtfully, instead, at the plate-glass central wall that now, seen at an angle from which the drop down into the atrium was cut off, looked stylish and unthreatening. A similar point of view could be said to apply to Mal Harris himself. But he belonged to that category of human beings who go so far not to advertise themselves that they are misleading.

This was what Giles Aston was reminding the committee, prior to calling Mr. Harris in. They should not forget that however unbusinesslike Mal Harris might superficially appear, he was the brains behind the recovery of Names' money from numbered Swiss bank accounts and anonymous trusts following the Ross-Gilbert scandal and was physically and mentally tougher and more distinguished than he looked.

In spite of this warning, William (Pill) Matthews was astounded when Mal Harris eventually walked into the room. Of the four members agents on the steering committee, Pill Matthews had the smallest list of Names whose allocations and general Lloyd's business he managed, but of them he had put twenty on the Keats syndicate. This meant that he was not in the best of tempers these days and tended to demonstrate with even more frequency than usual why it was that his colleagues had nicknamed him Pill, when Bill would have been a more conventional shortening of his Christian name.

When he was now introduced to Mal Harris and heard his Welsh accent, Pill Matthews turned down the corners of his mouth like a seaside landlady. He stared at the fellow, noted the Peter Rabbit country suit and placatory manners, and barely suppressed an audible snort of annoyance.

Needless to say, the qualities that aroused Pill's irritable spite didn't go unnoticed by the others, but they had a very different effect. Guy Smith-Levy had a definite twinkle in his eye, and Struan Gill the same, as Mal Harris sat gently down in his chair and turned toward them all a thin face with deep-set large eyes fixed in an expression of attention. Duncan Hope, the fourth man on the committee, leaned his huge shoulders back against his chair and sighed, but only because he wanted to go to sleep.

"Perhaps I'd better give a recap on why we decided to take the step of asking a man with Mr. Harris's distinguished record to undertake this task, which is basically little more than routine loss assessment," said Giles Aston. "This claim from Santhill is threatening to cause us all a lot of trouble." He paused and looked around the table. "Not only because of the size of this claim, therefore, and the complications surrounding it, but also bearing in mind the future threat that pollution holds out to Lloyd's, we are fortunate, I think, in having persuaded Mr. Harris to become involved."

Duncan must have felt a twinge in his shoulders at that point, because he braced them against the back of his chair in a gesture designed to loosen his own limbs but actually loosening the wood until it gave a sharp crack. He pulled his mouth down guiltily.

"Done too much shooting in my time," he said to Guy. "It's the right shoulder."

The chairman ignored the interruption.

"I suggest that we need to have a brief exchange of ideas and agree the parameters of this inquiry with Mr. Harris. Yes, Mr. Matthews."

"With respect," Pill said, using a favorite expression meaning its opposite, "I think that the activities of this committee and whoever we appoint should be limited to the losses on TT4."

"Nothing else is envisaged," Giles assured him. "All the same, among ourselves, it is as well to recognize that the American background on toxic waste is very dangerous to Lloyd's as a whole." He cast his eye at large over the table. "We all know that their land is geologically ill suited to disposal. Britain has a much better geological disposition; so that America, despite its size, is very accident-prone."

"That's true," said Guy Levy, "but Lloyd's is in the business of accidents. We can cope with accidents. It's not the geology of America but their law courts and those Mickey Mouse awards that are the trouble."

"No one's going to argue with you, Guy," the chairman commented, "but we must keep this meeting to the business in hand."

"My point exactly." Pill Matthews spoke in a peevish tone as if he had already tried to make this point and been ignored. "I don't agree with the idea that simply because this case borders on a landmine of quite different dimensions—I mean, look at the illegal trade in dumping in America. Do we want to get into that?"

"Correct me if I'm wrong," Giles Aston said, "but your concern is that we don't let ourselves in for the expense of blanket coverage of a general issue that's much bigger than the one claim."

"Precisely." Pill fidgeted with his tie, which was printed with a lavender-colored club logo. "Mr. Harris may have a great reputation—I'm not saying he hasn't—but we've got to treat this case tactfully, diplomatically. We want to end up with the lowest possible figure."

"That's fair enough," Giles Aston conceded. "All right.

Let's get down to the matter of exactly what we want Mr. Harris to do. We need the EPA's order scrutinized. The ground examined—that is, the toxic waste site in"—he pushed a sheet of paper aside—"the Mojave Desert. How about clearance?"

"That's the main issue, of course," Pill remonstrated with unconscious rudeness.

"Indeed," Giles said curtly. Pill was on the point of reducing those about him to their own lowest common denominator, as usual. But Giles made an effort and said courteously, "You're quite right. I should have said, how far do we want our assessor, Mr. Harris, to go in pursuit of the cheapest quote for cleanup? For example, there is probably room for negotiation with the EPA. There will definitely be scope for scientific debate."

"If I understand Mr. Harris's past involvements correctly," Pill persisted, with an edge to his voice, "he is more a fighter than a figures man."

"We must get on, Mr. Matthews," Giles Aston remonstrated. "What is the point you wish to make?" He half turned fussily to Mal Harris. "I hope you understand, Mr. Harris, your competence is not being questioned here."

"I merely wanted to stress," Pill said, feeling the familiar cold current of disapproval from his peers beginning to lap about him, "that we're *not* out to prepare the ground for anyone else. Not that I want to take a short term view"—("That chap has an absolute talent for inverse statements," Guy Levy said in private afterwards to Struan, and his friend said sharply, "Pompous ass!")—"but if we're not careful, Mr. Harris may find himself involved in more than he—or we—bargained for."

As usual, Pill had expressed himself with so little charm that his audience was instantly attracted to the opposite point of view. And the one and only prophetic remark he ever made passed without comment into oblivion.

*R*achel Grimmond was kept waiting for twenty minutes before she was asked to go into the committee room, but this was no problem. Her slipcase, as usual, contained the book she was currently reading, and as soon as she sat down, she took it out and became oblivious to her surroundings.

"The chairman has rung through, Miss Grimmond," Fred announced eventually. "I'm sorry you have been kept waiting. Will you go in now?"

"Thank you." She uncrossed her legs, crammed *The Bonfire of the Vanities* back into the slipcase, where it barely allowed the press studs to snap shut, and stood up.

"In here, miss."

Fred opened the door for her, and she gave him a broad and friendly smile. But seeing the men around the table, her heart hardened. Like a fox approaching a chicken coop, she just could not suppress her killer instinct at the sight of two or three businessmen gathered together.

She shook hands with Giles Aston and acknowledged his introduction to each of the others, including Mal Harris.

"Please sit down," the chairman said. Giles Aston was a good enough man and not at all unintelligent, but he still wasn't really used to working on equal terms with women, and Rachel was younger than his own daughter.

"There's no need to feel nervous," he said solicitously, "and we will not keep you long. All we require from you is a statement of the exact conditions you described to the underwriter when these years of run-off containing the Santhill claim were broked to him."

She lifted her face at a slight angle that at once conveyed—but only to someone disposed to analyze minutely what was going on around them—an ironical challenge.

"I took my orders from John Grise," she replied politely. "He is the head of my department in Steiger and Wallace."

Giles Aston smiled at her. With a little more encouragement he might have said, "Good girl!"

"Now," he actually said, "would you please recount to the committee what those instructions were."

"Perhaps I should explain," she began, "that I did receive those instructions secondhand."

"Why was that?"

"The broker who originally took the instructions couldn't place the business so he passed the slip on to me."

"Really! And you then successfully placed the business?"

"Yes."

Struan Gill wrote something down.

"Very good," Giles couldn't help saying. "Now please let us hear what the instructions were."

As Rachel briefly recounted the exact details, she allowed a minute tone of childish huskiness to enter her voice. The parody was fractional, and although it would have been hilarious to an intimate friend, it aroused no suspicion here. Only Mal Harris cast one glance of suppressed hilarity in her direction, and that went unnoticed.

"Thank you," Giles Aston said. "Now. What questions do any of you have? Mr. Matthews?"

"May I ask, young lady . . . ," Pill said. He paused there, unwittingly presenting himself as a target when his intention had been to give weight to his own words.

Rachel turned her face wholly toward him with a smile of maidenly venom from which he took no warning. "My name is Rachel Grimmond, Mr. Matthews."

He blushed. "Exactly," he said, fighting to reassert himself and feeling a smarting sensation on his cheekbones as if he'd nicked himself with his razor. "That's precisely the point I wished to make. Are you related to Sir Adrian Grimmond?"

"I am his niece," she said.

"With respect," he went on, "in that case we must address the possibility that you might have had a conflict of interest when you broked the loss."

"I did not," she said.

"Miss Grimmond," Giles Aston interposed hastily, "let me assure you that this committee is not questioning your integrity." He looked so anxious that her expression softened. "But Mr. Matthews is quite right," he went on, "to pose the question."

He looked coaxingly at her, and this time Guy Levy suppressed a smile.

"The answer is that Sir Adrian Grimmond is my uncle," she said, "but I don't work for him. I work as a broker for Steiger and Wallace, and Steiger and Wallace happen to be brokers who do a great deal of work for Grimmonds, since divestment. But I take my orders from John Grise, and I was not aware of anything"—she paused to glance dismissively at Pill, straight into the middle of his watery blue eyes, and then addressed the end of her sentence to the chairman—"not anything at all, contained in the run-off that could cause trouble. The underwriter has got the same idea as Mr. Matthews."

It was a very accurate barb. Pill's feelings toward women were at least as complicated as those of Bob Keats.

"So we understand," Giles Aston continued, unaware. "Mr. Keats claims that you must have known the underlying reason for the run-off."

"He has no grounds for that claim," she said. "The original underwriter, Stan Lacy, denies any knowledge at the time of handing the business over to Steiger and Wallace."

"Is that on record?"

She opened her slipcase.

"I have a copy of the memo here." *The Bonfire of the Vanities* fell out as she extracted a neat clip of papers and handed them over to Giles Aston.

"My boss, John Grise, took the order as you see."

"Thank you very much." He took it from her, glanced at it, and passed the paper down the table.

"You will see, gentlemen, that that includes a report on the background of the run–off package and a brief percentage break-down. We will study this, Miss Grimmond. Thank you very much." He emphasized the "very." "Our committee is grateful for your able cooperation."

She stood up, acknowledging the thanks of the committee with the signs of battle showing slightly in her pink cheeks. Mal Harris also rose. Looking at his watch to cue himself in, he said he had an appointment and made his excuses in time to accompany Rachel across the marble floor toward the elevators.

There was something pretty sharp in the way her high heels clacked against the hard floor, and Mal Harris followed in her wake with a certain mock humility as if it might be his fault. At the elevators they had to wait.

She stood in silence deliberately not fidgeting, her body locked into a pose like an irritated general forced to tolerate a delay. She held her arms clasped tight across the slipcase, her legs braced, her chin slightly thrust forward. The whole bank of elevators were engaged, the orange lights flickering laboriously over the lower floors.

"Well, I don't know," Mal said, breaking the silence as if continuing a conversation already comfortably begun, "It looks like being a thankless task, this one!"

She turned her head. "Not unique in that," she said.

"No," he agreed. He uttered the syllable with an expression of soothing enthusiasm that would have been comical if he had not seemed so sincere. She gave him a sideways look and said nothing.

"Now, my line in this is different," he said.

She looked very uninterested. She had no idea what his involvement was.

"You brokers do the dull stuff. Mind you, I wouldn't like to be rude. You probably find it very interesting."

She cast him a look of spiteful politeness and said, "Very!"

"There you are, you see."

At that moment the elevator doors sliced open. There was only one man standing inside the empty cage, but at the sight of Rachel his demeanor, which had been rather slack and sullen, sharpened. He cast her a look of unmistakable menace and took in at the same time the figure of Mal Harris standing beside her. He moved sharply out toward the middle of the elevator floor without disembarking, so that Rachel couldn't get in without passing near him, and simultaneously held the door button on "open." Mal waited. He saw Rachel hesitate, her fingers tighten on the binding of her case. She took a step forward. The man— Bob Keats—didn't budge.

"Miss Grimmond!" he said. "What a pleasure. If you were alone, we could have gone down in the lift together."

She didn't answer. She stepped past him in stony silence.

"Another time," he said threateningly.

It was a very brief scene. Within a minute it was over. Mal had entered the elevator. Keats had already stepped out, and the doors slammed. There was a pause while in the silence of the charged atmosphere the elevator, with a subdued vibration of power, began its descent.

The girl said nothing, but an angry tear brimmed over her lower lid. As if the feel of it on her own skin dissolved the fixings of her resistance, the tension of her body suddenly relaxed, and she gave an audible sob. Without hesitation Mal drew her over to the glass wall where she could stand with her back to the other passengers when they got in, as if interested in the view.

"This is a clean handkerchief," he said gently. "Use it quick before the doors open."

She took it from him without protest and blew her nose

hard like a schoolgirl. When the elevator reached the ground, she walked out with passable composure, but made no objection to Mal accompanying her.

"Would you like a cup of coffee?" he said.

"All right. Thanks. Not here though."

"We'll cross the road to Lutrec's then."

They did that. Mal ordered two coffees and a whiskey. When they got to the table, he set down the cups and poured the scotch into hers.

"I'm sorry," she said. Another dam of tears had piled up against the bank of her lower lashes and began to spill over, but she wiped them away. "I'm sorry," she said again.

"Don't you apologize to me," he said. "I should have hit him. I don't know what for, but I could see he deserved it for something. Have a mouthful of that coffee."

She swallowed some.

"He threatened to rape me," she said. She blushed as she said it. "And he meant it. If I meet him in the wrong place, that's just what he'll try and do."

"What on earth gave him that idea?"

"Because I sold him the run-offs that contained the Santhill liability." She looked at a point on the wall away from Mal Harris. "He thinks it's an appropriate punishment for a female broker, I suppose, because he reckons he wouldn't have stamped the line if he hadn't fancied me." She said this with such withering contempt that Mal very nearly laughed.

"I thought I recognized him," he said. "Bob Keats then."

"Yes." She drank her coffee. "What's your involvement with the inquiry? You're not an agent or an underwriter, are you?"

He explained it to her.

"Do you investigate insurance crime?"

"Yes," he said. "As well."

"When the underwriter or the insured has misappropriated funds or run some kind of a conspiracy? I remember now. You helped Leo Turner over that attempted fraud to do with tankers smuggling poisoned gas in the Gulf. My God!" she said suddenly, her eyes lighting up, "is that why they've called you in over Santhill? What on earth do they think has happened?"

"It's not the same," Mal said. "It's more routine this time. I do have to do routine jobs, you know."

"Don't mention routine to me," she said. She looked at her watch. "I was expected back half an hour ago." She reached out to her slipcase and pulled it toward herself on the bench. "But what questions exactly are you planning to ask Santhill?"

"I don't know yet," he said. "It's a complex scene, American waste disposal. A badly monitored and slaphappy past record, a powerful and draconian organization called the Environmental Protection Agency in the present, and a well-developed and violent illegal trade in illicit disposal operating in between."

"Sounds fun!" she said. "How long will it take in the States?"

The center point of his eyebrows went up a little, and he pressed his lips together, considering. "Two, three weeks."

"I've got to get back to the office," she said. "Thank you very much for the coffee—and for your help."

"It would be a good idea if you could come with me," he said, "to America I mean." He made the remark as if it was the most ordinary idea. "You broked the run-off. I could suggest it to Steiger and Wallace. It wouldn't be at all unusual. They've probably got some plan along those lines already. And from your point of view it would get you out of Bob Keats's way for a few weeks."

She sat down again abruptly.

"Yes, it would," she said. Her eyes were brightening with the suddenness of a starving child put on a saline drip. "Yes, it would."

"Shall I suggest it?"

"Will you? But what use could I be?"

"In these circumstances I've always got one of the brokers with me. You'd be as good as anyone else. You're the one who broked it."

He reached into the waistcoat pocket of his incredible suit

and brought out a card. He held it toward her between the first two fingers of his right hand. His fourth finger was bent sideways. It gave his hand a look of delicacy that was characteristically misleading since the finger had been broken by a bullet that ricocheted off the mast of a ship. Rachel took the card without much attention. She said, "Thank you. I'll ring you tomorrow."

She hurried out of the wine bar, looking again at her watch. It was about the same time as the officer, handsomely paid off, in the port authority in Naples stamped the documents that Vincent had had prepared for him, and the shipment due for America began its journey overseas. It was about the same time as Zack Webern, the lawyer, nudged away, in his sleep, the remains of his worry about the forgery. It was the same time as Time, to put it bluntly, seized hold the ratchet of the wheel of Fate and pulled it round another notch.

CHAPTER 16

*A*round the fifteenth of that month there was to be no moon, and night fell in the Mojave Desert around the Santhill waste disposal site with unusual silence. It was so still that the sound of the guard striking a match could be heard for half a mile. He cupped his hand around the flame, but he needn't have bothered. After the cigarette was lit, he drew on it with such emphasis he nearly choked himself, but when he had finished coughing, the silence settled down inexorably again all around him, like the silence of the grave.

His companion was inside the small lit guardhouse beside the gate, trying to fix the terminal of the telephone connection that seemed to have unaccountably developed a fault late in the afternoon. He came out.

"You fixed it?"

"Nup."

There was a long pause during which Pete looked around with his thumbs tucked in his belt. On either side of the guardhouse the high steel perimeter fence stretched away into the darkness. Only the faintest gleam of starlight crosshatched bits of it against the denser shadow. "What's goin' on here?" he asked.

Nothing.

Yet.

"How d'you mean?" Bob asked.

"Quiet!"

Bob nodded.

"Like before an earthquake or somethin'. You don't think there's goin' to be somethin' like that, do you, Pete?"

"Nup."

They were both silent again. And then a rustle in a bush about thirty yards away marked the first tentative movement of the returning wind.

"I've known it like this before," Bob said.

Pete said, "It happens."

The next phase of their routine would be to make a cup of coffee, lay out the cards, check the gates, and do a round with the dogs. Pete said, "You'll kill yourself with those things."

"Aw, for Chrissake!" The sound of Bob's cough was sharp in the uncluttered darkness.

The wind was up a bit now.

"I hear the wind," Pete said, "now you've done coughing." And, indeed, within the range of the gate light the inky shadow of a tamarisk bush quivered and swayed with a sudden elastic gyration.

"I don't hear it," Bob said.

"Listen."

They both listened. Bob said, "That i'n't the wind." They both listened—"Is it?"

"You can see it!" Pete said, pointing at the bush.

"Yeah. But listen."

Again they listened. In the far distance there was a sound like a big wind.

"It's a truck," Pete said, "coming from Stoddard's Well."

They listened again.

"One truck?"

One of the dogs—a German shepherd—which was crouched by the guardhouse, lifted its head suddenly, barked, and got to its feet.

"Shut up!"

More distinctly now, a distant roar sounded far over to the right.

"Sounds like three or four trucks."

"I don't see light."

At that moment either the trucks switched their lights on or a rise in the ground gave way to them and the full beam of the lead truck spilled suddenly into the darkness. By now the subdued roar of the engines dominated the lonely landscape, although they were still half a mile away.

"Where they making for?" Pete said. "It looks like they're off the track."

"Round toward China Lake?"

The truck lights swung inward instead of outward.

"They can't be coming here!" Bob said. "Aw, hell, you don't think that damn phone screwed up on us, and there's a transfer rescheduled?"

"I don't think so," Bob said. "I'll go try again, but it's closed now. I mean this place. They done transferrin'."

Up until the final EPA ruling, Santhill Chemicals had run a halfhearted and sporadic cleanup operation, trucking part of the crated waste for export east, in the hope of satisfying the agency that way.

"Look!" Bob said, before Pete had taken more than one step, "they're making straight for the fence down there."

"Jesus!"

An alarm went off in the guardhouse making a foul whine that split the eardrums.

"That's the number three gate," Pete shouted. "Sheeba! Crack!"

Both dogs were up and going, their barks like gunfire, their whole bodies tense with adrenalin, hair raised. Both men had their guns. Pete used his regularly to shoot at beer cans. Bob would hardly know where to find the trigger of his in a hurry. They ran for the patrol vehicle, got in, and with a backfire of loose gravel started to bucket down the inside of the wire with the two dogs racing alongside. Half a mile down the trucks were lined up at the gate, which was flapping wide-open, and the first had backed in on a wide arc that brought it in line with the excavation pits near the wire.

"You can't do that!" Bob shouted. He took hold of his gun as he leapt to the ground, and the dogs were going crazy. There was only one man standing on the ground by the huge lead truck, holding in his left hand a mask and in his right something that looked in the darkness like a Kalashnikov.

"Get that dog off," he shouted, "or I'll have to shoot him."

"Crack! Heel!" Pete loved those dogs. "Sheeba!"

Both dogs reacted as if Pete's voice was rope that held them against their will, and they barked in protest across the forbidden ground louder than before. The other trucks had now completed their manoeuvres bringing the three neatly into line, the drivers remaining in their cabs, their masked faces pointing outwards towards the two guards, their headlights dimmed but creating nevertheless a solid stage of light. Onto this stage two more armed men jumped down and joined the first.

"What do you think you're doin'?" Pete shouted uncertainly across the intervening space. "This is private property."

"We're off loading some waste, is all," the man shouted back.

"What waste? You can't put anything in there unless it's Santhill orders."

"We can put in what the hell we like," the man shouted back, "and you guys'd be better off makin' yourselves scarce unless you've got masks. It isn't healthy."

"You've got some nerve!" Bob exploded. "Get off this land now!"

He aimed his rifle at the intruder, and Pete made some play with the mobile phone unit, assuming these guys would think it was working. They didn't seem to think so at all.

"Don't waste yourselves," the stranger shouted.

"Hello, hello," Pete said urgently into the telephone receiver, although it was as dead as a block of wood and he knew it.

"Put down your gun. There are six of us here, all armed. Don't waste yourselves."

"What the hell we do?" said Bob in an undertone, dead scared. After a moment's hesitation he let the barrel of his gun point at the ground.

The three men advanced toward them until they were more within speaking distance. They all looked as physically rough as Bob and Pete. If a lot of money was being made out of the illegal dumping business, enough of it wasn't going their way.

"We've got three loads here," the leader said. "We're dumping in this excavated pit because the waste is semiliquid. When we're through, you will use your diggers to transfer soil from that area over there over the top of this pit. That'll deepen the second pit ready for our next consignment."

"Next consignment?"

"You're illegal," Bob said. "You're not giving us orders. You got no authority."

"Make him understand, Tim," the boss said, and his companion stepped forward and gave Bob a violent blow across the jaw with the butt of his rifle. He completed the manoeuvre with the effortless neatness of a dancer, and it was just the one blow, but there were plenty more where it came from.

"You understand better now?" the man said again.

Bob had staggered back without falling, and he wiped some blood off his face with the hub of his hand, but his eyes glittered with fright. Pete was no help to him. He was hanging on to his dogs like a mother protecting her children.

"We can't do that," Bob said. "We haven't got the machinery."

"Don't lie to me."

"It'll take us all night," Pete broke in. He flung out an arm, half turning to point back to the sheds where the machinery was stored and Sheeba sprang to attention, checked at the confused gesture, and barked sharply once.

The man dug into his pocket and took out a wad of notes tightly wrapped. "We thought of that," he said. He threw the money across. Pete nearly muffed the catch, but once he got his hand around it he noticed it was a sizable bundle.

"You'll get another one on our next trip. We know your duty schedules. We dump on those nights only. Wear masks when you're filling in or the stuff will kill you. Give him the card, Tim."

This last order was stuck onto the leader's other instructions without any change of voice and caught the second man unawares. He checked, like someone who had tripped in the dark, and then produced a white card and handed it over. "Give that to your boss in the morning."

"You mean"—Pete took the card, confused—"this *is* official?" The incredulity in his voice had an overtone of optimism in it, which was quickly extinguished. He tried to read the card.

"Now get movin'," the stranger shouted, turning his back and waving an arm to the truckers.

The man Tim remained with his eye still on Pete, his rifle held more or less loosely. He jerked his chin up and threw a peremptory look back behind Pete and over his left shoulder. He said nothing, but Pete began to move as if that one hostile sliding glance had marked out a tangible path for him to follow. Bob did the same. The leader who was striding back toward the trucks turned round to see how far they'd gone and shouted, "Further!"

Tim jerked the rifle again from where he stood now at some distance.

The two guards retreated further, until they and the dogs were out of reach of the fumes, and Tim, having pulled his own mask up over his face, backed over to the trucks. For fifteen minutes the gang of outlaw truckers were busy. Bob and Pete were far enough away now to only just see the moving figures and hear the whine of the pumps.

"We really got to fill in after those bastards," Bob said, "you reckon?"

Pete was undoing the wad of notes. He glanced up toward the lights. "They're goin'," he said.

The trucks were on the move. The two guards watched them drive out of the gate.

"Look, see here," Pete said, shifting his weight with a

sudden conversational emphasis, a more cheerful note in his voice. "You know what I reckon? It's not such a bad deal. These guys are only illegal dumpers. That's no such terrible thing. We got enough lousy stuff here, they can add to it for all I care. And here's what we get for it!" He held up the wad of notes. "See what I mean?"

"Yeah," Bob said, feeling his jaw. Nothing was broken. He turned his head and spat into the ground to get rid of the taste of blood.

"Sheeba! Crack!" Pete called, and started to walk. They were halfway to the guardhouse. The dogs went speeding past in the dark. As the two guards retreated, their figures looked smaller and smaller against the lit backdrop of the guardhouse a hundred yards away. For a while silence settled back down and it was as dark as before.

CHAPTER 17

*C*ome in, come in!" Sir Adrian exclaimed when opening the door to his niece once again. "My goodness, I can see you're pleased to be leaving London."

If Rachel looked a new woman, he wasn't the only one who noticed it.

In the interval since her last visit to the Grimmonds, the daffodils had faded into rusty rags, and instead of the opalescent gloaming of spring, the full glare of an early summer evening lay flatly on the tarmac and the grass. The sky should have been blue but it was a grayish white, and the birds, although they couldn't avoid flying in it, were far less likely to sing.

In contrast, Rachel stepped along without one hint of the office-weary stoicism that had characterized her when last she came this way. She walked so brightly that more than once strangers smiled when they saw her. From Sloane Street she turned into Pont Street, prancing around the corner so smartly that her hair was still going one way when her body was already facing the next, and the doorman of the Carlton Towers checked his step in the very moment that he was about to lean down to the passenger door of an incoming Rolls, the better to look. Between the black silken wraps of the Arab ladies who climbed out and the five-pound note the daughter held and gave to him as he escorted them to the main door, he managed not to entirely miss the flick of Rachel's ankles as she passed by.

"Look at the sparkle in her eye, my dear." Adrian carried on to Sarah, as he and Rachel entered the drawing room. "I told you she would not mind at all being sent on business to America. She's a modern girl, full of get-up-and-go!"

Speaking as one who had been given few avenues of life to explore herself, and those rather limited like Harrods, Ascot, and the passage between the dining room and the kitchen, Sarah merely said, "I know it, Adrian. I never supposed otherwise." And she kissed Rachel. She planted her kiss on Rachel's cheek just in time before Adrian snatched his niece back again.

"Now, Rachel, you take this"—he handed her a glass—"and I want you to tell me all about your meeting with the steering committee and that little fellow, Mal Harris."

"Oh!" She raised her brows smilingly at him.

"As the chairman of the managing agency that has caused all the trouble, Uncle Adrian, do you think you should be told? Committee meetings are confidential."

"By all means!" he said. "If I hadn't chanced to have a policy of getting rid of trouble before it happened to myself, that claim would have landed in my books, you know."

"Well, of course."

"Besides, Stan Lacy has already reported back to me, but he didn't catch a glimpse of Mal Harris. He's the one I want to hear about."

"Really," she said. "Oh, I'm sorry, Aunt Sarah." She had knocked a little ornament sideways as she sat and put her glass on a table, but it was unharmed. Sarah was already on her feet, but she only had to set the little box to rights.

"No harm done," she said. "Adrian rushes you so."

"Well, I want to hear about this man Harris," he protested. "What's wrong with that?"

"A little man, Aunt Sarah. Small, weedy, in a tweed suit that looks as if he had it made by a village dressmaker, and with a strong Welsh accent."

"Good gracious," Sarah exclaimed politely.

"He's the one I'm going to America with."

Her aunt frowned. "Well, you'll be quite safe with him anyway."

Adrian laughed. "That's just it! My dear, you simply don't know! This man's reputation for getting into dangerous situations and fighting his way out is beginning to be a legend in Lloyd's."

Rachel was looking at him attentively. "I don't really know much about him," she said. "Are you sure it's the same person?"

"Of course." Sir Adrian sat down on the large sofa, the silk damask cushions of which puffed up around him as his weight displaced the air. "You remember Dick Trene, Sarah?"

"That frightful, common little man who was Ross-Gilbert's partner when they did all that stealing and Jane Berringer thought she'd have to sell her house?"

"Precisely. Dick Trene apparently put out a contract to get Mal Harris killed—and failed three times. But what interests me even more is the gossip about the minister. You know all that, Rachel?"

"Yes, I do. You wouldn't believe it to look at him."

"Why?"

"So meek and mild. And then just as you're turning your attention elsewhere, you catch a look in his eye." She laughed, and held her hands outstretched. "He's a very amusing man to watch. I think he's brilliant."

"So you're looking forward to this assignment," Sir Adrian said indulgently. "And the pollution background—what about that?"

"I'm reading it up. It's a fascinating subject." In saying this, Rachel demonstrated the limitless caprice of human nature, as the subject of the chemical composition of toxic waste dumps might have been expected, in different circumstances, to have won from her a more than usually acid put-down.

In this case, of course, the whole matter had assumed a completely different importance, since it had become the means of her escape from her London desk and from the drudgery of day-to-day broking. And not only the repercussions of Santhill on Bob Keats's syndicate, but also the wider issues of pollution throughout America, became as interesting, on closer examination, as the wings and thorax and antennae of a wasp seen through a microscope. It was a wasp that was likely to sting Lloyd's again, as Adrian had become fond of pointing out in recent weeks to his colleagues in and around the market. There were many of them there who would find their syndicate accounts so swollen with stings that "the Names on the syndicates would have to poultice them with"—he paused to consider a figure, his hooded eyes glinting with cynical amusement at his own conceit (in the seventeenth-century sense of the word)— "forty thousand pound checks. No. One hundred thousand pound checks. The members would be having to write out checks of that order."

They were all in the dining room by this time and seated at the table, where on this occasion Carmen was serving dinner so that Sarah did not have to keep getting up.

"This Santhill claim will be contested," Adrian was telling them both, and Sarah was listening, but she was inwardly preoccupied even more than usual with a plan of her own. Adrian said, "Every insurance organization has to contest claims. They'll go over it with a toothcomb to find out exactly what Lloyd's is liable for. Why else are Rachel and the loss assessor from Shipping Investigation Securities going over to America?"

Had Sarah challenged that idea, then? Had she, in an attempt to make some innocuous remark aimed at demonstrating attention, accidentally hit a sensitive point? "Oh, I know that," she said. Her nerves were on edge, and she corrected herself with a little inward stiffening of alarm.

Adrian ate very little. He was still on the subject of this aspect of the market. "But," he said, and picked at his food delicately, "once that figure is decided, Lloyd's, in its three hundred year history, has never failed to pay in full. That's quite a record, you know."

"When do you leave, dear?" Sarah cut in, with unintentional abruptness.

"On Thursday, Aunt Sarah."

Sarah made an effort not to look as if she were thinking of anything beyond Rachel's own progress. Dinner was nearly over. She looked across the table at Adrian, seeing behind him the well-polished silver shining on the side table and the multiple refractions of cut glass from all the paraphernalia to do with the wine. She knew that Adrian despised her, in a kindly way, for what he himself had made of her. Was it lack of imagination or stoicism that made her able to live with that fact?

"Shall we have coffee in the drawing room?" she said, getting up. Her heart began to beat faster even as she pushed back her chair, but no one would have guessed it.

"Come with me a moment, Rachel," she said. "I've got something to show you, dear. Adrian, will you pour the coffee? We'll be back in a moment."

Rachel followed her aunt from the drawing room toward the bedroom. Her mind was only half on what she was doing. She thought it was of no importance.

Adrian and Sarah's bedroom was a frowsty arrangement of twenty-year-old Peter Jones designing. It was what a vast number of upper-middle-class English women call home, and stale memories of which even Rachel had lying undisturbed in the back of her mind. She followed Sarah with some restraint, never having much to say to her when alone. She stood in the middle of the carpet hardly seeing or registering the purposeful way in which her aunt closed the door and turned with furtive urgency to the dressing table. Rachel said for lack of any other ideas and vaguely feeling it was expected, "May I use your bathroom."

"Of course, dear. But don't be long, will you?" she said, causing Rachel to look back over her shoulder with a glance of puzzled politeness. Sarah had taken a key from one drawer and was unlocking another. When Rachel re-emerged, she found Sarah waiting for her. She was standing where the lamp on the dressing table cast a livid upward shadow onto her face. It was this, Rachel wrongly imagined, that made her aunt look so pale.

Sarah said, "Rachel, I want to ask you a great favor."

"Of course," Rachel said easily. "What is it?"

"Only this." She put the knuckles of her right hand on the dressing table to steady herself, but her wrist went into a spasm that she couldn't control.

"Are you all right, Aunt Sarah?" Rachel said with sudden anxiety. "Had I better call—"

She was going to say her uncle. She had half turned but Sarah, with anxiety screwed up to a point of speechless violence, lunged forward and seized her arm.

"Don't!"

"All right. I won't." Rachel sounded sharp, but on hearing her own voice, she at once corrected it and reiterated, "Don't worry, Aunt Sarah. Don't be so upset. I'll help you. Sit down."

She even went forward and put her arm around her aunt's shoulder and drew her down to sit on the end of the bed. Sarah allowed herself to be seated, but without relaxing.

"I want you to do something for me when you are in Los Angeles," she said. "Let me say this quickly now. Adrian mustn't know. He will never forgive me. But it isn't that. I can't . . ." She faded out but pulled herself together. "It's Charlie."

At the mention of his name her voice broke. "I'm being ridiculous. Please, Rachel, just fetch me a glass of water from the bathroom."

When Rachel brought it, Sarah took the glass with a hand that still trembled.

"Aunt Sarah," Rachel said gently. "If you want me to contact Charlie in Los Angeles, of course, I will."

The poor woman was trying to pull herself together. "Adrian mustn't know."

"I see," Rachel said, although she didn't fully appreciate now, and had never suspected before, that Adrian maintained any ban on contact between Charlie and his mother. "How shall I . . . ?"

"Wait until you come back to London," said Sarah. "Charlie mustn't write. Adrian . . ."

"I understand," Rachel said. "This is his address, is it?" Sarah was pushing a paper into her hand with speechless, distracted insistence.

"But, Aunt Sarah," Rachel started again, as she took it. "Surely Uncle Adrian—"

"Don't!"

Sarah laid her hand on Rachel's and held it in rigid silence for a moment, as if building her self-control like a house of cards that the least movement would scatter. "Just go and see him, and when you come back to London"—she paused as if halfway up a steep flight of stairs—"we will meet, and you can tell me about him."

She couldn't say more.

"Of course, Aunt Sarah." Rachel kissed the poor woman once on the cheek. The skin was deliciously soft without the elastic resistance of youth. It had the softness and whiteness of fifty years of expensive cosmetic care regularly applied night and morning, and the downy depth of time.

The manicured hands unclenched, Adrian's step sounded at the end of the passage, but he contented himself with calling, "Your coffee's getting cold, both of you."

Sarah completed the manoeuvre of pulling herself together. She stood up. "You go in, dear. I'll be with you directly." She went toward the bathroom, where she could moisten a piece of cotton wool with cold water and just touch the skin under her eyes.

Rachel walked slowly back toward the drawing room. She felt emotionally disoriented, as if she had witnessed an unexplained phenomenon such as a flame of passionate, thwarted love springing from the cold flesh of a statue carved in stone. If Sarah loved her son so much, Adrian's ruthless discipline in disowning him and refusing all contact was terrible. To Rachel, Charlie figured only as a once charming older cousin whose tragic addiction and disgrace had taken place when she herself was too preoccupied with her university life to give him much thought. The idea that in his mother he could inspire a love so intense shocked her. And it raised the question of how Adrian could so utterly rule his wife as to lock up the passion of a mother in that cold, conventional housewife.

On the threshold of the brightly lit drawing room she put her preoccupations aside. Unaware of the irony of what she was doing, Rachel, as Sarah had so often done in the past, cast toward her uncle a glance of speculation blandly concealed in a smile. "Here you are at last," he said. "Now, have some coffee." And he held the full cup toward her.

CHAPTER 18

A few days later, at a kitchen table in a suburb of L.A., a more fortunate mother sat with her child. The sun that was no longer more than a bleached shadow over Cadogan Square was here still in its prime. Finn Garrett had returned home from the office to give her little girl a meal before the baby sitter came to look after her for the afternoon. The little girl was at the table, alternately eating and arranging her food in heaps with her fingers. As she did this, she quietly sang a disjointed rhyme of some sort that she had learned or made up, and the sound of her voice belonged to that category of noises that soothe the heart: a cat purring, bird song, the whir of a lawn mower.

The window let the sun in, and it draped itself in flags and patterns on the wooden floor and plaster walls, and the mother, with occasional companionable remarks and smiles, made notes in a book. There was no master in the offing, and no traffic noise to speak of because the house backed on to what an English person might call scrub land. This land had bushes, trees, and grass, but it had never been used for cultivation or grazing. It had never been a farm; no hedges or walls had ever divided it into pasture; no plough had ever ploughed it. It had an untenanted look that had as little to do with the charm of the wild as a homeless dog. A local trucker had used one acre to store some consignment or other that had turned out to be not worth moving on. In this area, as in many other areas in America and in some everywhere in the world, the land fulfilled the same role as a swimming pool with no water in it: it was there.

"Are you finished, Daisy?"

Finn closed her book. The sunlight picked out spots of gold in her gray eyes as if the irises were freckled. She rested her chin on her hand and smiled at the little girl.

"I've got to get back to work now, sweetheart," she said, "and Marilyn's coming back for you." The doorbell rang. "Ah, here she is!"

The woman who rang the doorbell also opened the door and entirely filled the space between the hinges and the latch. "Am I early?" she said. "Is my little honey bun ready for me?"

Marilyn was a walking advertisement for the theory that fat is happy. Between pneumatic lips of bright red her teeth flashed with a smile that included a patch of shining gold, and the chaotic undulations of her clothes were full of color.

"Hi," Finn said. "Come in."

"You're always so quiet when I come here, you two," Marilyn exclaimed. "I've come from Betsy's, and the twins were both yelling. This time it was the dog, but it's always something. And I said"—she put down her sack bag on the floor and plucked Daisy out of her chair like a giant about to eat a fruit—"I said, 'We don't want to be late to fetch Daisy, do we?'" And she kissed Daisy, who swayed sideways under the onslaught and caught hold of a swinging lock of caramel hair to steady herself.

"We're going to see the rabbits."

"Oh, are you?" Finn said. "Daisy will love that!"

The little girl's squeal of agreement was drowned in the shrilling of the telephone, and the room was suddenly as crowded and as noisy as it had been tranquil five minutes before. Finn looked at her watch. It was half past one. "I'd better answer that," she said, as she made to pick it up.

"We'll be off," Marilyn said in an exaggerated quiet tone, but her beautiful lips stretching round the syllables as if to help someone lip-read over the shrilling of the phone or, as Finn picked it up, the voice of the caller. "See you this evening," she mimed.

"I shouldn't be late," Finn said with her hand over the receiver, and watched the whole amazing bundle—Marilyn, baby, sack bag, soft pale hair pressed against tawny curls, little body clasped in bulging folds—disappear through the door. She turned back to the phone.

"Hello," she said. "Yes, Dr. Garrett here."

"Dr. Garrett! This is Rat."

Finn looked for the second time at her watch in that familiar reflex that has to do not with verifying the time, but a subconscious attempt to protect one's own store of precious minutes by checking them out at the approach of a well-known predator. This person who introduced himself so oddly on the phone was an environmental chemist obsessed with his subject who had made a name for himself almost on arrival at the university by writing a brilliant thesis based on an analysis of all the traces of chemicals and bacteria on the footprint of a rat.

Finn said, using his Christian name, "I'm afraid I'm about to leave for a meeting, Stephen. I can't be late."

"But I've got some amazing news!" Rat shouted. He sounded delighted, as if he was getting married or had won the state lottery. "There are heavy traces of carbide acid in the field samples I took for this paper. Yes, exactly! Carbide acid. And the charge is negative, so there's a catalyst. It could be increasing at a rate of ten to fifteen milli osmils per liter per hour."

"Where did you take the samples? I thought it was C4."

She referred to the grid of the state of California that she used in her environmental studies and reports, and which her students used also.

"Sure, it's C4. And there's no mistake. I've checked it over. Carbide acid—CVX2 over ninety—tested with—"

"Look, Stephen, I've got to go," Finn said. "There's some

mistake here, and I'll sort it out with you later. Are you in this evening?"

"I'm telling you, Dr. Garrett—"

"Rat, I've got to go. I'll call you later."

She went out into the bright sunlight, got into her car, and drove along the freeway. During the entire drive and the following two hours the substance of Rat's phone call was never quite absent from her mind. Although she was ninety-nine percent certain he had made a mistake, the remaining one percent injected intermittent stabs of anxiety to the flow of thoughts directed elsewhere.

If Rat was right, the pollution emanated from the Santhill Chemicals site in the Mojave Desert. No location could be more inconvenient for a scandal right now. The contents of that site had been very carefully itemized by the EPA, and she, as its representative, was actually on her way to a meeting to negotiate with all concerned. It would not be an appropriate moment to air Rat's uncorroborated suspicions, but she could not help having them in mind as she entered the Santhill building and went up to the tenth floor.

There was an uneasy atmosphere from the beginning. The meeting was chaired by Dale Falcus. He presided with his personal assistant on his right and the company's chief scientific manager, Matt Prior, on his left, with Jim Faber beside him. The Lloyd's representative, who had apparently come over from London, and a female executive from the firm of brokers sat side by side. As Finn Garrett was introduced to them and sat with her back to the twenty-foot frame of the window, preoccupation with Rat's announcement snared her mind, as a strand of barbed wire hidden in long grass might snare the feet of someone intending to walk straight across a field. All the calculations to be made presupposed the chemical analysis to be as presently documented by Santhill and the EPA. But Rat's phone call introduced an uncertainty. Many of the calculations would be changed by it, if true, and these were the very calculations they were all here to agree to.

Dale Falcus, who was personally back in form since the discovery of the insurance document, was enjoying himself. His life-style as a successful businessman was as lordly and remote in its way as that of a British colonial administrator. More so. He arrived at work, for example, perfectly groomed and fed without having had to plan or gather for himself one single item of the goods he'd used: his soap, his shower, his clean towels, his toothpaste, his fresh clothes, the clean house he walked through on his way to the breakfast table, his coffee, his bread. His car was ready for him, and so was his secretary, whose very clothes and body were presented as a deliberate mirror for his successful manhood, that he could look at and feel fine, as he took in the details of the appointments she'd arranged for him. This afternoon, as he walked into the meeting with the notes that his P.A. had handed him, he looked, to do him justice, like a prince of sorts. He was relaxed and strong, with the strength of a man groomed by others. His mind, uncluttered with the overtaxing worries of making himself comfortable in other ways, gave the illusion of strength in business matters. He knew his way around. He had made the necessary introductions like a good host.

"Mr. Harris—Mal—meet Dr. Finn Garrett, who is authorized by the EPA as their local representative in this matter. Mal Harris, representing Lloyd's of London. Miss Grimmond from Steiger and Wallace, the broker. Matt Prior, you know. Is that all? Jim Faber you've met. Now, let us begin."

He took his ballpoint, discovered it had gone dry, and got as far as half turning his head before his secretary, seated on a chair behind and to one side of him, leaned forward and gave him a fresh one.

"Let us begin," he continued, "by going over the data to do with the actual chemical problem we have here and what the EPA—the Environmental Protection Agency of America"—he rolled that off his tongue and somewhere, buried deep, was meant to be a flicker of humor, although whether at the expense of Uncle Sam or Finn Garrett, one couldn't tell—"wants us to do with it. Now. Dr. Garrett."

He leaned back in his chair as a signal to others to take over.

The chair didn't creak, partly because it was a well-made reproduction and partly because he kept himself trim.

Mal Harris also sat back and listened. His eyes, large and very deep set, tended to catch the light because of something to do with the sculpted angle of his brow and the thin, high bridge of his nose. It was perhaps this that gave to his expression an unexpected alertness, which caught the average person a glancing blow just when they were discounting him from their calculations. Several times during her discourse with Matt Prior across the table, and notably when the thought of Rat's bombshell caused her to look for words to introduce a peg on which to hang a future caveat, Finn Garrett, who was anything but average, caught the glitter of this eye. She hesitated.

"Just a moment, if I may interpose here. . . ."

Dale Falcus seized an opportunity; not that he had to seize anything, as his tone of voice did imply, although in a style angled as if to deny it. Finn immediately turned to him. The glass wall, shielded from direct light, created something like an underwater luminescence in the room that fell in soft patches and picked out certain planes and colors. Finn's hair, for example, was rather bleached by it, but her face was painted in cinnamon shadow, like a watercolor. Where a large blot of light fell on the table, the wood shone a rich maroon that reflected a painterly line against Rachel's bare arm, which lay upon it. It also caught the tawny, hazel gleam of Mal Harris's eyes.

"The chemical analysis I can't speak for," Dale said, "but you're satisfied, Matt, I take it."

Matt nodded.

"And the cleanup program from a time point of view derives from that, and we have certain schedules that we are invited, but not obliged, to meet?"

Dale froze silently in position, to cue in the agreement he was sure of getting, and then moved his hands again and glanced down at his notes. "So why do we need this open-ended clause you're suggesting here, Dr. Garrett? We're dealing with the waste as is. We're sure of our facts, aren't we?"

"Yes." Finn managed to say that in a tone that included the

possibility of a no. Dale was genuinely seeking clarification, but above all he saw his chance to use a bit of muscle.

"You don't sound confident, Dr. Garrett," he said in a suddenly slightly bullying tone. "What I'm saying is that we have to be able to draw a line under this question of content before we begin. Otherwise we have an open-ended situation here, which is unacceptable to us and I'm sure is unacceptable to our insurers. Where is Zack Webern?" He brought his head up very suddenly and sharply as he asked this, and the belligerent tone deepened. "We need the firm's lawyer here, and he's ill. Did you ring and tell him to get here, Jane? Did you do that?"

"I did, Mr. Falcus. I did again half an hour ago. But Mrs. Webern said he was under sedation. And you said, sir, that he wouldn't really be needed."

"Well, I said wrong," Dale bellowed. He played this scene from time to time, and the restraint of those around him gave him the impression he got away with it. However, he had done Finn Garrett a favor. If she had had scruples, he had settled them.

"I'm not suggesting an open-ended clause," she said coolly. "Perhaps Matt understands me better when I say we must always allow for catalytic changes."

Matt Prior who, in spite of being forty, had what almost amounted to an adolescent crush on Finn Garrett, threw all his weight behind that with unsubtle promptness, and Dale Falcus made a note to do something soon to annoy him.

"Okay," he said for the time being. "Mal Harris, is that all right by you?"

"Well, thank you, I would like to put a point here," Mal Harris said. Finn looked closely at him for the first time. "The cover given by Lloyd's runs from 1955 to '62. Any waste or percentage of waste not deposited between those two dates cannot be included in costs met by Lloyd's for clearance. I think we all understand that?" They all nodded, expecting him to say more. "And the company is able to certify that the site in question was not used at all after 1962?"

Dale looked to his P.A. to answer that one.

"1962 was the last," he said.

"It is guarded, presumably?" Mal Harris said.

"Enclosed and guarded."

"Well, in that case," Mal said, "after such a lapse of time we don't need a clause for catalytic changes."

But Dale Falcus, whose purpose it was to get as much out of Lloyd's as possible, was not going to help him after all. He suddenly wanted that clause in if Lloyd's showed signs of wanting it out. Fortunately Matt Prior was alert to the same purpose and bailed himself out of his previous gaffe by citing chapter and verse about delayed chemical reactions in certain atmospheres and soil structures.

But this was not a meeting for hard and fast decisions. This was a meeting for sizing up the parameters. And it was also for sizing up the people. Finn Garrett, Mal Harris decided, had something on her mind. That beautiful, clear gray-blue gaze had a mote in it.

When the meeting broke up, he and Rachel Grimmond moved off less quickly than the rest of them. Dale Falcus, in hospitable mode after the business of the day, reminded them that he and Barbara were expecting them for dinner. He asked ritual questions about their hotel and the weather in England and had got as far as the door when his secretary reentered almost at a run and nearly catching him on the wrist with the knob. Something must have very much rattled her.

"There's an urgent message," she said, "from security." She obviously knew something of what this message was about. She was holding a piece of thin white card, but the unexpected juxtaposition of her boss so close to the door unbalanced her, and although she controlled every other reaction like the displacement of her hair and the need to catch her own step in mid-pace, she dropped the card. Mal Harris bent to pick it up and return it to her. He read it in the process. It was the card that Bob and Pete had been given by their visitors.

"I'll be with you in a moment, Jane," Dale said frigidly. The secretary effaced herself. If she could have reabsorbed the last five minutes of her life, she would have done so, and she showed signs of trying. When Mal Harris and Rachel Grimmond had gone, Dale called her in again immediately.

"What was that about, Jane," he said angrily. "Presumably there's something terrible going on and you wanted our important visitors to know about it."

"I'm so sorry," Jane said, "but there's a guard from the Mojave site downstairs in security, and I thought you'd want to see him right away."

"Why? Surely whatever it is, he should see Mr. Larson."

"But there's been a break-in," Jane persisted. "Armed men turned up at the dump!"

"*What!*"

"Armed truckers. This is what I've been trying to tell you. They've been dumping fresh waste."

"Who told you this?"

"Security called up. They've got the man there right now."

"Stephen," Dale buzzed his P.A. on the boardroom switchboard. "Stephen, get in here right away." He turned back to Jane. "You're not to speak of this to anybody, d'you hear. My God, this is all we need!"

His P.A. came through the door. "Stephen, we've got a problem. Apparently there's been an armed break-in at the Mojave site. I don't want anyone else to know about this. Not anyone. Do you understand that? One of the guards is down with the security officer. Get both men up, and don't let them speak to anyone else."

"Yes, sir," Stephen said, and went immediately.

"Jesus Christ!" Falcus said, his mind full of the debate he had just supervised around the boardroom table. "This could blow the whole thing. What *is* that?"

Jane had been trying to give him the card, but he was too panicked to take hold of it. Now at last he had noticed it. "Where did this come from?" he asked, taking it.

"The leader of the armed truckers gave it to our guard and told him to pass it on to the head management."

"One of the gang did this?" Dale said, still not reading the card. "The trucker?"

"Yes, Mr. Falcus."

He turned it over at last and read it. His lips moved like a kid with a comic. He read, " 'Call Zack Webern and mention George Cash.' "

"Is it blackmail, Mr. Falcus?"

"I don't know what the hell it's about," Dale Falcus said, "but there's an easy way of finding out."

And he walked, grimly, over to the phone.

CHAPTER 19

*W*hile this was going on, Matt Prior was accompanying Finn to the entrance of the building. He was making the most of it. Each time he pressed an elevator button or held open a door, he spun it out, to give himself more time. He was outlining the main points of a hypothesis he was currently testing in research, but when they reached the hall, he remembered something else.

"I saw your paper, 'The Environmental Tide,' was quoted in Congress," he said. His face glowed with vicarious pride. She smiled at him in response. Finn, who was tall, could look him in the eye, and on this occasion her glance, friendly and at the same time concentrated, seemed to pass straight through his retina and work some serious damage as it passed down the nervous system of his body. In fact, she was sizing up the pros and cons of mentioning Rat's phone call.

"Can I ask you about something in confidence, Matt," she said.

"Sure. Go ahead. Is it to do with this case at Santhill?"

"Well. Could there be any substance on that waste site that we've missed, and which could be capable of catalyzing . . ." She gave him all the details Rat had given her.

"No," he said.

She agreed at once. "Of course not."

"We took samples as well as the EPA," he said, "and it's bad enough, as you know, but nothing as dangerous as that. Why do you ask?"

"A student of mine rang up," she said, "but even the most brilliant can make mistakes. I guess that's what he's done." And when she had got this far she saw, over Matt's shoulder, the Lloyd's representative and Rachel Grimmond coming out of the elevator.

"I'd sooner not discuss this in front of Mr. Harris," she said. "He's coming up behind you."

Matt turned. Perhaps in obedience to Finn's wishes he scarcely even looked at the Lloyd's man, directing all his attention instead to the long-legged girl who was with him. She had a very un-American look, but she was glamorous and different, and the admirer of Finn Garrett could appreciate that. Belatedly, in reply to Finn, he said, "Silent as the grave. I won't say a word. Dale Falcus would kill me."

"Hello again," Rachel said. "We were just going to ask at the desk how to get to our hotel. We haven't got our bearings yet. Where is Bel-Air?"

"I can give you a lift. It's on my way," Finn said.

The reluctance she actually felt at exposing herself at close quarters to Mal Harris's penetrating observation gave way, typically, to impulses of hospitality, and Finn wasn't going to let the strangers find their own way to their hotel. She promised herself that as soon as she had dropped them off, she would call Rat and sort this matter out.

The three of them parted from Matt in the hall and left together. The glass drum of the door spun constantly, bringing people in and taking them away again. From the lofty flamboyance of the hall with the sound of footsteps and voices of people on business played back from the hard surfaces and roof with muted clamor, they stepped out and into the upholstered, air-conditioned intimacy of the waiting car.

Rachel sank into her seat with a sigh of exhaustion.

"Are you tired?"

"Oh no," she said. "Well, a bit."

"Flying this way is tough," Finn said kindly. Mal Harris looked at her thin, long-fingered hand on the steering wheel. His mind was on that hesitation, that almost fear that had interrupted the flow of her evidence during the meeting. But for the moment he sat very quiet, his eyes mildly fixed between the shoulders of the two women.

Finn drove smoothly up the hill with quick-witted but unaggressive dispatch. Hesitation and uncertainty were not characteristics of hers, then. So what serious doubt did she have about the status quo of that waste disposal site that had suddenly distracted someone so decisive during the meeting? This and the cryptic message on the white card were matters that interested him. He was prepared to take his time finding out, but as the car stopped and he was about to get out and Rachel was already saying her farewells, he felt a sudden foreboding. The unaccountable sensation took him completely by surprise. He looked instinctively to see if a cloud had blotted out the sun or something else was happening in the immediate vicinity, but the surroundings were as bright and bland as before. He got out, still feeling the inward vibrations of this unaccountable fright. Finn Garrett, sitting at the wheel, was looking up at him. The transparent intelligence and gentleness of her face prompted him to ask the question he had intended to hold back until later.

"I had the impression there was something you were not quite happy with at the meeting," he said. "Was it to do with the problem of Santhill?"

"Oh," she said, and let the air out of her lungs with a cryptic sigh. "I'll let you know if there's a problem. One thing the EPA is not at all into is any kind of concealment."

He believed her. But as her car drove away, he looked after it with foreboding on account of something else—he didn't know what.

*A*s soon as she drove away, Finn called Rat's number on her car phone, but getting no answer, she headed in the direction of the laboratory in the hope that he would still be there.

He was not.

The lab assistant, who was about to leave himself, said there was a note from Rat and some samples left out for her. She walked rapidly through the empty corridors, the woven soles of her shoes making very little noise as she went, the luminous shadow of her sand-colored skirt flicking through the quiet spaces like a mote of reflected sunlight. The work she found left out for her tallied precisely with what she had been told. The carbide acid precipitate was in a container for dangerous poisons, and the sample from which Rat said he had extracted it apparently came from an open section of the Santhill site in the Mojave Desert. It was only over this exact location that any question could be said to hang. She went over to the phone and again contacted Rat's private number. A friend answered and gave her another number. She tried it but got no answer. She stood motionless, weighing up the options. The meeting scheduled for the following morning would include Santhill's lawyer as well as the Lloyd's negotiators. If she went into negotiations with any uncertainty on her mind, her position would be impossible. The only alternative was to take a second sample from the grid area that evening and do a second analysis first thing in the morning.

With this plan in mind she left and drove home toward Barstow. She could expect, when she arrived, to find Daisy and Marilyn halfway through their evening meal and preparations for bed.

"Marilyn, would you be able to stay late tonight?" she asked soon after she got in.

"Oh, gee," Marilyn said, looking up from the side of the bathtub where she was crouched. Daisy looked up too. "I got a date," Marilyn said in a tone of voice between consternation and delight. "I promised to go watch football."

Finn came right into the room and sat on the wicker chair and spread a towel over her knees.

"I'm real sorry," Marilyn said. "I can stay half an hour or so."

"Don't worry."

Marilyn reached into the tub and took Daisy under the armpits, her own dimpled fingers sinking into the child's soft flesh as she lifted her out. As she swung her round to put her on Finn's knee, Finn said.

"I'm just thinking of doing a trip to collect a sample. But I suppose I could take Daisy with me." She ended up the sentence redirecting her voice for Daisy's benefit and making the child break into earsplitting squeaks. "After all, she's three now, and that's mighty big. Big enough to go for a ride after supper, wouldn't you say, Marilyn?"

"Ooooh!" Marilyn said, and her mouth in the process described an indescribably pneumatic O. Daisy gazed at her, waiting for what would come next. Marilyn picked up a corner of the towel and made a tickling dab at her nose. The child snuffled delightedly, putting up her arms over her face and her hair falling over her arms

"Where do you have to go?" Marilyn said to Finn.

"Oh . . . , to get a soil sample from just nearby, into the desert a mile or so. Daisy will enjoy the ride," Finn said. "And who's your date?"

Half an hour later she left with Daisy. It was a beautiful evening. The sky was violet colored, the dust track under the car's wheels golden as the cooling sun fingered it. Here and there among the scattered bushes one was radiantly in flower, and the crows that flew tipped their wings and swung against the backdrop of the distant mountains or swooped into them as if diving into a well.

It took half an hour to reach the chemicals site. The day-time shift was still operating. The man on duty made no diffi-culties about Finn's unexpected arrival and the informality of her inspection but simply took her over in the buggy, while his wife, who had come to fetch him home, played with Daisy.

"There hasn't been any new activity here has there?" Finn asked him. "Nothing since the fall?"

"No. Couldn't be," he said, looking at the area. The fill-ing-in done by Bob and Pete wasn't noticeable since it had not required turning over new earth. Finn identified the area in the grid and with gloved hands scooped up a sample and boxed it. The whole operation took less than ten minutes.

As they were returning to the main gate, a car approached and stopped. Two dogs leapt out, their barks of arrival ringing in the cooled air, the setting sun turning their ginger coats a darker smudge of gold. The men with them got out more slowly.

"Who's this?" Bob said. Chris's wife was holding Daisy out of reach of the dogs while ten yards away Finn and Chris walked from the buggy.

"She's from the state office," Chris's wife said. "Nothin' special. Samples or something."

She put Daisy down to open the door of her own car. "Are you ready, honey?" she called to her husband. "I promised Sue, remember?"

"Okay, okay," her husband said.

Daisy ran over to her mother.

"Thanks very much," Finn called to the other woman, and to Chris himself, "Thanks. Don't let me hold you up now."

When they were gone Finn, having put the sealed box on the backseat of her car, stood for a moment holding Daisy by the hand so that Pete could talk to her. The dogs who were never far from Pete trotted back and forth with their springing gait pacing out their territory again and stopping to nuzzle the child when Pete snapped his fingers.

"Bin here long?" Bob said. His small, sharp blue eyes had taken in the sample box anxiously, and he had trouble not repeatedly glancing at it in the car.

"Ten minutes," Finn said. "There are meetings tomorrow regarding the site clearance."

He would have liked to ask her which section she sampled from, but it might look suspicious. The buggy had been coming back from number 2 gate, maybe. Or number 3.

"Come on then, Daisy," Finn said, and made to go with a smile. Bob sucked in his lower lip and held it down with his teeth, looking at her. He was thinking. Pete straightened his legs and stood up. The child ran round to the passenger seat in the car, and her mother strapped her in and then looked back at the men. All three of them were more silent than they should have been. In the normal way Pete and Bob would have clattered about with the business of the place, and they would have asked the woman questions about where she lived and maybe made some comments about the car. Pete might have made Sheeba do her jumping trick to amuse the little girl, and both of them would certainly have responded to Finn as a woman and noticed her beauty. However, things being the way they were, they sized her up only in so far as she had that sample box on the backseat. They eyed her. They were quieter than they realized and through the gaps in their stilted conversation Finn felt the first subliminal warning of danger.

"I'll be going then," she said. "Good night."

A cold breeze whistled round the corner of the guardhouse. The sun, unnoticed, had let slip the hound of night. The last trace of warmth ran out of the colors of the surrounding desert with the quick and sudden movement of water escaping from a broken bowl.

But the men did nothing. Yet.

"I'll close the gate after you, ma'am," Bob said. He walked sullenly behind the car, and Finn heard the clang of the metal behind her as she headed for home.

For perhaps a quarter of a mile she drove gratefully away. Daisy was drowsily slumped in her seat, and it would have taken less than half an hour to get home if nothing had gone wrong. But at that point, with a sudden lurch to the steering wheel, the front off-side tire punctured. Finn cut the engine. In the sudden silence of the empty landscape the sound of the car door opening was the only distinct sound within hearing. Finn shivered. Although it was not yet quite dark, she realized she couldn't see clearly, and leaning in through the open window, switched on the lights.

Beside the guardhouse Bob, who had not taken his eyes off the retreating car, sprung to attention. "She's stopped," he shouted to Pete. "What the hell . . . ?"

Finn looked back to the perimeter fence and the guardhouse not far away. It was possible the men had seen her stop and would come and help her. She could hear the dogs barking in the distance, and the guardhouse light had been switched on. After a moment's hesitation she decided against shouting or attempting to attract their attention. She could change the tire herself without much trouble. She had a spare. She had a decent jack and a long-handled spanner to give the leverage necessary for a woman to be able to undo the wheelnuts even if they had been tightened by machine. She got going with it, hearing only the sound of her own shoes in the gravel, the scrape of the trunk latch, the sporadic scuffle of the night wind getting up, the muted bang of metal against metal as she lifted on the new wheel.

But then, as she was crouching there, suddenly, across the desert, she saw lights. Another track approached the area from the northwest, converging on the Santhill site, and along this route three sets of beams were moving. They dipped and lurched with the unevenness of the track's surface giving the impression, what with the intervening darkness, of perhaps traveling on water rather than land. She stared at them a moment, bent over the wheel that she was rolling round to the back of the car. She finished stowing it and stood up, staring intently again toward the advancing beams. It was three trucks, identifiable by the height, size and distance of their headlights, and there was no mistaking where they were going. They were heading for the Santhill site.

She reached through the driving window and switched off her own car lights. Then she got back into the driving seat and started up the engine. It was a Mercedes and quiet. With the lights off she turned around in a wide curve and drove back surreptitiously toward the wire. Bob had never taken his eyes off her. There was a pair of binoculars hanging in the guardhouse, and he had fetched them ten minutes before when he saw her stop, his movements brusque and urgent, full of anxious aggression. Calling her every name under the sun, he had clamped them to his eyes, and when he saw she'd got a puncture, he watched every move she made changing the wheel. He had kept up a running commentary to Pete whenever Pete was within hearing.

"Did you see that, Pete. Have a go. Look at that leg."

"Nup." Pete turned down the offer of the binoculars, as if not to look at her would make her go sooner. "I want that lady outta here. Those trucks'll be comin' any minute."

"Christ! Here they are," Bob said suddenly, almost in a whisper. Pete saw them too. His heart lurched. They advanced like the distant glitter of the fires of hell.

He'd been in half a mind not to show at work tonight, but his wife had talked him out of it, and then, there was the money. He'd decided to stick it out.

"Give them over here now," he said in a quiet voice to Bob, holding out his hand for the binoculars and keeping his eye on the trucks.

"Hang on!" Bob said, not moving. "She's seen them." He spat out the words. "Now what the hell!"

"Give 'm over here!"

Pete snatched the binoculars. First he checked the trucks and then swung over to the woman and the car. In the twilight after she had switched off the lights he could just still make out the dimly reflective surfaces of the Mercedes, and when he'd steadied the glasses and his eye had adjusted, the woman herself in her pale skirt, pale skin, pale hair. He saw her check, stare, get into the driving seat. He swung over to the trucks, now in full view. Back to the girl. The Mercedes was swinging round and coming very slowly toward the gate.

"The stupid bitch!" he said. "She's coming back."

"What'll we do?" Bob panicked. "C'mon, Pete, for Chrissake. If those men have to smash the gate in again, we'll have the repair to do like last time. C'mon. Leave the girl to me."

He dashed into the guardhouse and threw the switch to stop the alarm going off. Down by number 3, it being as yet still and quiet before the actual arrival of the trucks, the electronic lock all by itself retracted with a single, audible click.

Half a minute later the roar of the trucks breasted the slight rise in the ground and their lights began to hit the wire. The crisscross mesh sliced the beams up and deposited them in rectangles of light across the dirt floor. The gate swung wide.

"You stay here," Pete said. "Watch her." He leapt into the buggy and careened off down the inside of the perimeter wire to gate 3. Bob continued to watch the woman in the car. It was hard to see, but dimly he could just make out that she was no longer driving forward. She had come as close as she dared, and it was close enough to see what was going on. She watched as the three trucks went in at the gate. Sooner than she had expected the first truck came out again.

When it came out, it turned off the path it had originally followed. She waited in the darkness watching it anxiously. It was driving away from the gate at an angle not directly toward her but between the car and the further track. Stealthily, her heart jolting, she began to turn the car to drive away. At that instant the truck turned abruptly at right angles, coming straight at the Mercedes with a sudden roar and throwing the full beam of its headlights on her. The whole of the inside of her car was lit up like an electrified cage while the shadow of it was thrown in front on the desert floor. Close behind, the truck charged, its jaws full of noise and blinding light.

Finn threw her own main beam switch and stamped on the accelerator so that the overdrive shot the car forward, sending out a spray of gravel from the back wheels. Daisy woke with a squeal of protest that intensified into a howl as the car continued to crash forward along the track. The overdrive of the Mercedes, as it sometimes did, had stuck and locked the car into a low gear. The revs climbed up the clock completely out of kilter with the speed the car was doing, and the truck gained on them. When the distance between the truck and the car had narrowed, the man sitting in the cab of the truck beside the driver shouted, "Hit it. Give it a shunt!"

The Mercedes put on a spurt as the transmission momentarily freed itself.

"Don't let it get away!"

The driver's boot was flat against the cab floor. A pothole caught the Mercedes a sharp blow against the chassis. From the vantage point of the truck towering over it, the car was seen to crack down, but continued unslacking and still gaining from the truck. Ahead of her Finn saw another hole, and in the instinctive movement of however slight a check, the transmission locked again.

"Now hit her!"

The driver slammed into the back of the Mercedes, but not too hard. Daisy yelled, her voice shrilling above the crash of gears and the loud whine of the laboring motor. The front tires of the Mercedes bit into the dust with the impact of the truck, but Finn wrenched the wheels to the right and took off across the ground. It was too soft and hard in patches. Swerving to miss a tall shrub, she hit the path again.

"Clip the left!" The driver did what his boss said. He was enjoying this. He used the truck really neat. He went after the offside back light and clipped it hard. The metal crumpled. The shards of red plastic flew off into the desert, where they probably still are.

"Get alongside."

The truck crossed tracks and roared alongside, the cab fully four feet above the girl in the driver's seat of the Mercedes. The passenger in the truck who was giving all the orders leaned out of his window and looked down.

"Now get in front and stop," he ordered over his shoulder. The driver accelerated, swerved in front of the Mercedes, and jammed on his brakes. The Mercedes looped round the stationary truck just in time and made off across the desert, dodging bushes and scrub. The truck bore down with no trouble, crushing everything in its path.

"Hit it again," the man shouted. "Harder."

"Do I kill her?"

"No."

The two small blond heads below in the lurid glare of the headlights looked like moths.

The driver crouched lower over the wheel in the concentration of aiming and slammed the nearside taillights with the reinforced front bars of the truck. It looked as if the car would overturn, but Finn spun the wheel and made an attempt at accelerating away again. The car was hooked to the truck. The torn metal split with a bang and released the Mercedes. A second later the smashed wing that had sprung back dug into the revolving tire. There was a smell of burning rubber and the tire burst.

"She's blown," yelled the driver. "We've got her now."

He screeched the truck to a halt and left the motor running. The cries of the child could be heard at last above the din. The man said to his driver, "You leave this to me," and leapt down onto the track.

The woman was undoing the child's seat belt and taking her into her arms where she sat. The man snatched open the door.

"Get out," he said.

"No."

Her voice was unexpectedly steady, but it only checked him for a second. He'd seen the sample box that Pete had warned him about on the back seat. The door was buckled from the impact of the truck, and he pulled it apart from the body of the car with ease, and reached in and took the box.

"You might as well not take that," she said. "There's another sample in the laboratory."

He took it and tossed it up to the driver in the cab.

"Is that so," he said. "In that case, you're going to take care of it for us. You're going to keep your own mouth shut and everybody else's, lady."

He reached down. She didn't see what he was going to do until the last second. The skin on the back of his hands looked black, but it was only hair, oil, and dirt. He gripped the child round her body. Finn made as if to scream "No," and her lips formed the word, but terror struck her dumb. Although her lungs were bursting and she strained to scream as loud as she could, only a strangled whisper escaped her. Years later the truck driver, who was impervious to almost everything, remembered that, and it woke him up at night. Now the man pulled the child away, easily breaking the clutch of the little fingers and the frantic mother like tearing ivy off a wall. Finn's own hand ripped the child's sleeve. A whisp of Daisy's torn hair got caught in her ring. Daisy's screams split the darkness like the sound of a knife screeching on a plate.

"Speak one word of this," the man yelled, "and you'll never see this kid again.

He strode round the truck holding the child with one fist knotted in her hair. But if he expected the child's mother to just sit there and watch him walk away, he had a surprise coming. Finn leapt from the car and threw herself at him with a force that shocked, although it couldn't seriously inconvenience, him. The man turned and gave her a hard kick that looked as if it could break her thigh and sent her flying.

"I mean that!" he yelled. "You set up the alarm, and you don't see this kid again. If you see us right, I'll give her back when we've dumped the last load."

But Finn had again leapt up before he could finish speaking and threw herself at him as if she hadn't heard a thing he said, so that with his last words he gave her another kick.

"Why don't you kill her, Fratelli?" the driver shouted. "Look." He leaned across to where the other man had now got up into the passenger seat, either to hand something or pull down the glass, but the other hit his hand to one side.

"Drive!" he shouted.

The child flung herself toward the open window as soon as he let go of her hair and got halfway out, but he snatched her back in. Her face was cut against the ragged back of the seat.

Incredibly, the mother hurled herself at the moving truck. Between front and back were the usual coupling structures. On part of this, one hand got a hold. With the other she seized a steel strut that was sharp where it had come loose from a fixing and sank steadily into the flesh, as she gripped it. Her right leg dragged in the gravel. She hauled herself up like a tiger in a pit digging his claws into the wall of it, every muscle bunched for a leap. She got up onto the cab, the structure lurching under her, the wind of their passage beginning to lift her as if God himself would parody the snatching of the child and lift the mother out of the arms of the thieves.

"What the hell's that?" shouted the driver above the yells of the child, as the mother's legs banged on the roof over his head. Above him Finn clawed at a hold and missed. Her body jerked sideways. Her other hand slipped in its own blood. The driver stamped on the brakes, and over the windshield jerked the torn arm and bloodsoaked head of the mother still fighting for a hold, her hair tangling in the wipers.

"Christ, she's still there!" The man, holding the child to one side with his left hand, reached out of the window with his right and got hold of a piece of cloth.

"Kill her!" the driver yelled. "What's the problem, Fratelli? She can't say anything if you fuckin' kill her."

"Brake!" Fratelli ordered. The driver stamped again on the brakes. Finn's body shot off the roof of the cab and hit the ground with an impact loud enough to be heard above all the noise. Drops of her blood backlashed like rain on the windshield as she fell. Fratelli rammed a fistful of cloth against the child's mouth to stifle her screams. In the sudden comparative silence the driver said, "She's dead anyway. Why didn't you shoot her?"

"I wanted her alive to protect our interests," Fratelli said. "If there's another soil sample in the lab, they might know something. But if she's talking on our side, she can keep it sweet."

"She's not talking now," said the driver.

"Fuck!" said Fratelli.

ale Falcus, with the hairs standing up on the back of his neck, waited for Jane Webern to bring Zack to the phone. The lawyer's voice, when at last he spoke, sounded muffled and wandering, but Dale cut through the complaints or apologies without caring which they were.

"There's been a break-in at the old waste disposal site in the Mojave. Illegal dumpers," he said. "Do you know anything about this?"

"Do I know anything about this?"

Dale gritted his teeth. "I've got a good reason to ask you," he said. "I've got a message here. The leader of the gang of truckers that held up the security guard says—I've got it written down here—to 'Call Zack Webern and mention George Cash.' Now what is this, Zack? What the hell's going on here?"

Zack Webern felt a rush of something like a hot dark wind pour through every channel in his body displacing the blood, emptying the heart, so that it pumped on air with a sudden awful clatter.

"Zack!"

"I'm here, Dale. Give me time."

"Give you time? What the hell are you talking about? I'm asking you a question. We have an emergency here."

Jane snatched the receiver at her end a split second before Zack dropped it, and then attempted to catch him as he folded toward the floor. Dale's voice could be heard yelling from the earpiece as it lay on the carpet against the table leg. At last Jane picked it up again.

"What's going on?" shouted Dale.

"He fainted, that's what's going on. I have to go. I'll ring you."

She put down the phone without waiting for a reply, and Dale, his mouth dry, a bead of sweat beginning to run down from the hairline, replaced the receiver in his office. He waited five minutes without saying a word to anyone, and then the phone rang again. Zack's wife said, without preamble, "He wants to speak to you."

Dale's hand gripped the receiver round the throat until the lawyer's voice spoke again.

"I'll be with you in half an hour," Zack said. "Get . . ."

"Zack, I will not have you going out of the house!" Jane's voice broke in. She snatched the receiver.

"Dale Falcus. My husband is ill. He fainted just now. What *is* this? He is too ill to leave the house, I'm telling you. Since when does the firm's lawyer get ordered around like some office boy, when he's too sick to leave his bed? Dr. Zeigler has ordered—"

"Give me that phone, Jane," Zack said to her.

She gave it to him. She was frightened. The two red patches in her cheeks drained away visibly as she watched her husband arrange with Dale Falcus for an emergency meeting of the board of directors, and then hand the receiver to her as if he was too tired himself to put it back where it belonged. She began to say, "What's happened?" but heard herself say instead, "What have you done?"

At five o'clock Zack Webern walked into Charles Seaford's private office at last looking like a ghost. Zack, who had been thin already, had lost weight rapidly. The skin around his eyes had been sucked into the hollows of his skull. His mouth, always well defined, had a vermilion tinge to it. Charles Seaford said, "Sit down." It was an order. There was nothing of friendly solicitude in his tone. "Vincent, shut the outside door, will you." And with the flick of a switch, "I want no calls."

His secretary's answer through the intercom was cut off on the very utterance with just the sound of a quarter word.

"Now."

The lawyer faced them all. He took a step out of the nightmare that had confined him. "The Lloyd's insurance document was forged on my orders," he said. "George Cash is the name of the man who did it."

For the next fifteen minutes while he described the process of the forgery and details of George Cash's background, he took without flinching the barrage of questions and abuse that the other men threw at him. It was a relief to feel the impact of some of the punishment he had seen coming to him like a man who has watched a wave that is going to kill him build itself slowly up from the bosom of the sea. He was not brave. But he had a flame inside him that, just as it had never been particularly fed, neither had it ever been extinguished. This stubborn fire burned in him now, and when the deluge of their anger and contempt broke over him, this small flame continued, in defiance of all expectation, to burn.

This had some effect on his co-directors. Vincent Cordoba, for instance, felt some respect for him which he had never imagined Zack Webern could arouse. He himself was having to be careful not to overplay his part. This was the first crisis in his own covert exploitation of the Santhill conspiracy, and he produced just about the amount of venomous recrimination that he would have done if blameless. He left Dale Falcus and Charles to play the lead roles. No one there knew that Vincent Cordoba had anything to do with the armed truckers.

"Where does this leave us?" Charles Seaford said after an hour's talk. "Just look at the dangerous position we're in. A criminal gang of illegal operators are in a position to blackmail this firm into keeping silent while they dump a consignment of unknown toxicity on our land. And it's happening at the very moment when we were going to be able to get rid of that problem on our insurance, putting the insurance in jeopardy."

"Well, Charles . . . !"

Dale's reminder of the incongruity of what he had just said whipped Charles up into more anger but he held his tongue. Vincent let out a sharp contemptuous laugh that fortunately could take the brunt of more than one interpretation. These men were certainly no better than himself. They were more than prepared to keep the proceeds of the forgery if they could. Their indignation was all against it going wrong. The honest option—the turning over of poor old Zack to the mercies of the law and withdrawing the claim on Lloyd's—had been rejected in as much time as it had taken everyone to realize how much money it would cost. They would be back at square one, with Santhill being bled to death by the EPA.

"There's no danger that the EPA has heard of this, is there? Or the Lloyd's man?"

"No," Dale Falcus said. His mind swept bluntly over the afternoon's meeting.

"So, if we just keep quiet . . ." continued Charles.

As if mimicking their own program, they kept quiet there and then for perhaps ten seconds. Rather as Vincent had predicted: Charles, in a glum but stubborn and statesmanlike pose, with both hands on his desk full square; Dale, standing; Jim Faber, looking from one to the other waiting for them to speak; and Zack, locked into the hard silence of his humiliation. They were just as quiet as mice.

"That's that then." Charles broke the silence.

"Not quite." Dale looked across at Zack. "We've got to find out how these men got a line on the forgery. Who leaked this information? This fellow George Cash? You'll have to get on to him and sort it out." He directed his voice at Zack without calling him by name. "Can you do that?"

"God, what a mess!" Charles Seaford exploded. "If that guy—"

"Look, calm down, Charles. It was probably a bit of careless talk. He'd have nothing to gain by deliberately blowing his own scam."

Seaford rested his forehead on his right fist in a gesture of abdication.

"See to it, Zack," Dale rapped out.

What would he think, Vincent speculated, keeping his own face lowered and watching Zack out of the corner of his eye. What would he think if he knew his own son had done this? Vincent, who didn't by any means wish to pay for the profits from the toxic waste consignment by seeing the value of his stake in Santhill do a nosedive, made a mental note to speak again himself to Daniel Webern. To secure the authenticity of that insurance document against being blown, nothing would be more effective than a word in Daniel Webern's ear from his Uncle Vincent.

CHAPTER 22

*T*he following morning the participants of the meeting on Santhill's toxic waste clearance reconvened in the board-room with one exception: Finn Garrett was missing. Calls were made to her office both in the city and at the university, but drawing a blank as they did, the meeting had to be postponed. Dale Falcus was privately glad. He needed time to let his mind settle after the shocks of the previous day. He needed, as Vincent had pointed out, to watch it in front of that Lloyd's fellow.

"Mal," Rachel said, as they walked toward the front entrance of the building, "I think I'll go and visit Charlie. I told you about him. He's my cousin. I promised his mother to look him up."

"You go ahead," he replied thoughtfully. "I've got a few things to look into. See you back here at two o'clock."

A few minutes later Rachel was heading downtown in a cab with upholstery that reeked strongly of the ubiquitous American sweet raspberry spray. As this trip was taken on impulse, she had not telephoned Charlie to say that she was coming, and she could be lucky and find him in; or not, as the case might be. She didn't really care; she relished the opportunity to move alone through a city so new to her. When she arrived at the house on Fifth Street, there was a very long wait after she rang the bell, and she stood surveying the neighborhood. The streets of this poor part of town, loaded with grime and halfway through a divorce with European culture, threw up here and there the unbroken bones of a once splendid house. Charlie lived where skid row started, and in the evening the pavements were lined with queues of poor people waiting for the evening meal to be dished out by the nearest charity mission on Los Angeles Street and Fifth. Some, with a view of time that had transcended human illusions, never went away.

The front door was eventually opened in the creaking tempo of a horror movie and a very pretty girl stood in the shadow of the hall. Rachel peered in.

"I've come to see Charlie," Rachel said. "I'm his cousin. Is he in?"

"Yes, Charlie's here," the girl answered.

"Can I come in then?"

"Sure."

Marianne stood aside and Rachel walked past her.

"Are you from England?" Marianne asked, with a wide-eyed gentle look. Her tone seemed to set great store by the question. She had a breathy voice with a slight squeak in it, like a five-year-old child.

"Yes. I am," Rachel said.

The girl didn't move, but stood there gazing up as if she was in the zoo.

"Well, where is he?" Rachel asked.

"Oh!" the girl said, "I'm Marianne."

"Hello, Marianne. I'm Rachel."

The girl nodded silently and gave her a great smile. Her eyes were huge and pale in the shadowy hall. "He's in here," she said at last, twisting the knob of the door just behind her without turning and keeping her eyes on Rachel. The effect of this extraordinary choreography was unnerving. The girl's manner wove a dramatic web around the commonplace encounter calculated to make a visitor feel she might have her throat cut. Rachel took a step forward into the room.

It was in total darkness. Between the heavy drawn curtains a shaft of light struck through from the street and laid a swathe of dust-filled sun on the floor. The rest of the room was lit only as various surfaces reflected the sunlight. One of these surfaces was Charlie.

Charlie lay in a huge armchair, but he was not asleep. He looked out from under the dropped lids of his eyes toward the door. The room smelt, not entirely unpleasantly, of aromatic smoke and flowers mixed with food and dirty clothes. The flowers were fresh. Someone had put them in a jug.

"Is that Rachel?" Charlie said, as if she was a dream that he was experiencing.

"Hello, Charlie."

"My God! It's Rachel!" he said in a completely different tone. He laughed and stood up. "This is great. Christ, but it's good to see you. Here, let me draw the curtains."

He bore the traces of a recent shot of something, but the somnolence had passed and it would take time for his mood to accelerate again into agitation. He was as near to being coherent as Charlie Grimmond ever got these days. He stumbled as he walked across the room to the window, but only because things had been left on the floor, and drew back the heavy curtains. This was not the room George Cash had waited in. It was a less distinguished mess. The chair in which Rachel found herself invited to sit was the enormous companion of Charlie's—a brownish maroon velvet stuffed armchair of which the inner frame had splayed within the obese covering.

Rachel stepped back out of Charlie's welcoming embrace and sat down. As he had pressed his cheek against her face, the stubble had stuck into her skin. She felt the thinness of his body and the disordered vibrations of premature decay. And yet she was also aware, as she sometimes was with Charlie, of something else about him, something fine that could still be glimpsed by a person seeking it, as a lookout might glimpse an island on the very farthest horizon, faint with distance on a waste of empty ocean.

"Well, this is where I live!" he said.

"Do you have the whole house?"

"Yes. I must show you. It's not bad. Did you ever know Aunt Kessel?"

He yawned suddenly and deeply, throwing out his arms.

"Gee, it's good to see you." He was still standing but seemed not to know what to do with himself. "How long are you over for?"

"Just about a week probably. Maybe ten days."

"You didn't say you were coming. Did you? Did you write? I don't get them. Letters. They get lost."

He was looking for something. Under a loose jersey thrown on the window seat he found a packet of cigarettes. On the mantelpiece was a lighter. He saw it and began the journey across the room to light his cigarette.

"Where are you staying? Do you want to stay here?"

He stumbled against a table, lit his cigarette, and returned to throw himself back into the arms of his chair.

"No thanks," Rachel said. "I'm over on business so they're paying for the hotel."

"On business, eh!"

"Yes. Steiger and Wallace broked a big loss to Lloyd's, and I managed to get myself sent here with a loss assessor type that Lloyd's occasionally uses to examine dodgy claims."

"Dodgy?"

"Well, this one isn't dodgy," she said, with prophetic inaccuracy. "But they sent him because of other circumstances. It's a very big single claim, for example."

Charlie still wasn't interested. He had no reason to connect it, and he didn't immediately connect it, with George Cash's enterprise. Making connections was precisely what his mind couldn't cope with. Sometimes he couldn't even connect the beginning to the end of a sentence.

"What circumstances?"

"Oh. . . ." She prepared to explain as briefly as possible. "American liability cover of a chemicals firm called Santhill, written a long time ago, suddenly appeared like a skeleton walking out of a cupboard. Your father's syndicate wrote it originally, as it happens."

Then Charlie made the connection.

"What!" he said. The word came out like a bark as he jerked forward in his chair, his eyes suddenly sparking. The sudden movement made him choke, and as his thin body was wracked with coughing, he laughed as well, as if everything was shaken loose and thrown together.

"What's the joke?" Rachel said, smiling in strained sympathy. She found the overtones of mental disintegration that accompanied Charlie's manner unnerving.

"No joke." He'd remembered something about the need for not telling his secret: a confused remnant of what George had told him and what Rachel had said about a Lloyd's investigator. But he couldn't stop laughing. His delight was unstoppable.

"What's so hilarious about it?" Rachel asked. "Your father had bought a run-off, so he's not the one to pay, if that's what you're so pleased about."

Roughly thirty seconds after she said this, Charlie stopped laughing. He held his mouth in a characteristic expression, lips drawn slightly back, teeth almost together, tongue pressed against them, eyes a little flexed. His mind was searching for something amidst the chaos, inside there, but he looked, except for his ghastly pallor, like a young hero gazing out across an unknown land.

"Your mother sends her love to you," Rachel said. Perhaps she only wanted to change the subject. Or perhaps she saw, just then, what Sarah would have seen when with the eyes of passionate maternal love she imagined alive in Charlie those things that had been long dead.

He said, "My mother!"

"Well, what's wrong?" Rachel said. "It's rather hard on her."

If Charlie had been feeling well enough, he'd have got up at this stage in order to shake off, with the action of standing up, some unbearable connection in the idea. As it was, he made a quarter movement but collapsed.

"I don't want to talk about my mother."

"All right."

He took a deep drag on his cigarette, perhaps as if he was trying to suck something out of it that couldn't be found there. As he exhaled, he let his head drop back. His left elbow resting on the chair's arm, he held the cigarette high up. His hand in mid-air began to shake. Rachel's lips drooped. She could see the conversation beginning to be very boring. She looked at her watch and said, "Gosh. I'll have to be getting back."

He didn't seem to have heard her.

"The meetings are right up in Century City. By the way, there's a restaurant I passed coming down that advertises itself as the most genteel tavern in town. Genteel! I ask you!"

She could ask him anything now. He wasn't listening. Or answering.

"Charlie!"

She got up and went over to him. His head was locked back, eyes open. Inside the rims of his eyes the skin was exceptionally red, as if it had been scorched with nettles. A still integrated roll of ash fell from his cigarette. She took the rest of it from between his fingers, and he didn't move. She walked over to the fireplace and threw it in the empty grate. And then she quietly left.

*T*he next time Charlie hit a lucid patch, which was about eight o'clock that night, he at once remembered his conversation with Rachel. What he remembered most clearly was that "his" general liability insurance document had passed the scrutiny of the Lloyd's market and caused an uproar.

He was alone. The house around him was empty. Marianne was asleep. He began to laugh again in the dark. No one had switched the lights on. He crashed into something trying to turn on the lamp. It was the lamp. It smashed. He continued to laugh until he found the phone, and then the effort of concentration abruptly silenced him. He wiped the flat of one hand hard down his face and tried to think. He made a gesture of giving up but just then he got a hint of what he was after. He picked up the receiver and punched out a series of numbers.

Far away in England it was 4:00 A.M.—a deadly hour. Sir Adrian and Lady Grimmond were fast asleep in bed. The streets were empty. A cold gray gold light had just touched the silent sky, and birds in their thousands were about to sing in Cadogan Square. The heavy curtains of the bedroom cut out both the light and the sound from outside. But inside, suddenly, just beside Sir Adrian's very ear, the phone shrieked. He woke immediately, but was slow at first to work out what on earth was going on. Sarah's voice, sharp with anxiety and shock, cut into his consciousness more effectively than the bell.

"Adrian! It's the phone."

He picked it up with one arm and hoisted himself upright with the other.

"Who can it be?" Sarah hissed with dread. "It's gone four o'clock."

"Hello," Sir Adrian said. "Who's speaking?"

"Dad!"

Like the sound of someone throwing a handful of gravel onto the lid of a coffin, the sound of Charlie's voice made a desolate and dramatic impact on the silent room. Sarah gasped. In a gesture between protection and repression, Sir Adrian turned his back to her and shielded the receiver with his hand.

"Is that you, Charles?" he said. "You are not to ring here. Do you know what hour it is?"

"Oh! I forgot." For just a moment the paternal disapproval voiced on such practical grounds as a late phone call caught Charlie unawares and very nearly diverted him from his purpose. He began to apologize, but his father cut him off.

"I won't have you upsetting your mother. You are ordered not to call this number. Do I make myself clear?"

"But, Dad, I've got some news for you."

"What do you mean?"

"News. Information. It's about this general liability insurance on the American chemicals company. At least I think . . . What? Did you say something?"

"I see," Adrian said grimly. "Rachel called on you, did she?"

"It's not that."

Sarah was sitting up in bed behind Adrian's back with both hands spread over her face. Tears poured from between the fingers.

"I've got some news for you, Dad," the voice suddenly

resumed with a change of tone, singing out, "I've got some news for you. About that insurance claim, it's forged, Dad. I know because I helped to do it."

"Nonsense. I'm not going to listen to such rubbish."

"Why not? Don't you want to know how I did it? I had help. Professional help."

"You couldn't get LPSO forms."

"Got them sent, Dad."

"Sent!"

"D—Whoops. No names. Friend of mine sent me some in exchange for you know what. And then . . . What did I do then?"

Adrian held the receiver steady against his ear, muffled, his back to Sarah, his face grim.

"Did I say what did I do then? I put your syndicate number on it, Dad. Yours! See how the old bastard will cope with that, I said." And Charlie laughed. His laughter was strained. Even now he couldn't quite bring himself to speak in such terms face to face, as it were, with his father, and there was a note of almost normal childish embarrassment in the sound of it. Adrian's lips were white.

Suddenly Charlie's voice broke. He said, "Sorry, Dad." A choking ugly weeping echoed down the line. "Sorry, Dad . . ."

Slowly Adrian put down the phone. He kept his back to Sarah, but she heard it click into its resting place. Through a crack in the curtains a muffled burst of bird song broke into the silence.

"Adrian."

Sarah's voice, hoarse with grief, held a resonance that penetrated even to him. He reached over without turning and felt for her hand. She gave it to him soaking wet.

"I want you to forget this phone call, Sarah," he said.

"I can't. Oh, Adrian, please—"

"Sarah!"

She bunched her shoulders in a sob.

"You must forget this, Sarah!"

Anger flowed into him and the color began to return to his

cheeks. He didn't know how much of Charlie's words she had actually heard or taken in. She probably wouldn't have made out the individual words once he had his back to her. He needed to think.

Eventually Sarah was silent. She lay on her back staring with unseeing eyes into the half light. Beside her Adrian pretended to fall back to sleep. Consciously holding his body still to protect himself from interruption, he turned his thoughts to what Charlie had had to say. He brought his mind gingerly to bear on the possibility that Charlie had really forged the Santhill insurance claim, and knew that it was true. In spite of what he had said to Charlie the hideous tale had a ring of authenticity about it. The losses, therefore, which were currently being featured in the popular press in its ignorant way as the biggest yet suffered by Lloyd's on one single claim, were spurious. He could go to Lloyd's in the morning and pull the plug on the whole fiasco. He paused, thinking of who would have to be told. The chairman. David Greene, his own deputy, and Stan Lacy, Steiger and Wallace, Bob Keats. He cast the list aside and returned to basics. The news was that Sir Adrian Grimmond's son had committed a criminal forgery that had nearly involved the market in massive losses. But fortunately, like that of any common thief, his squalid enterprise had collapsed.

Sir Adrian lay there contemplating the progress of his revelations and seeing, in his mind's eye, the reactions of his peers. He thought about it for a long time. He came to the conclusion that he could not do it. He simply would not do it.

But in that case the payments would go ahead. Names who in some cases might ill afford it, and who in all cases had the right not to be robbed, would hand over huge sums of money. Nevertheless, when he had thought about it, he hardened his heart. It would be even worse if he himself had to hand over his pride and see his reputation and standing in the world dragged in the filth of his worthless son's wrongdoing. He would keep silent. He decided he would simply keep silent and let the matter take its course.

*T*he disappearance of Finn Garrett did not remain a mystery for very long; that's to say, her body, with some breath of life still left in it, was found. "We'll have to contact the EPA to appoint a replacement," Dale Falcus announced. His manner was frigid. A note of severity had crept into his tone when speaking to Mal Harris since he had become aware that his own company was cheating Lloyd's. He took the stance of the reluctant criminal who blames the victim more than he blames himself. At home on one occasion a huge iris had been blown over in a storm and he cut it. It had a stem at least an inch and a half thick, and carrying it round the garden was like carrying a beautiful woman by the neck. That, if he was going to commit a crime, was his sort of crime, not this messy cheating that he and the other directors of the Santhill board had been forced into.

Added to all this, he felt uneasy. Once things began to go wrong, you never knew what would happen. This attack on Finn Garrett was a case in point.

Mal Harris looked as if he had more to say than he was saying. Since the morning's adjournment he had been busy on his own account, but he held his tongue and Falcus was too busy and irritated to notice it. His P.A. had got a commitment from the pollution agency and they need not expect any serious hold-up if Mr. Harris and Miss Grimmond would just give them twenty-four hours. Mal nodded. Rachel said nothing.

"It's a disgrace, I know," Dale carried on, just to talk out the momentum of this necessary encounter. "Gangs of youths ride their bikes in the desert there. It's most likely she was set upon by them, poor lady. But it happens everywhere these days. I'm afraid every country seems to have its violent young people."

"Young men," Rachel said.

He looked at her. What the hell was she talking about? He ignored her.

"I mean," she persisted, "that when you say 'people,' you should say 'men,' because they account for ninety-eight percent of all violent crime. Women don't really come into it."

That was all he needed, a line of feminist claptrap thrown in with all the rest. He dropped the conversational tone and redirected his attention to Mr. Harris.

"If that suits you," he said, "I'll confirm tomorrow when we have a replacement, and we can carry on then. I don't think there's much point in meeting among ourselves without those figures and agreements if we can help it. We could make some progress, but it would have to be done all over again."

"Quite," Mal concurred. "As long as that's all right with you, Rachel?"

She agreed.

It suited Mal Harris very well to let Dale Falcus take the initiative in postponing the meeting. If he hadn't, Mal would have had to do it for him.

"Have you had any lunch?" he said to Rachel after they had left Dale Falcus and were on their way out of the building together. "Because I didn't have time myself, and I've got some information I'd like to talk over with you."

"Okay. Where shall we go?"

"There's a twenty-four hour Chinese place up the hill. Will that do?"

"Fine."

They set off walking.

"So what's this information?" said Rachel. "Who did you see?"

"I saw a man called Rat."

"Rat!"

"Mind out now. You can be prosecuted for jaywalking in this country."

A sour cop took his eye off them.

"Did you say Rat? He must be a bit unpopular."

"He's an environmental genius," Mal said, "who used the footprint of a rat to analyze the pollutants in an area and made a name for himself."

"Some name!"

"Well, he doesn't seem to mind it. And the point I'm coming to, Rachel, is that Rat has been working with Dr. Garrett."

"What did you say?" shouted Rachel. "Good God, the traffic!"

He steered her over to an open door hung with oriental signs. "Wait till we get inside," he said.

It was not only quiet but also, at first sight, almost dark inside the restaurant. Vases of plastic flowers in this fecund country where flowers grew in such profusion decorated the tables with lusterless splashes of color, and there was a smell of frying different from, but not less disconcerting than, a Yorkshire fish and chip shop.

"Will this do?"

"Yes. Fine," she said. "Tell me about Rat."

"He works with Finn Garrett."

"And so?"

When they were seated, he said, "You remember noticing that Dr. Garrett's manner at yesterday's meeting was a bit worried, as if she had something unresolved on her mind to do with the toxic content of the dump?"

Rachel thought back. "Poor woman," she said inconsequentially. "I really liked her."

"So did I, but that's not the point."

"What is it then?"

"There was something wrong," Mal said. "She was trying to provide for some alteration in the chemical content of that toxic waste that isn't included in the description notified to Santhill by the EPA in January. Now, why?"

"I didn't notice," Rachel said. "But it's quite cut and dried. The waste was analyzed and listed in the beginning of the year, and that, and only that, is the package insured."

"So you'd think. But she wasn't happy. And I found out why."

"How do you mean?"

"I went to the place where she works. She visited the laboratory after the meeting yesterday—went straight there after dropping us at the hotel."

"And?"

"Rat was waiting to see her, but she was late so he had to go. He left some samples out for her." He paused. "I want to take my time over this. I don't want Dale Falcus and the rest of the board to know about it until I have looked into it. Is that all right with you?"

"Yes."

"Well then"—he picked up a menu and made a gesture to the waiter to give them more time—"Rat had taken fresh samples from Santhill purely by chance, to lock in with another project. But he found new substances, and extremely dangerous ones from what I can gather, in the specimens from the Mojave Desert. Now, he rang Finn Garrett just before the meeting but she didn't have time to discuss it in detail with him. But she was worried about it during the meeting. After the meeting she went and examined the work he had left out for her. And after that she drove out into the desert. . . ."

Rachel said, "You mean there's something criminal in all this beyond just a casual attack?"

"Someone's tried to kill her."

"You mean Dale Falcus," she said, with mocking incredulity, "or that atrophied old meat loaf, Charles Seaford? I just can't see it. Or the lawyer, whatever his name is—the one who's sick."

"I don't know," Mal said, but in a tone of voice that meant he intended to find out. "There was that card, remember, that the secretary dropped on the floor. 'Call Zack Webern and mention George Cash.' "

"That's it" she said. "Zack Webern, the lawyer. I couldn't remember his name. Why should somebody give Dale Falcus a note telling him to ring his own firm's lawyer?"

"And mention George Cash?"

"Who's he?"

"He's an archive archaeologist. I looked him up this morning in the telephone directory. His occupation is finding old documents."

"Like insurance cover?"

They were both silent, thinking intently of the possible connections and unwittingly sending out the very signals to which a waiter is usually most apt to respond, when a customer is neither ready nor anxious to place an order. Now a young man who would have walked past someone dying of starvation without even noticing came purposefully up to their table and stood there holding his notebook. They chose what to eat hastily and at random.

"In that case," Mal began as soon as the waiter left, "I—"

"Good God!"

Rachel was staring over his shoulder, an expression of horror on her face.

"What is it?" he asked, twisting round to see where she was looking. A man had come in and sat down alone at a table near the door, with a newspaper that he was just folding up.

"Did you see?"

"No."

"I don't think I can have been mistaken," Rachel said. "Wait a minute. I'm going to ask him if I can borrow that paper."

She got up before Mal could say anything. The stranger saw her coming but thought she was making for the door.

"Excuse me," she said.

He looked up again, interested, friendly. "Yes?"

"Your paper," she said. "Do you think I could possibly have a quick look at it?"

"This?"

"Yes. Please. Do you mind?"

"You're English, aren't you?" he said, holding on to it. "Where do you come from? London?"

"That's right," she said. "But—"

"I've got a cousin living in Knight's Bridge," he said. "Do you know Knight's bridge?"

"Sort of. I live not far."

"Buckingham Palace and all that—and those regiments of black horses with red-coated soldiers on them with swords, trotting through the parks."

"It sounds different the way you put it," she said, "but that is exactly right, I suppose."

"And are all the girls slim and blond like you, with pretty voices?"

"Yes," she said. "And they all want to read your newspaper."

He held it out to her with a broad smile. She folded it back again to the front page. There was a large photograph of Finn Garrett, smiling with an adorable little child in her arms—a family snapshot. The headline read "Where Is Daisy?" And in smaller print:

> It has emerged that Dr. Finn Garrett, the environmental scientist and guru, took her child with her when she went into the desert. Dr. Garrett, now in the Samaritan Hospital in La Verne, was found bleeding and unconscious after having been brutally attacked. There were signs that a fight had taken place as she struggled to save her child and escape. Her car

had been rammed and smashed in several places. It is now feared that the attackers, who left the mother for dead, took the child. State police officials say. . . .

"Keep it," the man said. "You have it. I can get another. Really." He overrode her protests. "My mother always told me I'd go blind if I read at the same time as eating."

Rachel laughed. There was a smile still on her face when she came back to the table.

"That's all right then" said Mal dryly.

"Oh, no." She looked at him and handed over the paper. "I laughed because that man made a joke, but this is no laughing matter, as they say."

He took the paper from her and started to read. *"Diawl, mun,"* he swore quietly in his native language. "What a terrible story." He lowered the paper slowly and looked at Rachel. "We'll have to start putting ourselves in the picture," he said. "I suggest we begin this afternoon by paying a visit to George Cash."

CHAPTER 25

*G*eorge Cash was not in the mood to stay at home receiving calls. He had already had a visit from Zack Webern. Now that money had changed hands and the job that was commissioned had been done, each man would have preferred never to see the other again. And yet Cash found himself waiting once more for the lawyer's ring at the door, and this time without the stimulus, the incipient compensation, of money to be made.

When George met another man who he liked, he was capable of having some charm, but he didn't like Zack Webern. And just as George himself was identified in the lawyer's eyes with this phase of his irreversible undoing, so Zack looked like the devil incarnate to him. Had Zack always been that thin? And those eyes that burned out of bony sockets with such dead heat revolted him. George had done this forgery for money, for a nice clean sum; and he was fastidious about having that spoilt either by the contamination of having to meet a man like Zack Webern repeatedly or, worse still, by some stupid indiscretion. He listened with dismay to Zack's account of the break-in at the dump site and the gangster's warning. He himself had not been indiscreet. No one could have found out from him. He had not even mentioned the matter to Hugo, so you could leave Hugo out of it. On his side, that left only Charlie Grimmond and Les Deakin, the forger.

"But how about you?" he challenged the lawyer, in a tough reciprocal tone.

"Me?"

"Yes, you."

"How do you mean? I don't come into it."

The riposte brought out the belligerence in George Cash. The too closely knit joints in his small body bunched with choler, and his face flushed.

"How about the people in your office? Your wife? Your secretary? In order to blow something, you don't have to spell it out, you know. Other people can sometimes put two and two together. Who do you have working close to you?"

He asked the question as if he expected to be answered.

"No one," Zack said with fastidious hostility, "who could be at all interested in this matter." The thought of Daniel didn't even occur to him.

"That's not good enough for me," Cash said. "You forget you're not the only one who stands to lose here." And in the end Zack made a grudging short list of three employees in his department, which did not include his son.

No sooner had he left the house than George wrote out a hasty note for Hugo and set off downtown. He found Les Deakin without any trouble, in the basement that he had converted into a warehouse. The space had been created out of three shabby rooms in a 1950s high rise where the partition walls had been removed, and through tunnels of reinforced steel joists, perilously holding up the rest of the building, the daylight, back and front, was able to filter. It looked like a cross between a laboratory and an alchemist's library, with stacks of different varieties of paper, copperplates, chemicals, burners, pigments, photographic equipment, benches of fluid trays, tools hung up on the wall, brushes, tweezers, drills, and shelves of reference books, not to mention the bed and the table, always scattered with the remains of the breakfasts that Les ate three times a day. His official occupation was as a fine art printer. His country of origin was Australia. He had had to leave because in his experience, as he put it, there was no room for an honest crook over there. A good forger was wasted on the paperwork the business community passed around among themselves out there. But here in L.A. he was appreciated. "A decent forger grazes best in good pasture." He said this sort of thing as if quoting old proverbs passed down in the family, although his great-grandfather had been deported to Australia for sheep stealing, not forgery. His small but bright blue eyes seemed to look on George like one more good joke.

"You won't find a leak here, mate," he said. "I got no one to sneak on me except the cat." And he pointed at a dead animal in a large jar of formaldehyde designed for preserving fish.

But Charlie Grimmond, whom George visited next, was a different matter. The one amazing thing about Charlie Grimmond—so George reflected with contempt—was how far he had to fall. On his last encounter it seemed likely that Charlie had already hit rock bottom, but as if the impact of his fall had awakened some demon in the rock, the ground had rolled back to give him space for more. This time he was yet more physically decrepit, more wayward and confused. The detritus of his aristocratic background that George so much envied was now merely part of the rubbish heap of his existence—the smashed furniture, the squalid grandeur, the physique that was English and athletic and tall but too feverish to see straight or stand without weaving.

To make this junkie fool remember the incident of the Lloyd's document was, in itself, a risk. George hesitated, biting his lip. Charles, typically unpredictable, solved the dilemma for him.

"I hear our business enterprise prospered," he said suddenly.

George's heart stopped. "How did you hear that?"

This conversation took place in MacArthur Park, where George had had to come this time to find Charlie. It was a fairly safe hour of the day to be there, as far as anyone can ever be safe in MacArthur Park. The various criminals, drug traffickers, and addicts who haunt the place behave cautiously in daylight.

Charlie himself, sitting on his bench on the grass, looked not much worse than a drunken undergraduate—maybe Cambridge after a May ball: dawn pallor, stubble, trembling hands. How he did it, God only knew, but he seemed to have pulled himself up a little.

"How did you hear that, Charlie?" George had to ask for the second time.

"What?"

"About our little business?"

Charlie's expression changed from puzzled dislike as he looked at George to understanding. A playful smile palely lit his eyes. He drew in his lower lip and nodded with knowing satisfaction.

"The forgery."

George's glance snapped with irritation. "Don't use that word, for God's sake. You're not going to screw up on this, are you, Charlie? Have you told anyone?" He waited a minute for an answer and went on, "It's dangerous. No one must know."

"I didn't tell her."

"Her?" George was going from alarm to alarm. "Who the hell do you mean?"

"My cousin." And bit by bit George teased out from Charlie a more or less coherent account of Rachel's visit. His nerves were in shreds by the end of it.

"Did you tell her or did you not?" he damn near yelled.

"Nup."

"You didn't tell her?"

"Nup."

George let out a snort of air, bringing his shoulders down on it and turning his head away in an exaggerated parody of relief laced with insecurity.

Charlie giggled. The grass sprung green under even his feet. It was one of the best examples of what the Buddha meant by indifference: the indifference of the grass, an indifference that produced this fruitfulness even under the heel of decay. He moved his shoe slightly over to the right and tore out a few blades. By the time he looked up again, George was standing.

"I'll be seeing you," George said. It reminded Charlie of what he had been about to say.

"I'd like to see his face," he said, half laughing.

"Whose face?"

"My father. My *father*. God's sake, George, don't you ever listen to anything?"

Charlie gave one last draw on the disintegrating roach he had almost forgotten that he was holding, and threw it away across the grass. "I'd like to see my father's face when he finds out," he said.

"What do you mean?" George said with renewed sharpness, referring to the words "finds out." Charlie, laughing again, caught a glimpse of the crisp red hair and shaded face of George against the sky, but his own eyes were half closed.

"His face!" he repeated, shoulders shaking. "His face. I'd like to have seen his face when I told him we forged that insurance cover with his syndicate number on it."

It was George's face that Charlie should have paid attention to right then, but he was too busy laughing. If he had been in a fit state to notice, he might have seen a look in George's eye to make the blood run cold. As it was, he merely carried on laughing, and after another moment George Cash turned on his heel and left.

CHAPTER 26

*N*obody had seen Sir Adrian's face when Charlie had told him about the forgery, not Sarah, not anybody. He had kept his head turned away, and afterward, as he lay making up his mind what to do in the cold dawn, his expression was merely resolute and grim.

Beside him, Sarah stopped crying after a short while. She lay on her back, as still as Adrian. And also like Adrian, she reached her own decision. She intended to go to America immediately. She was going to Charlie. It was not only the heartbreaking experience of hearing his voice sounding so ill and pathetic and after all this time that drove her to the decision. It was also in obedience to an overwhelming, panic-stricken conviction that danger threatened him. The urgency of her instinct was so pressing she would have jumped from bed there and then but for the need to wait until Adrian had gone to work.

In normal circumstances one could have substituted the word "moon" for "America" as far as Sarah was concerned. Sarah never traveled alone. She took no decisions that were not domestic, and suddenly doing so now presented the most basic problems. For instance, where would she get the money for the ticket and the other travel expenses? She was ignorant of how to acquire a plane ticket, knowing only that they were not sold in any of the shops she normally patronized. In addition, the bank account that Adrian kept for her never had more than two or three hundred pounds in balance. On the day in question she found that she had ninety-nine.

When Adrian had left for his office, she dressed with all the usual care, with white-faced determination. Her skin, already taut and exhausted with shock and sleeplessness, received its full quota of grooming; Elizabeth Arden and Dior combined to dress the first wounds of this which was to be the most awful battle of her life.

At breakfast she remembered something; picked up the previous evening's copy of the *Standard* and found the flight advertisements. She made phone calls and soon discovered that she did not have enough money. Her purchasing power along the grooved track laid down by Adrian was prodigious. But she could not buy a plane ticket on her Harrods account. She could buy a coat costing two thousand guineas at Fortnum's, but what hotel or cab driver in Los Angeles would accept its card? Nor yet one from Peter Jones or Harvey Nichols. She did not have a Visa card of any kind. It had always seemed unnecessary. Adrian had a Visa card. That was good enough for both of them. The food bills, when not accumulated at Harrods or other suppliers with whom they had accounts which were settled monthly by Adrian, were small. An item here, an item there—a basket of particulary good-looking strawberries or flowers for a friend or a lunch with other wives—these were the things the bank account was meant to stretch to. It was not meant to finance a rescue mission five thousand miles away across sea and land and an indefinite stay in a foreign country.

She sat at her desk holding the telephone and listening to some nice girl say how much a plane ticket to Los Angeles would cost, and suggesting payment by Visa card.

"Thank you," Sarah said. "I'll have to ring you back."

She closed and locked her desk. Upstairs, Margaret was making the bed. As soon as she was finished and Sarah was alone, she unlocked the wall safe where she kept her less good jewelry.

The really valuable pieces had to be kept in the bank. Her fingers trembled as she looked up the combination, which she always forgot, and then fidgeted away at the dial. Behind all her actions, like the muted accompaniment of a frenetic orchestra, she heard the urgent discordant passage of time. She felt that she was in a race against death. If it were her own death, she would hardly have bothered to quicken her normal pace. But it wasn't. It was Charlie's.

She took a diamond ring that had been her mother's and an aquamarine necklace. On second thought she added a pair of emerald earrings. She put them in an envelope, the envelope in her handbag. She locked the safe, replaced the combination. What else? A moment she paused. She thought perhaps she should change her shoes in case these ones hurt her. She flexed and pressed her weight onto the ball of one foot. They'd do. And where should she go? Not to a jeweler where she was known. He might become suspicious or demand Sir Adrian's agreement. She had no idea what to expect.

When she got outside and had succeeded in flagging down a taxi, she told him to go to Gloucester Road, where she remembered a small but smart shop that sold gold chains and ivory baby's teething rings set in silver of the sort that she had once chewed on herself, and which she had held between the little sore gums of Charlie when he was a baby. She had held him then in arms rounded and firm, her shapely body proudly set off, her complexion beautiful. Now, as she got out of the cab, she held on to the frame of the door with an arm from which the wasted muscle hung in a soft roll.

She stepped anxiously into the shop, uncertain of the status of a stranger with an envelope full of jewelry to sell.

"Can I help you, madam?"

The girl in question looked quite unable to do any such thing.

"I wanted to sell a ring," Sarah said firmly. "Do you occasionally buy jewelry?"

"Mr. Collis may be interested," the girl said. "Mr. Collis," she murmured to a young man in the back of the room. "This lady would like you to look at a ring."

Mr. Collis thought that the girl meant that Sarah wanted to look at rings, not show him one. When he understood his error, he was less pleased, but braced himself and laid a velvet pad on the glass case top for Sarah to display her wares. She extracted the pieces and laid them out before him. He took them up one by one, his fingers touching for the first time the aquamarines that had lain against the skin of Sarah's throat and the diamond ring that her mother had had the habit of twisting round and flicking with her thumbnail, when annoyed.

"Yes," he said, and again "I see. Nineteenth century. This ring a little earlier, I think." And then, holding the stones up to look through his eyeglass, "Yes, well—if you can leave them with me . . ."

Sarah was appalled. "I wanted an immediate answer," she said. "I'm afraid I'm in a hurry."

His eye darkened. It obviously crossed his mind that the jewels might not be Sarah's to sell, but he had the sense to dismiss that idea. Nevertheless, the woman was blushing. What looked like almost a rash of speckled magenta showed at the base of her neck and a second later in the hollow of each cheek. He was not a particularly kind young man. Her agitation aroused only an undefinable suspicion. Intelligence was not his strong point, either. He looked again at the aquamarines. He sensed at the same time the extreme urgency of the woman and every instinct prompted him to assert himself.

"If I gave you the wrong price," he said piously, "it would not be fair to you."

Sarah said, holding her lips tight, "I see."

The young man, who took it upon himself to make the ruling that money was more important than time to Sarah at this moment, could see very well that he was upsetting her.

"Please," Sarah said. "Would you . . . ?"

He held the necklace consideringly. "Very fine stones, although I'd have to do a detailed examination; twelve in number. Aquamarines aren't popular just at present, I'm afraid. We don't sell them, but perhaps we could make an exception. A necklace like this could be worth fourteen, fifteen hundred pounds."

"But you can't make me an offer? I need the money immediately."

He had been about to reward her for her good manners, but this was too much. "I'm afraid that would be out of the question," he said.

She put the jewelry back into the envelope, her fingers trembling. She wasn't going to argue. She went back into the street. She walked all the way up into the park without seeing one free taxi. Her shoes had begun to rub. She stepped into Kensington Gardens in order to rest on a bench. To these walks and pleasant pathways, Charlie had often been brought when a baby. He had run after the birds and kicked a little ball along the grass. She jumped up. The overwhelming fear she felt for Charlie, the tyranny of her instinct, obliterated tiredness and discomfort. She went back to the gates and was lucky in securing a taxi almost immediately. She had decided to go to Bond Street, and as long as it wasn't Asprey's, where she was known, she could at least deal with a firm important enough to have the means to pay in cash. She rang the bell for entry at an establishment of which the name only was familiar to her. This time she asked whether or not an immediate arrangement could be made before showing what she had to sell. An older and wiser man dealt kindly with her, and an hour later she left with three thousand pounds in cash. Once outside on the pavement again she looked at her watch. It was three o'clock—well into the afternoon. With frantic haste she tried to reckon up what tasks remained to be done. She still had to buy the airline ticket, convert some of this money into—what? Dollars? Traveler's checks? Both? She had no idea. How did Adrian arrange these things when they traveled? She had left it up to him. She literally did not know what to do without asking. She flagged down another taxi and gave her bank's address. On arrival she asked the driver to wait. He settled in without grumbling, taking a sandwich out of the inside pocket of his cab.

Inside the bank, Sarah calculated that it would be too late that day for Adrian to call, since the bank closed at three-thirty, and therefore there was no danger of the manager or the cashier mentioning her visit to him. She braced herself to answer questions about her "holiday" to Mrs. Geoffreys or Miss Stevens. She took some delight in being able to say that she was going to visit her son. For a moment she allowed herself to wonder why she had never done this before, but then the very structure of her sanity began to crumble like a wall beginning to rain stones from its upper courses in imminent collapse. The reasons were too complex, the alteration between then and now too catastrophic. She signed all the traveler's checks with a trembling hand. The clock in moving forward caught her eye. The minute hand jerked forward at the completion of another sixty seconds. How many times had it done that since she came in. Thirty. Thirty minutes gone. She hurried out in disciplined panic to the taxi. She had scribbled down the address of the travel agency, but it was all the way round to Shepherd's Bush and down the Uxbridge Road. Her cheekbones became sharper, shadowed from below with the fluctuating blood of terrified apprehension, as the traffic held them up and the lights changed against them.

When at last she hurried into the agency, it was to find herself stranded once again in a human traffic jam, held stationary in a network of occupied telephones and computer screens. She thought her heart would hardly stand it. Each second began to have the corrosive power of an imprisonment. Her nerves were frayed as if some part of her were tearing at them in an attempt to get out. Each desk had a name on it. She looked for the name of "her" girl. Serena. The chairs in front of it were occupied by a man and a woman. Serena had the phone to her ear. Her eyes roamed around the room as she spoke. She uttered two or three short, clipped sentences, stabbing the keys of her computer between each group of words. After hours of crawling minutes the transaction was finished and the man and woman got up to leave. Unbearably, they exchanged a few pleasantries with Serena before vacating the desk. Did they not realize there were others waiting and waiting behind them? Sarah was so close behind them that the man nearly tripped on her as he turned. "So sorry," they both said, and Serena looked up with a bright professional smile and said, "Yes, I remember," as Sarah introduced herself. "This morning, wasn't it. Los Angeles? Right. Have you got your passport?"

"Passport?"

Sarah clutched at her heart. Her lips beneath the lipstick went gray.

"Never mind, never mind." Serena laughed kindly. "We don't need it. Just tell me the name *on* your passport? And what flight did you want?"

Sarah started calculating the time it would take her to get home, pack. . . . She wouldn't be able to go. Not today. Adrian might be home. She couldn't pack with Adrian there. She couldn't leave with Adrian there. He'd stop her. Neither could she take a particularly early flight the next morning for the same reason. Desperate tears flooded up her eyes, and her throat. "It can't really be a quarter to five," she lamented, but Serena said it was. She eventually left with the ticket for a twelve noon flight the following day, and from the Uxbridge Road she at last arrived home with the ticket and the money in time to supervise Adrian's dinner.

The next day, after a sleepless night, Sarah left the house at ten o'clock. Hands trembling, she had packed her suitcase and remembered just in time to take her passport from the locked desk. She found that in her previous morning's panic she had misplaced the key. The front door bell rang to announce the arrival of the taxi to take her to the airport.

"Take the suitcase," she said. "I'll be with you in two minutes."

In frantic haste she fetched a carving knife from the kitchen. She slid the blade between the flap of the desk and the top where it latched. When the blade bent, she pushed it further in. The wood splintered. The desk was an exceptionally fine example of the William and Mary period and had belonged to Adrian's grandmother. Sarah snatched open the drawer abruptly and the handle came off, but the passport was inside, and it was not out-of-date as she had half feared it might be. Leaving the evidence of her amateur burglary behind, she fled the house. And before her very feet, like the crack of an earthquake that runs along the ground faster than a horse can gallop, death raced toward Charlie neck and neck with his mother.

CHAPTER 27

*O*n the second day after she was found in the desert, Finn
Garrett recovered consciousness. The process was rela-
tively painless until her mind, pivoting in the new space, remembered the man's hands, black with dirt and hair, that seized
Daisy. There her mind stopped.

"She regained consciousness. I think she did," the hospital
nurse said in an agitated whisper. "But she's gone again."

But Finn had not quite gone. She had carried with her
down into the hermetically sealed space of her traumatized body
the knowledge of what had happened to her daughter.

An hour or so later the cabdriver who had picked up Mal
Harris outside his hotel said, referring to the hospital at La
Verne, "You won't get in there. But like I said, you pay and I'll
take you wherever you like."

"How do you mean I won't get in?"

"Publicity, man. That lady scientist's hot stuff hereabouts.
Look . . ." He twisted the steering wheel and braked, and a
bashed-up Ford completed a harmless manoeuvre to get out of
a narrow side street. "Did y' see that? Lousy driving. You got to
expect it. This place is half full of Hispanics."

He underlined his own illogical prejudice by clipping the
curb with his front wheel on the turn.

"What was I saying? Yup. Finn Garrett is hot stuff. And why?"

He looked half the time in the driving mirror, keeping his eye partly on the road and partly on that weird-looking little fellow in the back.

"Well, she's a mother, isn't she?" Mal offered.

The driver held up one finger. "That's one," he agreed. "Two, she's beautiful. Three, she fought nearly to the death to save her child. Christ, man, they showed her injuries on TV, and I was almost sick." His eyes flicked back between the freeway and the mirror. "Four, that's the cutest little girl, Daisy. You see her picture? Right."

The radio phone cut him off for thirty seconds of indecipherable static. He made a monosyllabic answer into the handset, and resumed immediately. "Where was I? Five. Yup. Five. She's not just some airhead, some good-looking dame. She's an intellectual, and—*and*—concerned with science and the environment. People are real keen on that just now, and she's been on TV, speaking up for things we care about over here, so she's known, right? She's respected."

"And the guru label? What's that about?"

"Well . . ."

The driver sucked his teeth and kept his eye on a red light. When it changed, he flicked a quick glance at his passenger's face in the mirror and then away again.

"I'm not so sure about all that. You know, spiritual perceptive extension they call it, or something like that. My wife's into all that. But if you go for it, Finn Garrett is the tops. She's the one they all think understands the secret of the universe or whatever. I tell you . . ." He took both hands off the steering wheel to make his point for a moment as well as an extended eye contact in the driving mirror. "Those guys who attacked her don't know what they let themselves in for. Let's face it, they were never going to be popular, but, Jesus, did they pick the wrong dame!"

★   ★   ★

The driver was wrong about one thing, namely, his prediction that Mal Harris wouldn't gain access to Dr. Garrett's bedside. Mal managed this with a combination of persuasion and chicanery so that when Finn Garrett next opened her eyes, he was sitting there, a white coat fitted over his country-made suit, a picture reminiscent of his great-uncle when he had kept the bakery at Nant-y-glo. Before she opened her eyes a small terrified clicking sound came from her throat. The nurse put her hand on her arm and said, "Dr. Garrett. Don't be frightened. You're in the Samaritan Hospital and we're looking after you."

The nurse pressed a bell with her foot, as she checked the dial on the intravenous feed, and almost immediately hurrying footsteps sounded in the passage and the door of the room opened. It opened softly, the way people open doors when they've got a paying customer inside.

"She wants to speak, Doctor," the nurse said.

"Who's this?"

"Oh, this is Mr. Harris. His presence seems to quiet her, and the nursing supervisor said that he had to be allowed to stay so long as her doctors agreed. It's something to do with insurance."

"Hmmm."

The young man assumed that the insurance referred to was the one that ended up with himself being paid. He busied himself extracting the plastic tubing from Finn's throat while the nurse eased the small of her neck. A cast covered one shoulder and the whole arm. Both hands were heavily bandaged. The light cover of the bed was held up on a cage.

"Daisy," Finn said. Her voice was gravelly and dry. A stream of tears fell out of the corners of her eyes across the temples and into the torn and bruised hairline that lay on the pillow.

"That's her daughter," the nurse said in a choked undertone to the doctor. "The little girl who . . ."

"Dr. Garrett, you're all right," the young doctor said in an unintentional parody of common sense. "Your arm has been operated on, and there's—"

"Where is Daisy?" Finn said. There was a pitiful note of hope in her voice, as if she misdoubted the reality of what might, after all, have been a dream. "Is she . . ."

The doctor looked at the nurse.

"They'll find her, honey," the nurse said, bending over Finn, her warm heart absolutely bursting with sympathy. "The police are out there now just waiting to talk to you, and they'll find her in no time. She'll be all right, honey. Don't ask me how, but I just . . ."

But to Finn the nurse's voice faded after the first few words. They lost all sensual definition and merged with the blocks of light and shade that made up the objects in the room. For a long time in the environs of Finn's awareness there was no sound at all.

Later, she became conscious of a man's voice. It had a soothing tone. He was not an American. There was a mesmeric rhythm in the way he spoke. She had heard it before. She began to concentrate on what he was saying. He was telling her that she must inform the police, as soon as she could get the strength to talk, of everything she could remember about the attack. She whispered yes. But in the very same breath, if it could be called breath—this pulse that hit the inside of her veins and seemed to wind her rather than give her strength—she remembered the trucker's threat. A word spoken could mean death for her child. Daisy had been taken as insurance against any information her mother might feel tempted to give. Mal Harris literally saw this fear leap up in her, flutter and blunder like something caught inside her body. He said, "Don't be afraid."

She tried to breathe. Her muscles seemed only to be able to work in spasm, threatening to choke her on her own wind. He said, "Try again." He had his hand on her wrist. She took another breath separating out the physical consciousness, the memory, and the future danger. She lifted herself on her breath until it forced her up out of the well of unconsciousness. And then—calmly—she opened her eyes.

The Lloyd's negotiator—Mal Harris—was sitting beside her. Apart from him the room was empty. The back of a man in state police uniform showed through the glass partition of the door. She couldn't move her head, but Mal Harris and the door were both in her line of vision.

"Dr. Garrett," he said, "I've been speaking to Rat, so I know about the new compounds in the waste area. Is that what you went out to investigate?"

"Yes."

"Is there any connection between that and the attack on you and your daughter?"

She looked at him. She felt her mind move with excruciating slowness. If she said yes, what would it cost her, bearing in mind what the trucker had said? She focused her memory on the trucker. His face was as clear to her eye—clearer—than that of Mal Harris.

"Could you describe the person who attacked you?"

Tightly curled black hair cut very short, dark eyes, white skin, but grooved and hatched with the blue-black growth and roots and stubble of facial hair and body hair; short and stocky; hands strong and short; a ring. The way he held Daisy's hair with that hand bunched into her head as if she were a thing, when he wrenched her over to one side. What must she have felt in her terrified little heart? Finn had not spoken. Her eyes followed with a dim and tragic attention, as her mind, in response to Mal's question, relived the moment of her own crucifixion on the truck staring through the windshield at the nightmare inside. She heard Mal say again, "There now, *cariad*. Just say if you could describe him to the police."

Her own voice whispered yes.

He waited a long time, and then she added, "Dare not."

Mal Harris got up. He moved out of her line of vision, but she was aware of him. She waited.

"I had better tell you," he said eventually. "I'm not a regular Lloyd's assessor. I belong full time to an organization that investigates insurance crime. So I have an unusual experience, you see; more useful perhaps, in this case, than your routine police unit. You see?"

He paused, looking at her. Normally when he explained

his role, he could bank on a good deal of adverse audience reaction. He was well aware that he looked more like a country chapel organist or a tubercular coal miner with a talent for poetry than a man capable of being dangerous to anyone. But then, this was America. He didn't know what to expect them to expect over here. It should have been reassuring for him in that case to see an incredulous smile just marginally lighten her face.

"We weren't expecting anything out of the way in this Santhill claim," he went on. "They sent me by chance, as it were. Big money, see. It often is in this business."

He sat down again. "I've spoken to Rat," he said after a pause. "I knew you were worried about something at the meeting, and I wanted to find out what it was. Rat told me." He paused. She had closed her eyes again.

"If you keep silent," he said, "the only one you're trusting is the man who attacked you, the one who took your child. You give him safe conduct through whatever he's doing, and he'll give you back your daughter, is that it?"

There was the sound of crepe soles, brusque and squeaking, in the passage, and the sound of wheels.

"You mustn't do it," he went on urgently. "Believe me, I know from all my experience their minds don't work like that. You must trust someone who can help you. Tell me who you saw out there and why, and then I'll have a chance to get to them before they know I'm coming."

"I saw the guards," she whispered, temporizing.

"The site guards, you mean? But it wasn't they who attacked you."

"No."

"You left? And then what happened?"

"I left the site with the sample I'd taken. The night-shift guards had turned up. Then we got a flat tire when the car was still within sight of the fence."

"So who was it who attacked you?"

"Truckers. They came when it was dark from the direction of China Lake. They must be tipping when the night guards are on. They are dumping this waste where the additional toxicity wouldn't have been discovered, if Rat hadn't happened to do that field study. But it's far more dangerous."

"Would Rat be able to trace it? Would he have any idea of the origin?"

She frowned, struggling in her mind to clear her normal channels of thought.

"He could," she said, "possibly."

"Is it Santhill themselves, do you think, who are doing it?"

"I thought so." She stopped to accumulate the strength to say more, and then added, "Not their compound."

"You mean the sample Rat took is not a product of Santhill's production line?"

"Not unless they're doing something very unusual. Or criminal."

She closed her eyes again. After a while she said, "They spotted our car, and one truck came after us across the desert." Her voice dropped into silence. Mal Harris got up. She opened her eyes and looked at him with renewed fear.

"Warn Rat. Not to talk."

"I will," he said.

"They'll kill her." She could hardly say it; the very idea pinched her vocal cords into a tiny monotone. "If they find out, they'll . . ."

Mal said quietly, "It's no good me telling you not to worry, love; but between you and me I'm far more dangerous than I look. And I'm going to get those men before they know I'm coming and before they can do the little girl any harm. And then I'm going to make them wish they'd never been born."

CHAPTER 28

*N*o less than the truck driver, George Cash had his reasons for what he was about to do.

Evening was falling. He sat in a neighborhood café on Fifth Street, conspicuous in his fitted white shirt that set off his tightly knit torso with unfashionable precision. From where he sat he could see the front door of Charlie's house. He had watched him come out and go off to score in the park. Three Cokes and a lime soda later, George saw him come back. He stood up.

In this district where many people looked like bundles of rags, no one noticed a nondescript, dirty, and inoffensive youth standing outside, who kept his eye on George. When George got up, the youth shifted that eye to the sidewalk where Charlie could be seen coming toward him. One arm was occupied with a bag containing some cartons of milk and a loaf of bread, and with his other hand Charlie fumbled in the pocket of an over-large linen jacket for a latchkey. When Charlie went up the steps to his door, the youth crossed the street.

George had come out of the café and walked off in the opposite direction, unobserved.

Charlie balanced what he was holding and leaned against the frame of the door, about to fit his key in the lock, when the youth came up behind him.

At that very moment Sarah, her mouth as dry as a thorn-bush, waited not many miles away by the baggage reclaim at Los Angeles International Airport. She decided to leave without her bag, but a customs officer politely stopped her. Her frantic compliance coincided with the moment when the youth came up behind Charlie on the step. With a knife the blade of which was almost as thin as a hatpin, he stabbed expertly, twice: once in the kidney and once in the heart.

The youth walked away from the collapsing body with no sign of emotion. When he was ten yards off, he was already indistinguishable from other people on the sidewalk. His gait purposeful but not hurried, he went in the direction previously taken by George Cash and found him waiting on the crossing between Spring Street and Fifth. While passersby glanced incuriously at Charlie lying in the doorway like any other collapsed junkie, three hundred yards away George Cash handed over the money he owed to the youth who had killed him. The youth took it with the same efficient and unnoticeable lack of emphasis with which he had committed the murder, and went on his way.

George Cash began to walk in the opposite direction. He walked—or so he thought—away from the body of his murdered friend, in the direction of Wilshire Boulevard. When he felt at a safe distance, he took a cab. Arriving home, he had a vile sensation suddenly, as he opened his own front door, that the distance between his house and Charlie's had contracted some-how, had been snapped up, as if the intervening road was no better than a length of measuring tape that had sprung-loaded itself back into its case, leaving just a yard or two between Brentwood and Fifth Street. He poured himself a large whiskey with a hand that was beginning to shake.

Hugo said, "You're damn late. Where've you been?"

On Fifth Street, passersby were beginning to notice the blood dripping out of Charlie, and near the airport Sarah Grimmond, her face ashen, said to her cabdriver, "Couldn't you please hurry. I'm terribly late."

"I can't hurry, ma'am," the man said. "There's no point."

He spoke a truer word than he knew. "Freeway's jammed," he said. "It's like this every night. We get there when we get there."

She subsided so quietly that he glanced in his driving mirror after a while to check her out. She looked desperate. He shook his head to himself, spotted a gap between two cars, and very nearly rammed his fender.

"Y' see!" he said.

She gave no response. He frowned and adjusted the driving mirror.

"Say, ma'am," he said. "Fifth Street and Spring is quite a rough area. You sure you got your address right?"

"Yes, I'm quite sure, thank you."

He waited, but that was it. She wasn't going to say any more. She looked about the same age as his mother, but there the resemblance absolutely stopped. Like the goddamn traffic. He ran the tips of the fingers of his right hand repeatedly over the ball of his thumb. It was getting too dark to see anyway.

Half an hour, maybe twenty-five minutes later, he cruised along Wilshire Boulevard and into Fifth. As he got toward the number the dame in the back had asked for, he came up on a bunch of cops and an ambulance. He figured on going round them. He peered out to check the house numbers.

"D'you know the building, ma'am?"

She was sitting straight as a ramrod, as if she had been struck by lightning. He braked to a halt, his eye still fixed on the rearview mirror, and then turned his body right round. He looked from her to the sidewalk. A cop waved him on, but he turned off the engine and got out and went round to the back door.

"Look, ma'am," he said.

She had a piece of paper with the address clutched in her hand. He gently pulled it out of her fingers and looked round to check the buildings, muttering to himself, "Jesus, now what?" and saying to her, "Come on, lady. You're all right, aren't you?"

"Move on" the cop said, coming up. "This is an accident here."

"What can I do?" the cabdriver asked him. "This lady wanted"—he looked again at the paper—"one sixty on Fifth. This is it, isn't it?"

"She asked for one sixty?" The cop bent and looked in the backseat. "Excuse me, ma'am, but are you known to the occupants of one sixty?"

There was quite a long pause.

"She's sick maybe," the cabdriver said.

"Where did you pick her up?"

"The airport."

"My son," Sarah Grimmond said.

The two men abruptly stopped talking to each other.

"Do you know the occupants of one sixty, ma'am," the police officer asked again.

Sarah began to get her legs out of the cab. Her eyes were fixed. Her right hand, without the glove, reached out to get a hold on the door frame. The policeman took it and clumsily supported her weight. He felt the thin papery fingers and the fine rings. When she was upright, she said, "Thank you," and began to walk toward the doorway, her senses almost suspended in the poisoned air of fear.

"Excuse me, ma'am, you can't go there," the officer said.

She stopped and almost turned to him. She spoke to him as if he were standing a foot or so to the right of where he actually was. She said, "I've come to see my son."

Just like that. It scared the man. He said, "Wait here, ma'am, please. Your son's name is?"

"Charles Grimmond."

While she obediently waited, he walked the few paces over to the doorway. The ambulance men had just laid a stretcher on the sidewalk and would soon move Charlie's body onto it. Sarah waited stock-still. He came back. He said, "Ma'am, will you come with me?"

She walked beside him up to the steps. There, lying on the stone, was Charlie. There was blood under his trouser leg and behind his left shoulder. There was some bread, other contents of a bag. The milk cartons had not broken open. Charlie's neck had fallen very awkwardly to one side. His head had nothing to lean on. She bent forward and very gently slipped her handbag as a pillow between his left cheek and the doorpost. He looked thin. Her heart, unable to discriminate between one grief and another, grieved that he hadn't been eating properly. There had been no one to take care of him, to love him. She picked up his hand. It was very cold. The cells of the skin felt compact, with an unfamiliar airless texture, like clay. Even her lips could not warm his hand. She gazed at his face. He was silent. She whispered intimately to him, "Charlie. Mother's here, darling." And waited for him to make a little movement, however small, even just the quiver of an eyelash or the faintest pulse, to show that he heard. She waited. But no stone was ever more still. With his hand gripped in hers, she let her face drop so that she was no longer looking at him.

"I tried to get here in time, darling," she said, as if she was late collecting him from the little nursery school he had attended in London before he was old enough to go away. "I tried to get here in time."

CHAPTER 29

I never thought," Rachel said, "that when people died, they got as dead as that."

She put down the mug of tea the policewoman had given her, let her head drop back against the wall, and closed her eyes for a minute. "Death like sleep," she said, "you know? Slightly dead—not answering and not hearing but otherwise the same. But instead, here is this crude and total change, an ex-live thing with the clammy coldness of putty and roughly the same consistency, totally utterly dead, not a spark of air or warmth or life in it. How can anyone doubt the existence of the spirit when the body without one is as dead as that!"

Mal Harris, who was used to death, listened patiently. After a pause he said, "How is Lady Grimmond?"

"Terrible." Rachel retrieved her cup and after a moment held the rim of the china against her forehead. "Poor Sarah."

In an adjoining room Sarah herself sat beside a trestle table on which lay the stretcher bearing Charlie. She had asked to be alone with him, but they had left one policewoman who was tactfully silent. Sarah also was silent. Eventually she got up and walked toward the door. The policewoman hastened after her with some vague idea of supporting her with a hand under the elbow, but although Sarah walked like a somnambulist, she was completely steady on her feet.

"Is my niece here?" she asked.

"Yes, Lady Grimmond."

She walked through the doorway.

"Turn left. It's the first door."

Sarah did as she was told, her mind locked into its own concerns. In the room she found Rachel and some sort of tradesman or person in business. Rachel looked well. Perhaps she had blond hair of that precise color because of being Charlie's cousin. His hair was exactly that shade. Ripe wheat. A lovely color. Rachel's eyes, on the other hand, were hazel. Adrian's eyes were hazel. It was Sarah and Charlie who had the blue eyes.

Rachel had said something. She had asked her . . . what? Sarah heard the inconsequential sentence on the echo, as the sound of the words receded through the empty chasm of her mind.

"I'm sorry, dear," she said, feeling Rachel's cheek against hers, the smell of her hair, the nice sensation of her embrace. "I don't think I heard you."

Sarah looked not so much like someone completely lost as like a person invisibly encased in an environment totally other than the one in which she appeared to be standing: the desert, for example, or a waste of snow. She looked, standing there on the threshold of what the Los Angeles police station called its hospitality room, like the only person not lost. However, if someone had made a real attempt to find out in what dimension it was that she was so firmly anchored, the answer was Hell.

"Aunt Sarah," Rachel said, "do you want to come and sit down?"

Sarah moved forward. There was a brown armchair. She sat. One of the other people put a chair close-by for Rachel.

"I have something to say to you, Rachel," Sarah said. "Listen carefully, because I don't want to talk about it again. I feel I should just mention it once. Your uncle spoke to Charlie on the telephone. Charlie rang up at four A.M. on Tuesday morning. Charlie was very distressed. Adrian wouldn't let me speak to him, of course. But I heard every word he said."

She stopped speaking as if someone had deactivated a switch. Rachel held her aunt's hand in hers. A few hours ago she would have said that it was like holding the hand of a corpse, but now she knew better. After a full two minutes in which she said nothing but simply sat listening in private silence to the sound of Charlie's voice in her memory, Sarah started to speak again.

"Charlie told your uncle that he had helped forge an insurance document for an American chemicals firm. That was a very wrong thing to do, of course. He put your uncle's syndicate number on it."

"Good Lord!" Rachel said. "Was it—" But she caught herself up, realizing the futility and perhaps the inappropriateness of anything resembling a technical question. Sarah gazed ahead of her and maintained another long and stony silence.

"That's all," she said at length. She turned her face toward Rachel, and after a while her expression softened very slightly. "You should keep your hair better combed, dear," she said. "It's rather common to let it get in a mess like that. Have you got a comb? I have one in my bag."

She picked up her handbag—a black snakeskin from Fortnum's, but the clasp was a bit shoddy all things considered. She took out a small Kent comb and handed it to Rachel. She watched as Rachel combed her hair and then took the comb and returned it to the bag. When she had snapped it shut, she kept her eyes on the clasp, as if forgetful of the next move. Rachel made as if to stand, but stopped, half braced against the seat of her chair, saying to her aunt, "Shall we go now, Aunt Sarah?"

Sarah looked up again. An expression of childlike desolation crossed her face. "What shall I do, dear," she said, "now?"

"I've taken a room for you in my hotel," Rachel said gently. "A doctor has been called, and he will give you something to make you sleep."

"And then ring Adrian," Sarah said.

Together they walked out of the room and into the police car waiting to take them back.

★ ★ ★

When, an hour later, Rachel made that phone call from Los Angeles, it brought to an end three days of painful uncertainty and anxiety for Sir Adrian Grimmond and replaced them with worse. He had been able to see, because of the smashed desk flap and the drawer where the passports were kept, that Sarah had gone abroad, and he guessed that it was to America. But the absolutely unprecedented anarchy of her behavior posed quite a challenge. Should he just bide his time and wait for her to come home? The one overriding anxiety was that matter of the accursed forgery. And then, just before he was about to leave the house for work, the phone rang.

Adrian listened to the bad news of Charlie's death and the not unexpected information that Sarah was in Los Angeles with gloom.

"I'm so sorry," Rachel said. "it's a terrible shock for you."

"How is Sarah?" he said, not denying it. "How is she taking it?"

"She's sleeping," Rachel said. "A doctor has seen her and given her a sedative. She's here with me, at my hotel.

"And . . ." He hesitated. "Charles?"

"His body is being held by the authorities at the moment. Of course, they have no idea who killed him, but the police . . ." Rachel's voice tailed off. "Uncle Adrian, I'm very sorry to have to mention this, but Charlie said that he had forged this general liability claim for Santhill."

"What!"

Adrian sounded so genuinely shocked that Rachel, unable to see his face, didn't know what to make of it.

"I'm sorry," she said. "I thought you knew. I only mentioned it because I assumed you would have . . ."

"Knew what! Some harebrained addict's fantasy? How should I know?"

"Sarah said that Charlie telephoned on Tuesday morning and told you."

"You can't take notice of what Sarah says at the moment."

"It's not true then? Sarah said Charlie called to tell you

what he'd done and that he gave your syndicate number on the document."

Adrian maintained a brief but furious silence and then changed his tack. He said, "May I ask who else knows this?"

"At the moment, beside Sarah, only Mr. Harris and myself," Rachel said. Her voice had lost its tone of familial confidentiality. "But naturally we weren't visualizing a situation in which it would remain concealed."

"Meaning I was!" Adrian said.

"It wouldn't be possible," she said evasively.

He could see that now. The mortifying fact did not endear her to him. She knew that he had been aware of the forgery since Tuesday and had done nothing, and therefore he began to dislike her. He could not stop her coming to the correct conclusion about what he had intended.

"I will have to meet my board to explain this before leaving," Adrian said frigidly, "and I may hope to be able to get a flight this evening. My secretary will ring and let you know."

Rachel tried to get back onto something like their old terms before putting the phone down, but he wasn't having any. With the prospect of humiliation before his own board and the Lloyd's directors ahead of him, it was no consolation to Sir Adrian that only Rachel need ever know that he had contemplated keeping quiet about the forgery. When he arrived in Los Angeles to take over the management of Sarah and of Charlie's body, he and Rachel would have a new relationship.

"I know what's going to happen," Rachel said with ironic prescience, when she had recounted the conversation to Mal. "He'll make out, when he gets here, that I've become unattractive as a woman; I'll have lost my femininity or something like that."

"Well," Mal said, looking at her and shaking his head slightly, "twenty-six *is* quite an age for a woman!"

For a second she stared at him with an expression as if the milk jug had just bitten her, and then he laughed. "Don't you worry," he said. "Real men like beautiful women with brains and wit best. I should know."

*D*uring this same day the reports of Finn Garrett's progress and the efforts of the police to trace her daughter had continued to fill the local papers. Barbara Falcus was distraught about it. It was just absolutely typical of Dale that he did not feel as she did. To Barbara, Finn was a sort of messianic figure, whereas to Dale she was just the EPA rep on the cleanup order for Santhill. And his entire response to the tragedy now surrounding her was limited to worry that the paperwork for the insurance claim was being held up by it. He assumed, as Barbara did, that local youths were behind the attack. But although his uneasiness wasn't exacerbated by any suspicions that she might have clashed with the illegal dumpers at work on the site, he was uneasy, nevertheless, simply on account of the delay.

The EPA itself, although at one time viewing the cleanup as a matter of desperate urgency, seemed to have lost all sense of time and to be prepared to settle down to a pace comparable to the movement of a glacier.

"Okay," Charles Seaford said, when Dale expressed his worry about the lack of progress, "so the Lloyd's fellow and the broker will have to go away and come back again. It's no skin off my nose."

"It wouldn't be," Dale said. "All things being equal, Charles, it wouldn't be. But all things aren't equal here, are they? We've got a ticklish situation on our hands."

That brought Charles down to earth. "You mean . . ." He bunched his lips together and frowned. For somebody of his weight, the feeling of thin ice was not pleasant, but he could hardly complain when his second-in-command reminded him of it. And without a doubt, in such circumstances, getting from one side to the other quickly was just common sense. Even though the forged document seemed quite safe, it got safer with every piece of corroborative paperwork, and safest of all when it had been processed through.

"What can we do?" he said.

Dale walked over to the plate-glass overhang, and glanced at the view of Los Angeles.

"We should put the screws on the EPA local office to produce a replacement and get the paperwork wrapped up. Who's our best man on government relations? It's Vincent really, isn't it. He's got some of them in his pocket."

"Get him on to it then."

"I don't know if he's back."

"Back from where?"

"Italy."

"Italy? What's he doing in Italy again? Was that work for us?"

Dale shrugged eloquently. But he did find Vincent Cordoba back at his desk. He walked in and slapped a copy of the local rag down on the tanned leather surface.

"Did you see that?"

Vincent hadn't. He'd been away, ostensibly discussing a marketing franchise with a pharmaceuticals firm in Naples, but of course the negotiations had provided him with the opportunity he'd needed to tie up his own affairs. As far as he knew, the top loading of the Santhill waste dump had gone without a hitch so far and promised to be extremely profitable to himself. And then he saw the newspaper Dale had put in front of him, and he immediately started drawing very different conclusions from those that were automatically assumed by his colleagues.

Vincent had not forgotten Finn Garrett. Since the Seaford's party her image had a trick of returning to his inner eye. He was successful with women, but had never found one capable of being successful with him. He never gave his heart to bimbos and playgirls like some of the men. Or high school romances turned matrimony with types like Barbara Falcus, who had "woman" written right through them with the utterly boring consistency of a stick of rock candy. But Finn Garrett was another matter. For the last ten days when his white teeth showed like that just between his lips, and the crease—not quite a laugh line and not quite a dimple—that cut down his cheek deepened, he had been thinking of her. When his long black eyelashes were lowered against the intrusion of everyday surroundings and behind them his eyes took on a deeper reflection as if the image of a beautiful woman had stepped right into them, that woman was Finn Garrett.

He picked up the paper and said, "What's this?" But he could see what it was. It was a photograph of Finn Garrett before and after the attack; and a photograph of the child. "When did this happen?"

Dale, leaning with his fists on the leather, jerked upright and said, "Two days ago. Three. While you were away."

"What was she doing there?"

"How should I know?" It was the first time Dale had thought of it. "She makes a lot of trips into the desert. Barbara tells me she's got a thing about it."

"Have you checked whether she had been to the Santhill site on this occasion?"

"What do you mean?"

"What I say, Dale. Watch my lips."

Two runnels of broken veined color appeared on Dale's cheekbones. "Don't you be so damned smartassed with me, Vincent! What the hell do you mean? You're not suggesting she . . ."

Vincent suddenly realized he'd sooner not suggest any such thing to Dale. It was only the shock that had made him speak out when the idea occurred to him that Finn, with her habit of visiting the desert at all hours, might have witnessed the illegal dumping. And in that case he didn't know what his truckers might not be capable of.

"You mean that damned business that Zack got us into?" Dale said.

"No. It can't be anything to do with that," Vincent assured him. "What do you want me to do?" he asked distractedly, with half an eye still on the column.

"Get onto Kabe Geary and hurry up a replacement."

"Right."

"So that we can get the agreement signed and sealed. Charles wants that Lloyd's money locked up."

"Very well," Vincent said. "I'll get onto it right away."

And he did. But when he'd put the phone down on Kabe's senior staffer (Kabe was out), Vincent came right back to that newspaper article and read it over slowly. With the fingernails of his right hand he flicked back the leaves of his desktop day calendar. He sneaked out his pocket diary and checked a number there. By his calculations he was deeply unhappy. He rechecked the night in question. And tomorrow? He hesitated over a phone number. It was a call he didn't want to make; it was unprofessional and risky. But he had to know. He punched in the numbers. When the man at the other end answered, Vincent spoke in Spanish, not Italian, and arranged a grudging meeting, which would involve him in driving out of Los Angeles when the day's work was over.

Early that evening, leaving his 1959 Oldsmobile Classic in the garage of Century Hall, he drove along the freeway toward Bakersfield in a rented Pontiac that he sometimes used when he didn't want to be noticed. In this he could drive around the back of the settlement near Loraine and make his contact without exciting attention.

He went past the houses of the nearby town, marveling, as every frequent visitor to Europe must, at the building standards here and the way each fellow threw up what he needed for the following three years and then left it for the next man. Barbara and her sort said, in answer to any criticism of this aspect of American civilization, that it was the weather: meaning, if it doesn't rain much, who needs a proper roof?

Vincent knew the tone in which his grandmother would have pointed out that in classical Greece and Italy the weather was just as good. For all intents and purposes the uninhibited squalor of the shack at which Vincent finally drew up was preferable to him. Indifference to civilized standards was preferable to trying and getting it so terribly wrong. Here at least things were what they were: three men, in crumpled dark blue shirts in which they slept, and rooms smelling of piss and beer. In the butterfly blue light of dusk Vincent walked over to the wooden table standing on the scuffed grass by the door. The trucker who had come out to meet him slammed down two cans of beer. "So what's up?" he asked.

Vincent took out from the inner pocket of his coat the page from the local paper. The trucker glanced at it.

"Yup," he said.

"Did you do that?" Vincent asked him.

The man's eyes narrowed.

"Who's asking?"

"I am," sneered Vincent.

"B'cos I thought y' might be, y' know. It's not Nightly that sent yer?"

"No one sends me," said Vincent. "I'm the one who pays."

"And we're the ones who do the work," the trucker shouted suddenly, with the readiness of his type the world over. He hit the table and moved his jaw sideways in a gesture copied from crass cinematic clichés while little flicks of white-gray static could be seen in the half light through the open door where his TV prompter was running overtime.

"Is the child here or isn't she?"

"The kid's with Dicey. Dicey's Lee's girl so there's no sweat."

"And you did this?"

"What else!"

His jaw bunched and bristled with aggression. "We find some interfering dame—not just a dame, but official, nosing around where she'd no right to be. What do you expect us to do?

"Kill her maybe."

"Yup. Well, Lee said so. But if she keeps her mouth shut and watches our backs until we're through, that'll be okay, won't it? Two more runs to make: T'night and Friday."

"Why should she watch your backs?"

The trucker stubbed the picture of Daisy with his finger.

Vincent took a look at the man. "You jerk," he said. He spoke with such uncompromising venom, his tone so hard, he took his opponent's breath away. The man stared angrily back without daring any response.

"You're going to have one hell of a job not killing that child even if you try," Vincent went on. "Don't you see what this rag says? She's three. You can't slam around a three-year-old like a tin can."

"She's bein' well looked after," the trucker said.

"And if you weren't going to kill the mother, why the hell did you hit her so hard?"

"What is this?" The man took a step forward. "She fought like a tiger. I couldn't get her off! No dame I ever came across fought like that."

"Maybe because she's a mother, and you were taking her child away."

"Maybe. An' maybe she's just an exciting wild baby, Christ, imagine getting somethin' like that in the sack."

Vincent looked at him. He folded the paper smoothly up and put it back in the inside pocket of his coat, as if trying not to disturb a viper he had nestling inside there.

"Be careful," he said. "You've fixed it so that the desert's getting watched, so you'd better be very careful tonight and Friday. You stick exactly to your schedule. Friday's dark. You don't use lights. You don't waste time. And you bring the child.

The trucker said, "Right."

"As long as that's understood," Vincent said, "I'll be going."

CHAPTER 31

*M*al Harris, at an early hour of the morning and before going down to breakfast in the hotel, telephoned the university office and left an urgent message for Rat. He then called London and got through to his own headquarters, where he spoke to the twenty-four-hour duty officer.

"Why did you do all that?" Rachel exclaimed when they met at breakfast. She looked only half rested. Her cousin's death, which had been, the day before, so senseless and unexpected that it had hardly shocked her, had changed the contours of its meaning during the night, and she had not slept well.

"I feel confused," she said. "Where are we now? Where do we stand?"

"Are we out of a job, you mean?"

"I suppose we are."

"We've still got steps to take in the matter of giving notice to Santhill."

"About the forgery."

"Yes."

"That should be fun," Rachel said ironically. "I'm not sure that I'm looking forward to walking into that building and telling five extremely powerful American businessmen that I know they forged their insurance claim."

"I am," Mal said.

She gave a slight laugh. "So why the melancholy visage then?"

He sighed. "The forgery's only half the story now, isn't it. I'm not going to leave Finn Garrett to the mercies of this lot." He tipped his finger to the folded sheet of the day's paper lying beside his plate.

"But if we're no longer involved in the clearance claim . . ."

"Exactly."

"Is that why you called Rat? And London?"

He bunched his napkin up and put it beside his plate. "We've only just scratched the surface of what's going on here."

"But if it's not our business anymore what can we do?"

"I've asked my firm's permission to use our watcher."

"What's all that about?" Rachel asked. "I've never heard about any watchers except in the Lloyd's sense of local people employed part time to watch the entry and exit of shipping in local ports and log their times and condition."

"It's a similar idea," Mal said. "Our firm copied it. We keep a network of local people—usually businessmen or traders of one sort or another—who are registered with Shipping I.S. and hold themselves available to help any officer who comes to that town on duty."

"I see."

"I've sent in a request for a contact, and to be given an extension of duty covering the Mojave Desert attack."

"But what about me?" Rachel said. "Steiger and Wallace will expect me to go straight back to London."

"They won't expect you to turn around in two days. We've got to meet the Santhill board. Then you'll have to get a flight. Three or four days is all I need."

"And what do you want to do?"

"I want us to get Finn Garrett out of this," he said. "No one else will. She's frightened to death. She can't speak to the law about the illegal dumping that's going on for fear the truckers will kill her child."

"When they finish the job, they'll give the child back,

won't they?" Rachel said. "Can't we all just keep very quiet until they've done it?"

"And let them get away with the poisons they're tipping without pinning down the source, or the truckers, or their principals, and leaving them free to do it all again?"

"Look," Rachel said. "Harvey Sanger—you know, that property tycoon who's been in the news here? He has a scheme to cover a hundred acres of a beautiful local hillside with a hideous building development. No thanks," she said to a waiter who went away with a tray of waffles and syrup. "A few hundred gallons of anthrax poison, or whatever it is, added to existing pollutants on the Mojave dump seems preferable to me."

"Well, there's something in what you say," Mal agreed, "and I think a lot of developers are a form of pollutant in their own right. I know of one developer in Penarth who should be made to rendezvous with the next load of poison for dumping in the Mojave and made to drink it. Then they could bury him in the ancient, lonely little churchyard he wants to cover with executive dwellings." He said this with bloodcurdling sincerity and then added, "For now though, we've got to concentrate on possibilities."

"Aren't we risking the child's life if we interfere?"

"That's not the way it works," Mal said. "If you sit back quietly, the villains don't return all the counters to the right squares."

A pageboy stopped at their table with a message.

"Rat is in reception," said Mal. "What time is Sir Adrian arriving?"

"Midday," Rachel said, getting up. "But I'll have to remain fairly near to Sarah until he gets here."

They both rose and were walking toward the exit. The crowd of tourists and business people was thinning, but the dining room still rang with the glitzy chatter of voices starting a sunny rich day in close proximity to the exotic gardens that glamorously spread outward from the plate-glass wall.

Reception, in comparison, was shady, and Rat, leaning

against the desk in a pose more reminiscent of a disintegrating stick insect than a rodent, was chatting up a glamorous clerk. She was giving him a reasonable rate of return. Leaning on the desk with his elbow caused his shoulder bones to jut out of his jacket. He wore a pink tie that matched the sunburn on his hairline and thick spectacles in the lenses of which both tie and burn were fragmentally reflected. When he saw Mal coming toward him, he tried to do a race date booking with the clerk, whipping a small diary out of his inner pocket with an intentness of purpose that grotesquely collapsed when, just behind Mal Harris, he spotted Rachel. He returned the book in mid-sentence, his eyes glazing over, and took a step away from his playpen.

"Morning, Rat," Mal said. "Thank you for coming over. This is Rachel Grimmond, my colleague."

"Oh my! Oh my! I little thought . . ."

"Good God," she muttered.

He blushed.

"Come on, Rat," Mal said. "Over here. It's your brains we're after, I'm afraid. Body next time."

The three of them settled in a corner.

"Coffee?"

"Oh, yes please." A waiter was already beside them. Rat said, "I'll have a black in eclipse with two shots of lightning."

"What on earth's that?" asked Rachel as the waiter, apparently quite satisfied, went off to prepare it.

"Double expresso with Strega and a layer of cream floated on top."

"For breakfast!"

"Of course," he said. "Now, Mal, I've got that analysis you asked me for." He dipped two fingers into the right-hand pocket of his coat, which was sewn on as a patch without a flap, and tweezered out a fold of paper. He passed it over. "It's not just the chemical pollutant that's the problem," he said.

"What else?"

"It's catalytic properties. It's mixing with what's already there."

"How bad could the result be?"

Rat's eyes lit up at first as he contemplated the question, but he let himself get distracted. "Man," he said. "There was a consignment going begging in Italy. They humped it around like the black death, and dockers went on strike rather than handle the stuff, and the local people turned out in strength in England and forced the cargo vessel back out onto the high seas. I wonder if this is it!"

"Could it be?"

Rat's coffee arrived. He prodded it into a nice position and took a tiny sample bottle out of another pocket. It looked evil, and it was labeled with precision. He upended it with great care, and one drop of liquid fell from its lip into the coffee cup.

"Did you hear me, Rat," Mal said. "Do you think the notorious load of toxic waste you refer to is the one being dumped?"

"It could be," Rat said.

"Could it also be a by-product of any Santhill activity?"

"Yeees," Rat said. "But not a legal by-product. They make—but hang about there; I mistake me. That's a different chemicals company—Camberwell." He took a firm sip of his concoction. "My guess is that this will be the Italian stuff. In which case there's not a great quantity of it. It will have come through at A—where there's a crooked customs official called Sego who lets in about a quarter of a million dollars' worth of commission to himself in illegal imports per year. And shall I tell you an interesting item?" Rat gazed round at the two of them with gloating incredulity. "He declares it for tax, all up front. He calls it commission loading. He's not scared of the law, but, Jesus, show him a revenue inspector and that man's jelly."

"How do you know so much about it," Rachel demanded, "when this whole area of illegal pollution is about the most violent and ruthless in modern America, excluding the drug scene, I suppose."

"I'm not involved," Rat said, shocked. "I just put the picture together, as a hobby."

"Dangerous hobby!"

"Pollutants, toxins, and poisons need their human equivalents and support structures," he said. "Take a simple example. Take anthrax. That stuff can't walk, at least not until it gets into the sheep, and then not far. It needs the anthrax human being to make and administer it. How about dimethyl acetate, the main legal ingredient at the Santhill site? That's a by-product of the manufacture of baby's diapers, but only *if*'—he held his finger up to his audience—"*if* you reject the option that gives *only* a fifteen percent return on capital. For that lower return on capital the process can be different and doesn't have the toxic waste. But the dimethyl acetate human microbe speaks up for the more toxic process and the higher return. Get it?"

"My God," Rachel said, "I can't bear it."

Rat pushed the remains of his coffee aside and put his arm around her shoulder. "Lean on me, baby," he said. "I can stand it. I've got the head for it."

And just for a fraction of a second, like a movie frame arrested under the hand of an editor, he was beautiful. His teeth didn't catch the light. His glasses lost their opacity. His impossible frame was graceful. As in a hologram, the scientist for an instant vanished beneath the image of the poet.

CHAPTER 32

*S*ir Adrian, arriving at Los Angeles airport at midday, would barely have time to meet Sarah before the Santhill conference scheduled for the afternoon. But he was not unpracticed in the painful art of relegating her needs to second place. Nor was it entirely the prospect of confronting those scoundrels in the American chemicals company with their own crime that weighed on him. There would be enough satisfaction, possibly, to offset the mortification of admitting the means by which he came by the information, namely, the dishonesty of his son. But there were other considerations that caused him to look from the car at the approaching outskirts of Los Angeles with a jaundiced eye. And when he reflected on his meetings the previous day in London with Lloyd's colleagues, remembering also that he would here encounter the too-knowing scrutiny of his niece, his cup of bitterness was full.

The cab turned left off Sunset Boulevard and started to mount the pleasant foothills of Bel-Air. Shortly after, it drew into the gates of an exotic garden, and he found himself getting out in a shady grove of tropical plants and flowers that led to the imposing entrance of the hotel. The splendor of it all caused a small dry smile to sketch itself into the corner of his lip as he submitted to the dutiful embrace of his niece, who was waiting for him.

"Rachel" was all he said in acknowledgment, and he gravely gave Mal Harris a fractional nod when he held out his hand.

When twenty minutes later he reappeared, he was ready to leave for the meeting, but he stopped on the threshold of the foyer with a slight frown. "Are you coming too then, Rachel?"

She had just returned from the desk with the reply to a fax from Steiger and Wallace, and was literally caught bending as she reclipped the lock of her document case.

"Why, yes."

"Are you needed?" he said. "It would be kind if you could look after Sarah until I get back. I think she wants someone at hand, you know."

"Of course, but . . ."

He was looking at her with an expression of judicious solemnity. His handsome face was impassively lifted so that his glance was directed on a downward slant. With the tips of the fingers of his right hand he was putting an engraved card into the small pocket of his waistcoat. He injected a fractional flow of warmth into the contour of his smile then and waited for her answer.

Ostensibly so polite and small, this move on his part cut her to the quick. With it he retracted all the avuncular pride he had expressed in the past in her intellectual talents, the egalitarian generosity with which he had commented on her career in the city. A housemaid treated as a friend for twenty years and suddenly sacked for breaking a cup might have felt the same.

"I should like to very much," she said, "but I'm afraid it would be difficult to justify to Steiger and Wallace if I was absent."

Her recovery had been quick but not seamless. It was not entirely without satisfaction to Sir Adrian to have got the stab in, even if she had parried it in the end.

"Very well," he said, and on the strength of his own permission he led the way out to the car.

They drove after this brief passage of arms almost in silence down into the city. There the directors of Santhill, who were expecting Mal and Rachel, were not expecting Sir Adrian. Failing the active participation of Finn Garrett, Vincent had succeeded in getting paper certification from the EPA office, which they were hoping could form the basis of the first settlement. When reception announced the inclusion of Sir Adrian Grimmond in the Lloyd's group, Charles Seaford's secretary was instructed to show them into the chairman's office, and Charles himself and Jim Faber, who had been in conference, put other business aside for ten minutes in order to receive them. Dale Falcus, who had arrived to chair the meeting in the adjoining boardroom, was called through, and likewise Vincent, who was presenting the EPA certificate. Only Zack remained at large.

"Give us five minutes, Dale," Charles Seaford said to Falcus. "Ten. That'll be enough. Jim and I want to get through this program by four o'clock."

"Sure." Dale frowned uneasily. "What's Sir Adrian here for?"

"Not trouble," Charles said. "Don't let's ask for it, Dale. Everything's taken care of."

By the time the heavy mahogany door was swung wide by Charles's secretary and the three visitors walked in, the entire team, except for Zack, was assembled. They made an impressive picture: four tough, good-humored, prosperous captains of American industry under the not necessarily mistaken impression that they ruled the world. Into the splendid room the sun shone, tempered with tinted glass and the ingenuity of modern architecture. Charles Seaford was on his feet. Taller than Sir Adrian by only half an inch but rugged everywhere that the baronet was smooth, from the pitted grooves of his face to his springing hair and strong hands, he came forward with masterly address.

"Sir Adrian," he said. "A pleasure to meet you, sir. I am Charles Seaford. Let me introduce my board here. Dale Falcus. Jim Faber. Vincent Cordoba."

Sir Adrian made his greetings.

"It's certainly a pleasure to meet you, sir!" Jim Faber said. "I think I'm speaking for my colleagues when I say I don't know what we'd have done without you." And they all laughed with bluff good humor.

"Is your trip over specifically to deal with the liability, Sir Adrian?" Dale asked.

"I had some family matters to see to," Adrian said noncommitally. Dale liked it better that way. It figured.

"Prosperous, I hope," he said. "This is a fine time of year to come visiting us."

Zack Webern at this moment walked into the chairman's anteroom. Nothing warned him that he was about to find himself in the presence of the man whose son he knew George Cash had had murdered. When he heard the name, he let out an actual cry but managed to turn the sound into a cough. Sir Adrian, as he shook his hand, looked into the martyred hollow of the lawyer's eye, but the moment was passed off as Charles said aimiably, getting down to business, "Now, what can we do for you, Sir Adrian? You'll sit in on the meeting, I take it. Then if you have any further briefings in mind . . ."

Sir Adrian said, "I'm afraid my unexpected appearance is going to cause some inconvenience."

"No," Charles said. He'd picked up the charming flat contradiction from watching George Bush on TV. These things got around. "We're very happy to have you come by."

"That's not quite what I meant," Sir Adrian said. "Perhaps 'inconvenient' was not the right word. I'm afraid I have to tell you some unpleasant news."

"Oh, really?" Charles said. He kept a strong front, lifting his chin and letting the toughness of his reaction show immediately as his lower lip slackened.

"I'm afraid," Sir Adrian said, "that the insurance cover document that was presented on your behalf is a forgery."

"A forgery!" Vincent was the one who stepped in there. His sardonic incredulity, delivered with a strong smile, acted like a shock absorber for the others. Dale looked steadily at Sir Adrian, but he felt the impulse of the dreaded accusation ricochet along the pathways of his nerves.

"This is an extraordinary charge!" Charles said. "I don't know that I am prepared to discuss it. Zack?"

Sir Adrian didn't defer to this cue to the lawyer. "Gentlemen," he said. "We are not accusing you personally. I have no doubt that you know nothing of this. Some other member of your staff may have perpetrated the forgery without your knowledge."

"Hold on here," Dale said. "What forgery? Who says that it is a forgery? Is it Lloyd's that says so? We've received no notice to that effect."

"You will," Sir Adrian said.

Charles was about to reply, but Zack with a dry finger touched his sleeve and silenced him. "If I may, Charles," he said, his burning eye fixed on Sir Adrian. "On what grounds is this extraordinary accusation made? Has the Lloyd's office rejected the document?"

"Not yet," Sir Adrian said.

"In that case this discussion is premature, to say the least."

They seemed to remember for the first time the presence of Mal Harris and Rachel Grimmond.

"Mr. Harris," Dale said, "you'd no hint of this in our previous meeting?"

"No."

"Miss Grimmond, you broked this cover?"

"Only the run-off," she said. "The document purports to be part of an old package of business without a modern record."

Dale made a gesture of impatient contempt. He began to see that they could win this one. He looked at his watch. "Charles," he said, "I think we should consider getting on with our meeting so that we keep to schedule, and then if there turns out to be any truth in this"—he paused and drew a breath through his teeth—"this melodrama, we can deal with it in its proper place."

"I agree," Charles said. "Mr. Harris and Miss Grimmond, are you willing to deal with it in this way?"

Mal, who had been watching the play around him with the coldest and most placid eye, said, "I think it would be a waste of time." He paused. "Sir Adrian's own son was employed in the forgery. He telephoned England and confessed to his father what he had done. This is why Sir Adrian is in the position to be so certain of his facts."

Charles frowned, and Dale, with a doubtful stare, fixed his eye on his colleague.

"Well, this is most embarrassing," Vincent began, but Adrian cut him off. "Please." He held his face up to quell his audience with a look. "If you would kindly disregard the personal side of this. I don't want to inconvenience you with my own feelings as a father. But I assure you, my son did telephone me in London and confessed to this forgery."

"Can he repeat that?" Zack said. He said it like a man who utters, with his last breath, a message that he has galloped through enemy fire to deliver. The sudden intervention struck a false note even in the ears of those members of his audience who had no idea that this essential witness had been killed. Mal Harris looked at him sharply.

"No, he cannot," Sir Adrian said.

Charles, sensing layers of intrigue, looked in silence from Mal Harris to Zack.

"Cannot?"

"He is dead," Mal said. "He has had an accident."

"Your son, Sir Adrian?" Dale said this, his fit and heavy body arrested in a gesture of unbelief. "Well then . . ."

"I don't understand," Charles said. "How then can he testify?"

Mal Harris's attention was fixed on the lawyer, whose calculated question had unleashed this line of argument.

"Perhaps Mr. Webern can best answer your questions," he said quietly to Charles Seaford. "He seems to know a great deal."

But Charles couldn't take so much in. Between the obligations of civilized concern for the father and possible relief at the elimination of the only witness, the ground was too uncertain. He could see Zack's hand in this, and for a fraction of a second he spared a thought for the blood that might be on it.

"Let me understand this better," Dale suddenly said with determined crudeness. "Sir Adrian's son confessed to having forged this document, but he is now dead and we have only Sir Adrian's word for it that the document, which Lloyd's accepts as valid, is a forgery."

Adrian nodded once, as one who acknowledges with cold restraint the mistakes of those who know no better.

"In that case," Dale carried on vigorously, "I think we are entitled to place our faith in the cover document itself, which, after all, is mere paper and not subject to any form of psychological or other pressure. If it's forged, Lloyd's will pick up on it when the cover given doesn't tally with the records, isn't that so?"

He made this statement disingenuously, knowing damn well, as Zack had so anxiously pointed out, that underwriters of the vintage of this piece of cover kept scanty records.

There was a momentary silence. It was broken by Mal Harris, who said, "I would advise accepting that, Sir Adrian."

"Quite," Sir Adrian said, bunching his lips, as if he held the proposition between his teeth.

"If we consider," Mal continued, "it is obvious that while the bona fides of this document was unquestioned, it passed as genuine. But now that there is cause to reconsider, any number of discrepancies are bound to show under scrutiny."

"Indeed," Adrian said. "LPSO stamps out of sequence, or the bureau number. They'll discover a mismatch between the broker's number on the policy and the bureau number."

It sounded too real by half, and resentful apprehension sent a rush of angry blood to Charles Seaford's head. "I propose that we cross that bridge when we come to it," he said forcefully. "Now, do we proceed with this meeting or not? Do we get the paperwork ticked up now, or do you guys have to come all this way again, with all the added expense to you and delay to us that would entail? Let me warn you, we will expect compensation if our expenses are exacerbated in this way."

He had not intended his speech to veer over into an angry tirade, but he was carried past himself, and, indeed, in different company he might have appeared formidable. But Adrian's hooded eye and sauve hauteur allied with the unexplained solemnity of Mal Harris more than matched him.

"Perhaps we had better leave it at that then," Adrian said. "We will say good afternoon, gentlemen," and with ironic courtesy he led the way out of the room.

CHAPTER 33

*D*efinitely the Italian," Rat said. "It's the consignment of toxic waste I told you I suspected."

He was standing as he spoke on one side of Finn Garrett's bed and on the other stood Mal Harris. "I've looked up all the formulae and circumstances. I'd go for that one hundred percent. Everything figures."

Finn watched Rat's face with gaunt anxiety as he spoke. She no longer had a drip attached to her arm, and her body was healing rapidly. Her hair had been reduced to a ragged halo where it had been cut to suture the injuries to her head. But there was an expression in her eyes that almost contradicted the idea of her survival.

"Shall we take that as our starting point then, Finn?" Mal said.

"Yes," she agreed.

"We don't have to do it," Rat said.

A bleak smile curved the edge of her lip.

"I can't let my silence be bought."

"You don't have to," Mal said. "Rat will do it. He's going to tell the police that he made the deductions about the illegal dumping and your having tangled with the gangsters involved in it from the starting point of the chemical sample he analyzed. You warned the truckers that there was a duplicate."

Looking at her as he spoke, he noticed, with vivid compassion, how around her right eye the bruising was almost the same color as the iris. "Our best way of protecting Daisy, at the same time," he went on, "is finding out who's the organizer before the police cause a reaction. If Rat's right about the country of origin, all we need to know now is who is the Italian company's contact over here."

He pulled up a chair and sat down.

"Tell me, Finn," he said. "Of the dealers that you handle on the licensing side in the EPA office is there anyone—anyone at all—who looks suspicious? Or who has applied for licenses for waste disposal from European sources before?"

She was silent for a moment.

"Well, of course, there are quite a few, but not of this type."

"No one from Santhill?"

He made the suggestion on the off chance. It would have greatly pleased Vincent Cordoba to know that Finn had no recall of any connection between himself and ExMetals—or at least, not at that moment. She shook her head.

"I'll check that out," Rat said.

"But how will you do it in time," Finn protested. "The police won't delay beyond tomorrow. As soon as we tip them off, they'll start one of their so-called undercover surveillance operations. I've seen them do it before when some Mexican illegals were dumping near Death Valley. If the truckers spot them, what will they do to Daisy?"

"We'll get to them first," Rat said. He laid a clumsy hand on her shoulder, all fingernails and an outlandish watch resembling the inside of a telephone plug. "I swear it."

And she smiled at him.

Mal Harris thought about that smile later as he drove himself and Rachel toward Dale Falcus's house on the next stage in their strategy. It made him unusually silent, and Rachel shifted uneasily in the passenger seat beside him.

"We could have walked this," she said.

"Then you wouldn't have had the car phone to use to call Dale Falcus at the time we've fixed."

"That's true."

They had turned in through an ornate entrance and up a short drive, and Mal now stopped the car on the gravel sweep in front of the door. Mal prepared to get out.

"You know what you're going to do? Don't forget to disguise your accent."

"Of course," Rachel said. "I've got the phone under here, and I ring at nine o-five and tell Dale the story as agreed." He nodded. "But, Mal, are you really sure I can't be seen through this glass? What if someone spotted me?"

"They won't," he said. "It really is one way. They hire these cars out to film stars. I should know. SIS is going to get the bill."

She looked uneasily through the tinted window. No one at that moment seemed to be about. The evening sun was drawing longer and yet longer shadows from the bushes and flowers.

"Right. I'm off," Mal said.

He got out of the car and slammed the door behind him. The sound of his feet crunching on the gravel was distinct against the background hum of traffic down the hill.

The door was opened by a maid who led him across a small stone-tiled hall into an open area that was abruptly close carpeted, with graceful variations in floor level and pillars instead of dividing walls. A huge, carved marble chimneypiece of French origin was grouped with a set of sofas upholstered in raw silk and a low table scattered with magazines and flowers. In another area a staircase furled down in a curve like a peacock's tail, and in another an alcove of books and a television led to an elaborate drinks table and what looked like a game of chess in progress, although no one had touched it in years. Here Dale and Barbara, when at home, came and went in the anchorless space, answering phone calls and filling in the gaps with TV.

When Dale made his appearance, he did it with the air of a man who, although he has agreed to talk, can think of better things to do. Mal Harris had asked for a meeting, and Dale had responded with a view to keeping communications open for the eventual deal that Zack insisted would be forthcoming. He wasn't sure of that himself. Basically, he resented the forgery. He wasn't ashamed of it, but he resented Zack's dreaming it up, and more than that, he resented the need for it. It was Dale's fault that no bona fide insurance existed with Lloyd's, and Victor had made sure the other directors knew it. In the general muddle of Dale's emotions, anger was uppermost. Whatever Mal Harris had come here to say, Dale behaved as if he was damn lucky that anyone would listen to him.

"Well, here I am," he said. "What can I do for you? I thought we'd reached bottom this afternoon, but if you have something to add right now, I'm listening."

He got no further before the phone rang.

"Help yourself to a drink, will you," he said, indicating the table ranged with glass bottles and decanters. He picked up the phone.

"Hello. Yes. This is Dale Falcus."

He listened in silence for a moment and then said, in a tone of cautious anger, half turning his back to the room, "What do you mean? This is nothing to do with me. Who's speaking please?" and then, "Are you a journalist?"

He was silent briefly.

"You what? What was that you said? Look, I assure you, whoever you are, that Santhill is not involved in this. I can't imagine how you got the idea there is any connection."

But despite what Dale said, the news that Rachel was giving him—namely, that Dr. Finn Garrett had been nearly murdered and her child kidnapped by the truckers involved in illegal dumping on Santhill land—rang horribly true to him. It was almost as if the information had lain dormant in his own mind, only waiting to be activated by the voice of this woman telephoning him. It all fitted in. His instinct was to play for time, but he was not to be given the chance.

When the phone rang, Barbara had been upstairs, and with practiced caution picked up the extension to listen in. She was always on the alert to catch Dale having affairs, and when she heard the sound of a woman's voice on the other end, she thought at first that this time she had scored a bull's-eye. Seconds later, her fury at the revelation that her husband was involved with the animals who had attacked Finn Garrett and stolen Daisy knew no bounds. In that instant all the fears of her years of marriage and all her hopes for a rebirth of the happy state of the first years of their relationship, which, even more than fear, had contributed to her willing enslavement, went up in smoke.

"Dale Falcus," she screamed down the phone from the bedroom, "you'll pay for this. My God, that wonderful woman! That poor child! My God!" She threw the phone down on the bed and stormed down the stairs to confront her husband in person.

Barbara was a woman who was never seen without what she called her war paint, but this time she happened to be between applications when the phone rang. She wore makeup to bed. She combed her eyelashes with a fresh layer of mascara after brushing her teeth, and Dale hadn't seen her without blue eyelids for fifteen years. She had always said that when the earthquake hit L.A., her last act would be to check her makeup in the mirror, but this revelation about Finn Garrett and the child evidently got a higher rating.

Dale himself hardly recognized her as she came down the stairs. She looked like a different woman, her eyes flashing in the limpid shadows of a real eye socket, her cheeks flushed with a color that came from her own blood.

"Dale Falcus," she said again, not yelling this time, but he was already looking at her, "I'll never forgive you for this."

Dale slammed the phone back down on its cradle, oblivious to the woman at the other end now that he had this one to contend with.

"Barbara, I didn't know!" he said. "Do you think I imagined for one minute those bastards were responsible for what happened to Finn Garrett and her child?"

There was almost a break in his voice, but she didn't even hear it.

"You know who's done it then?" she said. "It's to do with you and your miserable business. Finn Garrett might as well come from another planet as far as all this mess is concerned. You'd never bother to listen to what she had to say outside the administrative function of her office. Some sort of crank is what you thought her, as if truth and beauty were just diversions for the feebleminded. I wondered if you were right sometimes. Christ! You made me feel like some idiot at a card game who's got a hand loaded with rubbish, like love, womanliness, spirituality, compassion." She told the items off on her fingers with such passion that she bent them back almost to breaking point. "And you've got masculinity, money, commercial influence— all the trumps! Shall I tell you something, Dale Falcus? I thought yours looked like a handful of shit the whole time, but I didn't trust my own judgment."

"Barbara!" Dale shouted. He managed to get heard, and so he carried on, "I didn't know! I did not know that there was any connection between the illegal dumping that was going on at the Santhill site and the kidnapping."

This sentence bellowed with all the strength of his lungs, was followed by a sudden silence. Then Barbara said, "What illegal dumping?" and Dale remembered the presence of Mal Harris. Mal was standing, as he had been since he came into the room, with his hands in his pockets and an expression of quiet attention on his face.

"I had an appointment to speak to your husband this evening on this very subject, Mrs. Falcus," he put in.

"On this subject? What do you mean?" Dale turned aggressively on him. "Your remit was confined to the insurance cover, Mr. Harris, and while you choose to renege on that commitment, this other matter is certainly nothing to do with you. Just exactly what concern of yours is it?"

"Your wife has just explained to you," Mal said, "that not everyone limits their involvement to money making. Like her, I was was struck with Finn Garrett's remarkable personality, and I'm not leaving her to the mercies of whatever criminals have been attracted to feed on the corruption with which you and your colleagues in Santhill have surrounded yourselves."

Dale glared at him.

"What the hell are you talking about?" he exploded.

"That forged document," Mal said. "You're not still making out it is genuine?"

"*What* forged document?" Barbara demanded to know. Dale would have told her to shut up, but he no longer dared.

"There's no point in you continuing to deny forgery," Mal said. "You've been overtaken by events."

Dale wavered. "I'm calling the other members of our board," he said, taking a step toward the phone.

"Don't pick that up," Mal said, without himself moving an inch.

Dale paused, bewildered. "Who do you think you're ordering about? Why should I not call them?"

"Because one of them may be responsible for the illegal dumping and therefore the kidnapping. You say you didn't know about it. You didn't know about the forgery in the beginning, either, did you?"

"What forgery?" Barbara said again.

"Zack got a document forged," Dale said at last without looking at her. "We were short of the insurance cover that should have protected us against the costs of the cleanup order from the EPA, and Zack got one forged. It was his idea. The rest of us didn't know."

"Gee!" Barbara said. "What initiative. I'd never have thought Zack had it in him."

"Well," Dale said, "someone—we don't know who—found out about it and used it to buy our silence over some illegal dumping on the old toxic waste location in the Mojave."

He sat down with a tired grunt. "These guys just turned up at the site," he said, "threatened the guards and sent a blackmailing message to us about Zack Webern. Naturally there was nothing we could do."

Barbara looked at him.

"I didn't know they were responsible for trying to murder Dr. Garrett and kidnapping her child. What do you think I am, Barbara?" He looked so desperate that she could see he meant it. "Do you think I'd have gone along with all this if I'd known? I can stomach forgery, but give me credit for stopping short of child murder!"

At least he had succeeded in convincing Mal Harris. "Have you any suspicions," he asked, "who might have set this up?"

Dale considered. "You could do worse than look at Vincent Cordoba. That guy's got a toxic waste disposal outfit called ExMetals. He keeps it very quiet, but if there's one person I know who would slit his own grandmother's throat, it's him. He could have learned of Zack's forgery somehow."

Mal Harris turned the name around in his mind. "ExMetals?"

Dale gave him a snappy look and said, "Yes. Now what do you expect from me? Am I to tell the rest of the Santhill board about all this? If not, how do I sit around and let them make fools of themselves over that forged document?"

"Can you give me two days?" Mal said. "As of tonight, the police have been set on the right track. They're still questioning bikers, but only as a blind to mask the surveillance they're setting up to ambush the truckers. But I'm worried—very worried for the child."

"So you should be," Barbara said cryptically.

An almost undetectable spark of surprised amusement flickered across Mal's eye.

"I'll be going then," he said. He ducked his head with the self-effacing solemn farewell of a mourner leaving a deathbed. Barbara's eyes narrowed suddenly, suspecting a joke. But he was gone.

CHAPTER 34

A bloody silly way of doing it," Rachel said, "if you don't mind my pointing it out!"

"No, no. I don't mind."

"I sit there for three quarters of an hour outside Dale's house with my ass getting sore and nothing to do. Why didn't I go in with you in the first place?"

She slid the limousine neatly into place in front of the hotel and then stepped on the brakes so that the weight of the chassis shot forward on the stationary tires and the entire body, smoked glass and all, did a kind of stationary St. James's curtsy.

"Don't be angry," he said. "Look! Dale Falcus might have been placed quite differently. Once you'd got him on the line, he forgot about me. I could see his reaction for what it was. Then, he didn't know there were two of us, and you were outside. If we'd needed to stop him in his tracks, I was going to speak to you on the intercom, remember, and you would have gone for help."

She stepped out of the door being held open for her and handed the keys to the garage attendant.

"All right," she said, "but now I'm going to bed."

Mal walked behind her into the foyer, and when he had

said good-night, he went on past the Louis Quinze console tables and through to the piano bar. There was a black musician at the piano doing something interesting to Chopin in the half light. Mal sat not far from him, and when the waiter came by, he ordered a malt whiskey and something for the pianist. Until there was a break in the music, he thought about Finn Garrett. It was a very quiet evening. Thursdays were often quiet; tomorrow once more people would start to arrive. Tomorrow—Friday—there were a lot more things scheduled to happen, some of which Mal knew about and some he didn't. He looked at his watch. The heavy scent of cooling flower petals wafted in from the garden, where the plate-glass wall stood ajar.

"Mal Harris?" a voice said beside him. "How d'ye do. My name's Bossy Baker. Thanks for the drink, man."

The pianist sat down as he introduced himself and pulled out a pack of cigarettes. "I got your message," he said. "Bel Air to Pasadena via London. What can I do for Shipping I.S.? No one's been in touch with me for eighteen months except for some circulations."

"It's a long story," Mal said. "You'll have read in the papers about this local guru of yours, Finn Garrett, being attacked in the desert."

"The scientist lady. What about her?"

"Her daughter's being held by a gang of illicit waste disposal truckers as security against Dr. Garrett telling the police they're dumping in the Mojave Desert. We want to know who these truckers are and the date and time of their last drop."

Bossy shook his head and did something with his eyes that made the lower lids sag outward in a way that was definitively expressive of the negative.

"They don' advertise, man," he said. "You know where the load came from?"

He seemed to ask the question without much optimism, but when Mal said "Italy," he came suddenly to attention as if someone had jerked him upright with a rope. "Italy!" he repeated. "Italy? Say, that's different."

Mal made a discreet gesture with brows raised, like a conductor quietening a boisterous section of the orchestra. "How different?"

"Like Shipping has had a certain load watched since New Year. This'll be the one, and I'll tell you why. Our watcher in Naples signaled a transfer four'n a half weeks ago. Not many loads are worth transporting over here, but this one was so bad it figures. The Italian disposer was Nove Desta. It's just a question of looking up the registered American correspondents. I'll give you your answer tomorrow, man. I gotta go back and play now."

He ground his cigarette butt in the tray and stood up.

"If it's a local business man who's done the deal," he added, before walking away, "then I can suss out the boys he uses, no problem. We'll get it so tied up timewise we'll have them going from A to B like jackals answering the dinner gong. All right, all right." He waved to the bar man, who was pointing at the dial of his watch across the floor.

"I'll call you tomorrow," Mal said, also standing up. "And thanks."

Bossy moved across the floor in all innocence, quite unaware that those jackals he had in mind were already on their way. The moon was on the wane. Tonight it scarcely spared a silver splinter for the frangipani blooming darkly in the hotel garden. Tomorrow night it would be pitch-black.

Mal went to his room, but he felt jaded without being tired and the idea of sleep was uninviting. A submerged awareness that he couldn't quite grasp irked him. He flung himself down on his bed in his shirtsleeves and rummaged through the shadows in his mind. An hour later, he got up and went downstairs. The entire hotel, by this time, was quiet. Bossy had gone home. The piano was closed. The one clerk at the desk looked up and said, "Good evening, sir," in a quiet but lively voice. "Can I do anything for you?"

"I'm just going out for a walk," Mal said. "Will I be able to get back in later?"

"No problem, sir. Just press the small bell here on the right."

Mal walked through the garden lit with muted low lamps along the path. When he reached the road, he turned to the right. The city still vibrated under the accumulated effort and heat of the day, but with a dying fall. It had not yet reached that lowest point from which it would reemerge with the new day riding it like a gadfly.

As Mal began the long walk down to the ocean, his mind trawled the dark waters of events, urgently aware that somewhere in the depths lurked a killer shark. If he could not tune his instincts to forestall this predator and catch him unawares, then he would not save Finn Garrett or her child. Whether it was this starry night, or the sight of the billows of the Pacific restlessly milking the pale steep contours of the shore, he felt oppressed. He leaned his elbows on the rail, and looked out to sea.

A man standing by the water's edge not far away below him, moved suddenly. He did not show up against the general darkness until he moved. But when he started to walk back toward the embankment, Mal's attention was drawn by the sound of his shoes in the shingle and the denser blackness of his moving shadow. This combination of effects—the waves, the footsteps, the weaving black shadow where a man walks on soft ground—made a sinister and also a very timely impression. Mal watched his approach, still turning over his preoccupations of a moment ago and letting the images merge between his inner and outer eye. When the man reached the ground directly beneath where Mal was standing, the investigator straightened up and said, "Vincent Cordoba!"

Cordoba stopped. He was wearing a light black coat and trousers. With sinuous calm he adjusted his balance so that he could look up without too much twisting his neck.

"Mr. Harris!" he said. He abandoned the idea of speaking more than two words from his present position and made for the nearest set of steps. He reached ground level looking at his watch.

"What a coincidence!" he said. "I often come down here but the same can't be true of you, Mr. Harris."

"Sleepless times," Mal said.

"Yup." Vincent made the characteristic gesture that showed his white bottom teeth, while the long black lashes of his eyes dropped to a noticeable angle. "I got a phone call from Dale Falcus about an hour ago. Shocking business. You can't think too well of us."

He looked hard at Mal Harris as he said it. He encountered only a noncommittal expression.

"It's Finn Garrett," Mal Harris said, "who worries me."

"So I gather," Vincent said. "She's got a real talent for getting under the skin."

"Yours too?"

A hardness closed against Vincent's eyes as if metal replicas of the iris had slotted over the real ones.

"Maybe," he said.

Mal appeared not to particularly notice the terseness of his reply. "My concern is that as soon as the police start looking for illegal waste disposal cowboys instead of young bikers, those criminals who took the child will get very nasty," he said.

"Your concern? How come this is your concern?"

"I'm free to concern myself with anything I like, Mr. Cordoba," he replied. "For example, ExMetals. You might say I've got no reason to be interested in ExMetals, but I am. I am very interested."

A look of astonishment first hit Cordoba's eye to be instantly snuffed out with ice-cold rage. "Who told you about ExMetals?" he demanded.

"Let's just say I found out."

"What the hell has ExMetals to do with all this?"

"You tell me, Mr. Cordoba."

Vincent took a pack of cigarettes out of his pocket and lit one. He dropped the match on the tarmac, where it would have gone out without any help from him, but he trod on it, grinding it under the hard sole of his leather shoe. The unconscious symbolism struck a chill into the night air.

"I'm not telling you anything," Vincent snarled, "except this: don't get so carried away by your concerns. You need to look where you're going." He turned on his heel and walked back to where his car was parked alongside the ocean front. Mal Harris watched him get in, and then he began the long walk back to the hotel.

CHAPTER 35

*W*ith the dawn Sir Adrian Grimmond, in his room in the Bel-Air Hotel, rose to make the last preparations before leaving for England. Charlie's body could not accompany his parents on their homeward journey as it was the subject of a yet-unsolved murder inquiry. But although short of one corpse, Sir Adrian was not to be deprived altogether. Sarah's body, albeit with Sarah still nominally alive inside it, would be with him.

Even now, Sarah kept the expiry of all that had made life sweet to her as much to herself as she could. Despite her grief, she asked for no attention. She got herself up, she dressed, and she did not complain. In fact her behavior was so much as it had always been that a more sympathetic companion might have been tempted to speculate on how such a capacity for endurance had developed in the first place.

As Adrian poured her a cup of tea from the tray that had been brought up to their sitting room and took it through to where she sat at her dressing table progressing very slowly with her usual morning routines, he said, "Here you are, dear. This will do you good."

She nodded coldly at him in the glass. He turned away, saying to himself that time would heal. It would certainly do the trick in his own case. In time people at Lloyd's would forget the farcical element of this story, and they would surely forget that he had been in any way personally involved.

Even so, someone observing him now as he moved back into the sitting room in somber style would have marked a difference in him and perhaps put it down to grief. The habitual expression of lofty mocking good humor was missing. His eye was still commanding, but it was dull, and when he heard a knock on the door, he called "Come in" with a peremptory inflection in his voice, as if he knew and intended to discourage his visitor. He was half expecting Rachel.

Nevertheless, when she opened the door, he feigned a slight surprise, as if inconvenienced in the middle of doing something of private importance.

"Good morning," she said, with a tentative smile. "I came to see if I could help you at all, or Aunt Sarah."

"No. I don't think so," Adrian said. "Come in. . . ." He let his voice peter out to make it plain that for his own part he couldn't think of any reason for her to be there.

"I don't want to be in the way," Rachel said.

"Not in the way. I'm ready, and Sarah is just dressing. Can I offer you a cup of tea?"

She looked at the tray and saw only one cup. He followed her eye. "I'll ring for another cup." He said this in a tone of resignation that was exactly judged. Rachel let him ring the bell, suppressing her involuntary impulse to apologize.

"Sit down," he said. "Sarah won't be long." He sat down himself, but she remained standing.

"Do you mind if I . . . ?"

"No. Do carry on," she said. "You need to have something before leaving so early."

There was a silence between them, broken only by the sound of Adrian pouring himself a cup of tea. Eventually Rachel said, "You know, Uncle Adrian. . . ." She paused. He wasn't helping and instead kept his inflexible attention turned away from her until she eventually added, "You've been so kind to me always. I'm most awfully sorry about all this."

He moved his head in a frigid half circle until his eye rested on her. "Please don't let us discuss it, Rachel," he said.

It wasn't at all what she expected. "How do you mean?" she said, suspecting that they were perhaps talking at cross-purposes. "I—"

"You've apologized, Rachel," he said, cutting her off. "Let that be enough. I don't want to discuss it."

She turned a puzzled look on him, the first spark of anger providentially putting a stop to the idea of tears.

"When I say I'm sorry about all this," she said, "I'm not apologizing for anything that I have done. I'm not aware of having done anything that calls for an apology of that sort. Am I wrong?"

He refused to answer her. After a moment's pause she said again, "What I meant was to express sympathy."

"For what?"

"Charlie's death."

She saw the cloth of his waistcoat heave silently with an indrawn breath, whether of exasperation or disdain it was impossible to tell.

"Has my behavior called for an apology?" she persisted.

"I've told you, Rachel," he said, "I am not prepared to discuss it. Presumably you're not intending to continue to work in the City?"

"Why not?" she asked in astonishment.

"It isn't suitable for you," he said.

"How do you mean? I'm good at it. I will probably not carry on in broking, but I haven't decided yet where to change to."

"I am your trustee," he said. "You know I control your finances for some time yet, but we are both aware that you don't need to work."

"I dare say," she said. "But when you were my age, you also could have eked out a living on your private income if that had been your idea of yourself." Her voice was heated, but even though she was a novice compared to Adrian, she had enough courage and quickness to control her temper.

"Sit down," he said.

She rested one hand on the back of the sofa that hid the long curve of her bare legs. Embedded as Adrian's mind was in a novelettish concept of women, for once he was unaware of her physical attractions. His need for dominance stood between them as solidly as any furniture. She did not sit. She looked down on him, her cheeks reddened but only enough to highlight the flashing of her eye.

"Do you have it in mind to do anything about this opinion of yours?" she asked. "Are you planning to try to force me to give up my job?"

He refused to answer. His silence was not defiant. It was too assured for that. It was the silence of a parent whose remonstrances have been ignored by a badly behaved child.

"Uncle Adrian?"

"I will do as I think fit," he eventually said.

She was too astounded to reply at once. "On the contrary," she eventually said, and there was a complete change in her tone, so that he stared resolutely at her with an expression of challenging inquiry. "I won't put up with any interference of that sort," she said. "I'm sorry, but if you say one word or do anything to affect my work or reputation, I will let it be known that you were informed of the forgery several days before you disclosed it." She stared straight at his face and had the satisfaction of seeing the shock of realization hit him. "I'll let it be known that your own intention was to conceal the facts: as we both know it was your intention."

"How dare you!" he said.

"Unwillingly," she replied. "But you can absolutely count upon it."

After a moment's pause he stood up. "I wouldn't have expected this hysterical behavior from you, Rachel," he said.

She took the misogynistic term of abuse without comment, just as he would have done if a prostitute called him mean. He turned in silence to the window where the half-drawn curtain showed, between the ten-foot high swathes of padded blue linen, the sun of early morning.

"Very well," he said.

"What should I take that to mean, Uncle Adrian?" she said.

"You know perfectly well."

"We have an understanding then. You will do nothing to harm my reputation at work nor put any pressure on me to resign."

He grunted in assent with his back to her, but then he turned. If he had given the flicker of a smile, or the slightest warmth of the old admiring mockery had shown in his eye, she would have been unable to resist him. But he ranged himself to face her with the hauteur of settled dislike as if he had despised her for years.

"But don't expect," he said, "to be on the old terms with your aunt and me. I want that understood." He scrutinized her face for signs of the hurt he hoped he was inflicting. But her features were set hard.

"I've treated you like a daughter since your parents died," he said. "My house was always open to you. But under the circumstances I'm sure you will understand if that arrangement has to end."

"How about Aunt Sarah?" Rachel said. "Does she have any say?"

He disdained to answer her directly but said, "Don't let us have a vulgar quarrel please."

"Of course not." She met his glacial stare without attempting to match it. "In that case I'll say good-bye."

She went into the bedroom where her aunt, sitting at the dressing table, had heard every word.

"Good-bye Aunt Sarah," she said.

Sarah reached up behind her own head, looking at Rachel's reflection in the glass, until her hand found and closed over a tress of her hair. Gently she pulled her down until the girl's cheek rested against her own smart gray locks and Rachel could breathe in the scent of perfectly laundered clothes and Diorissima. She said nothing, as if her heart was too full for words, or as if perhaps her heart was too empty for them. Rachel kissed the poor, loving, wasted woman with the first real understanding that she had ever felt for her.

"I'll ring you as soon as I get home," she said quietly. "Don't worry. We'll lunch together, and you must come to my flat."

Adrian had made himself scarce. When Rachel returned, he was not in the sitting room. She let herself out and went, with relief, down to have breakfast with Mal Harris.

CHAPTER 36

*M*al Harris, after a sleepless night, felt the hollow of his eye with a tired finger. From his predawn encounter with Vincent Cordoba he had gone to rouse Bossy from his bed, and what weighed on him now as he sat at the breakfast table at the hotel, was the fact that in their night time researches they had not been able to find any lead on the team of drivers used by Vincent Cordoba for ExMetals.

"Say, man," Bossy protested, "wait till morning and I'll get it for you easy. Why the sudden rush?"

"As I said," Mal reiterated with a look of mild apology, "I can't explain. I just feel there isn't any more time owed us. If the drop is tonight and we can't identify the truckers before they set out, God knows what the police will get up to. Interception in the desert will be the only choice left. If the child's not with them, that'll be tough enough. But what if she is?" He stopped short, pulling his lip between his fingers, his eyes focused in a blind blaze of inward speculation. "I know it's Cordoba," he said. "He must have just changed his team."

The telephone, by means of which they had dragged four watchers in widely separated areas of the country from their beds, sat on a stack of papers. An empty file drawer on the floor caught Bossy's foot as he crossed over to the fridge. It bounced off the front of his sneaker and skidded on the tiles.

"All right," Mal said. He looked at his watch. It was six-thirty in the morning. "I'm sorry."

"Don't apologize, man. You got experience that I don't have, and if you think time's runnin' out, you're probably right."

Mal got up. "Can you be available tonight? I need a car, and I need you with me."

"What for, man? The answer's yes, but just outta curiosity, y' know. What for?"

"To drive into the Mojave Desert and keep a watch."

He nodded. "When?"

"Say eight o'clock."

"Sure. I'll get Speed to do the Bel Air." He yawned hugely clenching his fists as if squeezing out the long-drawn breath in a paroxysm of enjoyment. "And I got a recording this afternoon, so I'll sleep now, okay?"

"Can you give me a lift back to the hotel first?" Mal said.

"You look terrible," Rachel said, when she reached the breakfast table. "Are you all right, Mal?"

"Why? What's wrong with me?"

"Well. You seem to have cut yourself when you shaved, and the cut shows you've got green blood instead of the normal stuff. And your eyes look the sort of blue the sea would go if someone boiled it. What's happened? Tell me about your troubles, and I'll tell you about the fight I just had with my uncle upstairs."

He laughed.

"So what's wrong?"

"You know what's wrong, *cariad.*"

"But you're going to save her," she said. "You're going to save Finn Garrett and the child. Leo Turner told me that you had nerves of steel. What's gone wrong?"

"Well . . . , I'll tell you." He held her eye for a minute. "There's a series of paintings by Botticelli in the Prado. Hunting scenes they are."

"Go on."

He sighed shortly and cast a glance wider afield across the dining room before coming back to her, and saying, with the hint of a smile as if expecting her ridicule, "It's women they're hunting."

She said nothing.

"In one picture there are women running screaming in front of men with dogs; in another they rape the women; in another it's knives. Sport, you see. It stuck with me. I realized something that isn't changed by the fact that I don't share it myself—that a depraved instinct to prey on women is widely felt still by a lot of men, and always was. I found the idea depressing."

"You and me both," she said. "But it's changing. Look at the row I just had with my uncle. I won."

A spark of humor lit his eye for an instant at what she'd said.

"Well," he said lamely.

"Well what?"

"I suppose this brutal attack on a gentle intelligent beautiful young woman like Finn Garrett has marked a change in my view of things like the paintings in the Prado," he said.

"You're used to violence in your job, I thought."

"Strictly masculine violence. It's different. Compared to this, it's all been good clean fun."

She gave an ironic laugh and said, "You go around with that sparse modest air to get everyone to think that you live on the margins of things."

He held up his cup of coffee and looked at it.

"What was the name of that drink that Rat ordered?"

"A black in eclipse with two shots of lightning."

"Waiter," Mal said at once, seizing an opportunity. "A black in eclipse and two shots of lightning."

"Coming straight away, sir," the young man said.

"You're not going to drink that?"

"What else do you suggest I do with it?" he said.

When it arrived, he picked it up and said, " 'We go our ways—I to die and you to live.' "

"I'm watching with bated breath," she said. "And when you've drunk up your hemlock, I think you ought to go and get some rest."

He got as far as raising it to his lips when the telephone appeared at his elbow with a caller on the line. Mal took the receiver from the waiter, expecting to hear the voice of Bossy Baker but instead he encountered Rat's harsh college drawl.

"Mal," he said, "how's Rachel?"

"She's all right," Mal said, with a glance across the table. "Why? Were you expecting otherwise?"

"No. I always like to ask after beautiful girls."

"Okay," Mal said wearily, "I suppose that's not all you have to say. Go on."

"Listen." Rat followed the command with a dead silence, and Mal let his eyes close once in a weary gesture. "Are you there?"

"Waiting."

"Just to say I got what you asked for, and it'll be at the hotel desk midday."

"Thanks, Rat." He rang off. "That was Rat," Mal said, in response to Rachel's look of inquiry. "He sent you his love, and he's delivering me some protective clothing for tonight."

"Why? Where are you going?"

"Into the desert with Bossy Baker," Mal said. "There will be no moon, and it might be black enough to seem convenient for our poison friends."

CHAPTER 37

*B*ut I simply don't know how it could have happened!" the hysterical nurse was saying. "Dr. Garrett can't walk on her own yet."

"Please don't cry, Nurse Lowensky," her supervisor commanded, but the order fell, as it were, on stony ground. With tears pouring down her cheeks the nurse turned her face to camera, and there was a sharp cry from one journalist to his photographer, "Get a shot of the one who's weeping."

"Who was the last visitor in here?"

"Nurse Lowensky can't remember, doctor. It's no good asking her."

"Will you get the press out, please!"

It would have been a lot easier said than done but for the fact that there were only minutes to go if the reporters were to make the late evening editions. When the room was clear the doctor, the nursing supervisor, the security guard who had been on duty, and the nurse were alone.

"I've never known anything like it," the supervisor said. "They just don't give up."

"I guess they're glad they didn't know," the security man

said with some bitterness. "They camped on the doorstep long enough, and they finally got a peach of a story. 'Badly Injured Local Scientific Guru Vanishes from Hospital Bed.' "

"I need a list of all the people who these flowers are from, nurse," the guard added after a moment's pause. He picked up one bunch that was on the end of the bed; it consisted of a mass of white daisies and roses. The guard started reading the card.

"Had Dr. Carter seen this patient this afternoon?"

"Yes, doctor." The supervisor leafed through the logbook. "And here's his record. He'd endorsed the existing regime, and she had stitches removed from the left leg this morning."

"Then if she couldn't walk, she must have been carried— right past you, Officer Best."

The affronted man was about to protest, but his portable phone crackled into life at that moment with a demand from his chief for news on the emergency, and he stood there with Vincent Cordoba's card, still unread, in his left hand and his entire attention focused on not losing his job.

The light faded outside the hospital while they were still arguing, and around the men and vehicles involved in the police operation to intercept the truckers in the Mojave Desert, darkness also began to fall.

Even so, Bob, driving in to the guard's night shift at Santhill in company with Pete and the dogs, spotted the third police patrol car drawn off the track and concealed with the subtlety of a full-scale battle rehearsal before they'd even reached Stoddard's Well.

"Shit!" he said. "What the hell's going on?" One of the dogs in the back got up on all fours, scrabbling for balance with his claws on the seat, and let out a shattering bark.

"Sit, Sheeba!"

But the German shepherd had also spotted the police and gave another volley before subsiding as they left the patrol behind.

Bob said, "They're staked out."

"No." Pete shifted gears with his face slewed round and his jaw distorted with a corresponding twist. " 'Tain't nothin' like that."

"What is it then?"

But although Pete had made his mind up to it, an explanation wasn't forthcoming. "They'll be gone," he said, "when it's dark. There's no need to worry."

However, when the daytime guards, relieved of their shift, passed that way again half an hour later, the patrol cars were still in place, although they could no longer be seen for the darkness. If the patrol cars had waited until darkness before moving in, Pete and Bob would not have seen them, either. As it was, Bob nagged on long after the two of them had relocked the main gate and turned the lamp on in the guardhouse.

"What if they've got a surveillance on? You know? T'night?"

"Will you just belt up, Bob," Pete said, "and find where the hell those guys dumped the can opener."

"Why can't you feed the dogs before you come out?" Bob said, or was going to say, but his words were cut off by the sound of an approaching helicopter flying low. "What's that?"

Pete hit one of the dogs briefly on the nose to quiet it, his face turned upward like Bob.

"It's the cops," Bob reiterated with angry agitation. "Didn't I say. The place is crawling with them. What if—"

"Aw, shut up!" Pete snapped. "Could be anyone." But his voice lacked conviction. "Look," he added more reasonably, "if they're still here when the bastards come it's their problem. We're out of it."

"You say that," Bob came back at him, "but what about the number 3 gate? Do we open it? Huh, Pete?" He was following Pete around again by this time, as the other man looked in the guardhouse and turned over boxes and papers hunting once more for the can opener. "But what do we do if . . . ?"

His voice carried on as the darkness, more and more

densely, descended mote by mote and cloud by cloud, gradually blackening out the land. And on the rim of this moonless nightscape appeared Vincent Cordoba's car, with Vincent at the wheel and Finn beside him.

CHAPTER 38

*V*incent drove the 1959 Oldsmobile slowly, although Finn
Garrett gave no sign that the unevenness of the desert track
aggravated the pain of her injuries. He kept the old-fashioned
dashboard lights on, and their dim glow threw the faintest swath
of light upward and sideways on her face so that he could see it.
The sight had the effect of silencing his self-doubt at what he was
doing.

He cut the main beam switch, and the view of the road
ahead contracted and shortened, but he still saw the telltale bulk
of another patrol car parked too near the track. It was the third
he'd spotted.

"I told you," he said, "I heard a rumor on the grapevine;
and I thought if I could help you in any way—in any way at
all—to get back your child, then I must do it."

She gave him a look of gratitude. Even in the semidarkness
of the car's interior her clear eye seemed to reach right into him
and turn over a few stones.

"You're beautiful, you know," he said.

The remark was an uncharacteristic miscalculation. But this
whole enterprise—this taking her from the hospital into the
desert, casting himself in the role of rescuer and friend, from

which he calculated at a later date to be promoted—this whole enterprise was an uncharacteristic miscalculation. When he had heard the rumor of the intended surveillance, Vincent's original intention had been only to suss out the police presence. But he soon plotted a more complex scenario, and he was now making for the point where the trucks coming in could be intercepted just as they branched off the road from China Lake.

He glanced at Finn now to measure her reaction to his praise. In his own face the unfamiliar traces of sincere feeling mutated by force of habit into the gestures of exploitation, and he looked outwardly as he always did. She, on the other hand, was changed. It was not so much her physical injuries in themselves as the way she dealt with them that accounted for the change. Just as Houdini had learnt, in order to survive his arduous escape routines, to reduce his pulse and heartbeat so that his life force needed almost nothing to support it, she also in her determination to retain the capability of protecting her child, had disciplined her being into an extraordinary lightness, like someone walking on a floor of muslin stretched over battens of hazelwood. Her breath was light and shallow, and her presence seemed to weigh nothing. The fear and suspense that in its force, unchecked, would have been enough to destroy her was mastered. It sparkled like the visionary flames of marshfire over the landscape of her immediate life, without the power to burn.

"How did you know," she said, "which path to take back there?"

"What path?"

"There was a fork in the track."

He made a play of being willing to turn back. "Do you think we should have gone the other way?" he asked, braking. "I don't mind."

"That's all right," she said. "I realize you know where you're going."

He let the car speed up with a slight jerk, and a spray of small gravel scattered in the dark. "How do you mean?"

"What are you going to do?" she said.

"I'm going to get Daisy back for you."

He couldn't quite make out whether she had seen through his story. He'd been careless with the track back there, and now he didn't quite know how things stood.

"I know," she said.

He looked at her. Her skin shone very pale, the curve of her lip, the cheekbones, the throat reminding him of how like a statue he had thought her when they first met in the Seafords' garden. He had never completely managed to forget her since.

"This isn't what I planned," he said. He emphasized the "I" in his sentence. "Being violent to women and children: do you think that's my style?"

She said nothing.

He realized with fury that he had somehow fallen over the edge of a confession. He hadn't been looking where he was going, where his words were taking him. Now he could feel the air rushing past as he fell, and the little roots of past moments of truth and decency in his past were as useless as heather and saxifrage growing on the cliff face; they offered no handhold strong enough to break his fall. He considered turning the car round there and then, but that option was no longer open, either. He had no doubt that Finn's resistance would be implacable. She might honor a contract of silence if he recovered the child, but he would have to kill her if he decided to turn back now without rescuing Daisy.

He saw ahead of him a group of low bushes that marked the point where he had planned to wait. He let the car coast forward on its own momentum. There was a stealthiness in its almost silent progress, as the pale bulk of it glided fathoms deep in the darkness, like the shark Mal Harris had been looking for. It stopped, and he cut the engine and turned toward Finn.

"I don't know what the hell I'm doing here," he said, with dangerous bitterness. Except for his own voice the silence was absolute. The wind was still. They were alone, as if there were only the two of them in the whole night. He reached over suddenly with a gesture half appealing and half aggressive and took her hand in his. Immediately he felt the shock of contact strike her, and a tremor like a trapped moth under the skin, fluttering. To his surprise the sensation excited him almost unbearably. He felt his senses leap with unexpected force, and he snatched the hand to his face, laying it against his cheek and his mouth as if he would devour it. He could see a frightened pulse beating in her throat. It was too much. It sent him wild. It had all happened so fast. He had never seen anything so beautiful. Like a cat mesmerized with the fluttering of a sparrow, he savored the panic beating of her heart with ravenous excitement.

Nothing would have stopped him. He would have been blind and deaf to everything except the intoxicating struggles of her body and the gasping of her breath—but for one sound. Out of the night ahead of them came the thunder of an approaching truck.

The noise cut across his senses with a sudden and almost ridiculous abruptness. He looked through the windshield to identify the source of the noise with eyes that still glittered with the heat of unslaked desire. He gave a curse under his breath. His body snapped upright, and he switched the lights on and off with three rapid stabs into the darkness.

The unlit trucks were almost on top of them before they could brake at the signal, and Vincent was out, slamming the car door behind him, holding out the flat of his hand toward the lead vehicle. Fratelli threw open the passenger door and jumped down. In the lackluster shadows the eye accustomed to darkness easily made out the pale gleam of flesh and the occasional pallid glint of starlight on metal.

"What the shit!" Fratelli cursed with muted violence as he recognized Vincent Cordoba. "What you here for? Has something gone wrong?"

"Keep your cool," Vincent said. "There's a police cordon of surveillance around this side of the waste site."

"Then how the hell we get in there?"

"You'll have to take the track right round to the south."

"What is this?" The question came from two men who had jumped down from the second truck, while the driver leaned from the first cab calling, "Fratelli! We unload here then. I ain't running no gauntlet of cops with this load. Who the hell's he think we are?"

"That's right," Fratelli said. "Why not?" he continued to Vincent. "Last load. We can just pump it out and run for it."

"You can't pump *that* out!" Vincent said.

"Who says?" The man who spoke came up from the last truck. He held his mask dangling from his right hand. It was uncanny the way every word spoken by the men could be heard with such clarity in the still dark night air. They had started with their voices low.

"Look," Vincent said. "Let's not have any disagreement about this, guys. I've driven through, and you know what the cops are like. You can get round south easily. I'm telling you."

"But why bother?" the last man said again. "We don't need to risk it. This spot is as good as any, and we can get the hell out with empty trucks while the going's good. It'd be different if we had another run, but this one's the last."

Vincent was like a man who has not yet fully realized that the machinery he is handling has got a dangerous grip upon his person. The news that the truckers had attacked Finn Garrett and kidnapped her child was the first warning. The snare that was winding around him had consumed almost all of its slack. He could still feel, like blood on his tongue, the sickly, bitter flavor of the unfinished rape, but his mind had no time to taste it. Now came the suggestion that a deadly poison should be emptied here in unmarked desert, and he was powerless to resist it. The men formed up in agreement against him, and at last he realized how he was placed.

The words he was about to use to attempt to persuade them were that minute drowned by the sudden noise of a police helicopter over to the west. It flew with searchlights sweeping the ground beneath the swollen belly of its undercarriage. The pools of light swung in apparently narrow tracks and receded in the wrong direction, but it was enough for the truckers. Vincent didn't have a chance.

"That's it!" Fratelli said. "Get moving."

They responded at once with the businesslike drill of men who knew very few routines, but this was one of them.

"Where's the child?" Vincent shouted after Fratelli.

The trucker was striding round the front of the cab to put the pumping mechanism on half hold, while his partner grappled further back with the coupling. He was in a hurry, and he pointed to the last truck and said, "In there." Fratelli scarcely intended to give Vincent a glance, but just the involuntary gesture that brought his eyes up gave him a view of something else, and he came to a halt with a muscular punch of his fist in the air and said, "What's that?"

Vincent spun round to look where he was pointing. Standing on the gravel like a ghost, Finn Garrett—her pale clothes and paler skin gray and faintly luminous—was enough to scare a superstitious man.

Fratelli was not superstitious. "What's she doin' here?" he demanded. "Who the hell is she?" He didn't recognize her.

At that moment, from the other end of the truck, the driver shouted, "Fratelli! What you doin'? Switch on, I said." He looked round the end of the bulk carrier and saw the woman. His mouth dropped.

"Get her away!" Fratelli shouted.

Vincent was out of his depth. This wasn't the place for him, either. His patent leather elegance and sardonic ruthlessness cut no ice in this company.

"Give her the child," he said. "The job's finished now!"

But Fratelli, coming to the conclusion that he didn't need to bother a damn, ignored him. He leapt up into the cab and threw the switch. He pulled the mask that had been hanging round his neck over his mouth, and on the other side of the vehicle, away from where Vincent was standing, the eight-inch-caliber pipe locked to its housing on the container began to disgorge its contents in measured bursts like a severed artery rhythmically pumping the blood out of a human body.

Vincent took a white handkerchief out of his pocket and held it hard against his face as he dashed down the line of trucks. The men, all occupied on the other side, couldn't see him, and he reached the last truck and jumped up on the metal foothold to wrench open the cab door. The little child was asleep. She was jammed between the two seats, with her head lolled over to one side. They'd put a mask on her, but the elastic was too loose, and it had slipped or she had pulled it off.

Vincent had to haul himself further up to get a grip on her. He tried not to breathe while he couldn't hold the cloth to his face, but it took too long. He wrapped his arm as far as he could reach around Daisy's body and pulled her toward him, pushing the mask back in place at the same time. She woke with a little yowl of distress, and he almost lost his balance. He gripped her tight and swung backward onto the ground, just making it without falling. She struggled out of his arms. He was willing enough to let her break loose, because he was choking, needing to snatch the cover back over his own mouth. He felt a wave of nausea surge round him. He needed a lungful of clean air and threw himself away from the trucks, staggering drunkenly ten or fifteen paces into the darkness. He hardly knew what was going on for a moment. The child, screaming soundlessly in the din of the machines, had run back behind the trucks, making for no-where in particular.

It was then that the blaze of headlights suddenly flooded the scene. After so much darkness it was dazzling. In a single instant the trucks and the hellish activity surrounding them were awash with light.

The men had grouped at a slight distance to protect themselves from the foul air while the pumps were working. They turned now toward the lights in a body, as did the solitary figure of Vincent on the other side. He saw his own car moving forward, lights blazing, with Finn at the wheel. Fratelli's voice bellowed above the roar of the machinery, "The lights! The lights!" But she was no more listening than he had in times before. She had seen a glimpse of the little staggering figure of Daisy making off into the darkness, and she—and only she—had heard distinctly against all the other noise the sound of the child's voice.

"Turn off the lights," Vincent screamed from his side.

The car covered the twenty yards up to the line of trucks, and Finn, momentarily uncertain whether to round the pumping or the blind side, saw the faint glimmer of little legs running back toward the light and the widening pool of poison that seeped over the ground.

She wrenched the wheel over in that direction. The men scattered as she drove toward them. The patrolling helicopter had taken only seconds to lock on to the sudden blaze of light and was already overhead. And over to the west and the southwest the headlights of two cars going at top speed raced over the desert.

Vincent Cordoba, running like a madman between the trucks, saw Fratelli holding something in his hand and raising it.

"Don't shoot," he screamed. "Fratelli! Don't shoot!"

The car had reached the other side of the pumping area and full in the lights the figure of the child suddenly showed up running wild, the mask flying loose like a little white scarf, the mournful square of her screaming mouth and even the tears on her cheeks illuminated in the white glare of the lamps.

Vincent saw the car stop, and Finn, flinging open the driving door, raced out toward the child. She snatched her up into her arms as Fratelli took aim, and Vincent threw himself across the intervening space and hit the trucker on the back of the shoulders. He stumbled and fell as he pressed the trigger. The police patrol car and the second vehicle driven by Bossy Baker with Mal Harris in the passenger seat, screamed into view at that moment when the impact of the bullet hit the stony ground wide of its mark and ignited the combustible poison in a blanket flash of something worse than fire.

In the putrid glare of the intense heat they saw the awesome sight of Vincent Cordoba standing silhouetted in the core of the fire. For a long and ghastly moment he stayed upright, but when he sank down he seemed to melt visibly into the fires of hell. Fratelli's body had already vanished.

"Get the car!" the police officer shouted to his passenger, thinking that there was an escaping trucker inside there, as Finn in a frantic zigzag drove away from the blaze. The marksman beside him rested his elbow on the sill as the patrol car was propelled forward, and fired. With the first shot he missed. With the second he hit a back tire. Vincent's car started to slew, and the marksman was ready to have another go, like a rabid tourist with a self-winding camera.

He only stopped when Bossy, driving straight at him on a converging path, screamed to a halt inches from the police vehicle, and Mal Harris leapt from the passenger seat shouting for the fifth time to the intoxicated marksman, *"Don't shoot!"*

But the man was stubborn. He said with infuriated accuracy to his driver, "What's going on? I don't know what the hell's going on."

"Get out of the way," his companion shouted at Mal. "You're in the field of fire."

"You bet I fucking am!" Mal uncharacteristically shouted back at him, but without being heard. More important, he ignored the order to stand aside. Vincent's limousine had come to a stop up ahead, resting on the hub cap of the shattered back wheel. Mal Harris, his figure lit up against the looming background of the further desert, was running toward the car. If he'd had the breath to pray, he would have been praying. He saw a figure slumped behind the wheel and a smaller bundle half smothered beside her. He wrenched open the driver's door with despair in his heart, and at that moment she turned. She turned her head round and looked up at him, her eyes gaunt as if about to turn inward into her skull, her lips hanging open. And yet, when she saw that it was Mal, she smiled. All the running and the chaos came to an abrupt end. He felt the momentum of terror past throw his body up against this sudden peace, and he said, "Hello, my lovely. Can I give you a lift anywhere?"